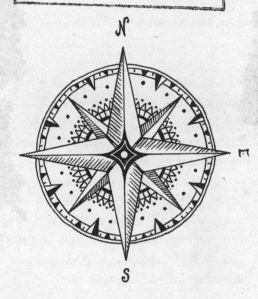

Have you ever felt that plants were trying to speak? I know I have. Friendly herbs wave from their beds while wild briar patches are spiky with warnings. But the heroine of *The Map of Leaves*, Orla, *truly* taps into the language of the plants. If she listens, she'll hear of a terrible poison, a great journey and the possibility of healing – for her and for her world. This novel is a fantastic all-action adventure, but it's also a vitally important story about nature and the care we owe it. Yarrow Townsend is a passionate new author – and a wise, funny and exciting talent!

BARRY CUNNINGHAM
Publisher
Chicken House

The MAP of LEAVES

YARROW TOWNSEND

Chicken House

2 Palmer Street, Frome, Somerset BA11 1DS
www.chickenhousebooks.com

Text © Yarrow Townsend 2022
Illustration © Marie-Alice Harel

First published in Great Britain in 2022
Chicken House
2 Palmer Street
Frome, Somerset BA11 1DS
United Kingdom
www.chickenhousebooks.com

Chicken House/Scholastic Ireland, 89E Lagan Road, Dublin Industrial Estate,
Glasnevin, Dublin D11 HP5F, Republic of Ireland

Cover and interior design by Helen Crawford-White
Cover illustration by Marie-Alice Harel
Typeset by Dorchester Typesetting Group Ltd
Printed and bound in Great Britain by CPI Group (UK) Ltd, Croydon CR0 4YY

FSC
www.fsc.org
MIX
Paper from
responsible sources
FSC® C171272

1 3 5 7 9 10 8 6 4 2

British Library Cataloguing in Publication data available.

PB ISBN 978-1-913696-48-1
eISBN 978-1-913696-66-5

For Bridie Watts

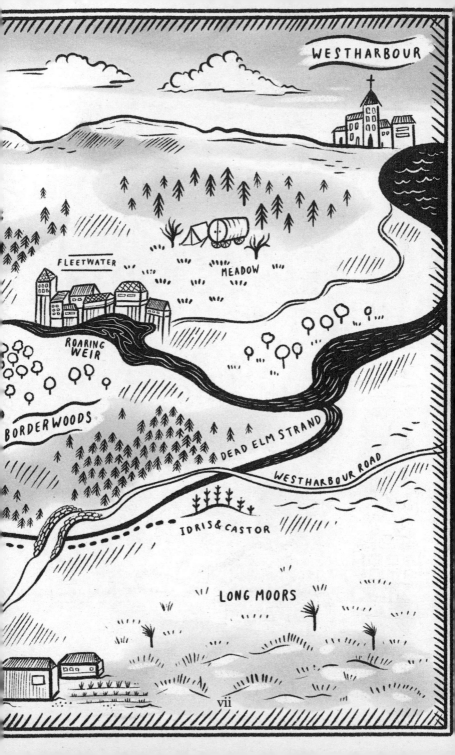

1

Comfrey *Symphytum officinale*
Leaves: for a poultice against inflammation and infection.
Also known as knitbone.

The village of Thorn Creek should have been abandoned long ago. It was a shivering, damp, dead end of
a place, where wooden houses huddled together along a
marshy river, as though afraid they would fall into the
churning stream or else be swallowed up by the forest.
It was not a place for children, out among the foggy
woods and wild marshes. The winters were long and
dark and impossibly grey; and no one in the little
village looked forward to spending their days swamped
by river mist, wrapped in two woolly jumpers, stacking
firewood and collecting fallen pears. No one except
Orla Carson.

Twelve-year-old Orla had dark-brown hair, bramble-scratched hands, and a determined frown. She wore a pair of boy's breeches that she never changed, an oilskin coat that smelt of beeswax, and a pair of thick leather boots. Her home was a small wooden shed, once used by a farmer to store his firewood. It stood at the edge of the village, in the shadow of the forest, in a tangle of blackthorn and apple trees, long forgotten by the farmer. Orla had lived in the woodshed with Ma, and now that Ma was dead, she lived there alone, with no help from anybody. She looked after the wild garden, and the wild garden looked after her. There was no need for anyone else.

That afternoon, in the goose-grey light, Orla found herself knee-deep in nettles, peering into the undergrowth. It was the first day of September, and the seasons were changing. The fog settled low on the river, and the bracken and comfrey at the end of the garden were draped with jewelled cobwebs. Around her, the plants whispered, their voices sparking through the tangle of leaves and stems.

Take it from the stem! called the dock.

You need more than two leaves, said the milfoil.

No – just a little from the tip! insisted the nettles.

'I know how to make the ointment,' said Orla, choosing which nettles to cut, and carefully pruning them with her knife. She caught the plants as they fell, plucked the leaves from the stems before they could sting her, and stuffed them into her pockets. Her horse, Captain, was tied to the porch of the woodshed, looking forlorn. His hoof was half-rotten and she needed to draw out the infection before it got worse.

Goose-grass! called the purple toadflax.

Chickweed! chirruped the honesty, its seed pods like silver moons.

'Hmm,' said Orla. She pushed on through the scraggly patch of nettles and into the brambles, which snagged her oilskin coat and grabbed at her breeches. 'Maybe. We'll see about that, shall we? Excuse me, please,' she said, peeling the thorny stems from her coat. 'You know I've got an important job to do.'

She wound her way down through the patch of twisted old apple trees, towards the creek. 'Nettles, comfrey, clay. That's all I need.'

Comfrey always works, echoed the comfrey proudly.

By the water's edge Orla wiped the mist from her nose with her sleeve and cut the comfrey leaves. She knew them well – broad and green, with a fine fur of prickly hairs. In summer the plants were adorned with a spray of pinkish bells, sometimes purple and sometimes white. But it was the thick leaves that she used for medicine – for burns, for bruises. Once, she had patched up a sparrow with a gammy leg by soaking a comfrey leaf in honey and wrapping it round the leg like a bandage, just like Ma had shown her, feeding the sparrow on porridge until it flew away again.

Comfrey always worked.

Third time lucky, said the plant.

Orla bit her lip. 'Let's hope so,' she said. Captain's foot had gone bad three times this summer, and each time she'd made the old remedy, just as she'd been taught. It shouldn't be coming back *again*. The first time, she'd mixed in a mountain of dock from the ditch by the hedge. And last month she'd stirred in a chunk of honey from the bees in the apple tree. That should have sorted it.

Not those – not good enough! More dock! said the blackthorn hedges.

More milfoil! cried the marigolds.

'All right, all right,' said Orla. 'I *am* listening, you know.'

She pushed her damp hair away from her eyes and examined the comfrey leaves in the gloom. They were smaller than usual and flecked with black marks. Orla tried to rub the marks away with her finger, but they seemed to be part of the plant.

Bad leaves, said the moss beneath the apple trees.

They'll still do! said the comfrey.

What you need is some pine, said the wormwood.

Pine sap and resin and tar. Pine tar! echoed the garden.

'Pine tar, indeed,' replied Orla, her mind still on the comfrey. She pocketed the leaves and trudged back up to the woodshed. Captain was peering up at the hedge that separated the garden from the lane, sniffing the air. His mane was tangled with burdock spines and his patch-work coat was dappled with mud.

'Stop thinking about blackberries,' she said to him, scratching behind his ears, just where he liked it. Then she picked up his feathered leg to examine the gammy hoof. Captain struggled a little, but Orla shushed him and patted his bony side gently, before peering at the hoof. It smelt terrible and there was something oozing from the heel. Gently lowering Captain's foot, she pulled the bundle of leaves from her pocket and tried to pick out the ones that didn't have black splodges on them, while Captain sniffed enthusiastically.

Pine would be better, muttered the wormwood.

'Let's try my idea first,' said Orla, pulling a stone mortar from beneath the little bench in the porch. She tossed the leaves into the mortar and hammered them to a pulp. 'There,' she said, adding the greyish clay and watching it turn green, just like it was supposed to. 'That'll do it. There's nothing wrong with the leaves, they're just a little past their best, that's all.'

Hmm, said the dock leaves by her feet.

Are they? said the wormwood.

Orla chewed her lip. 'It'll be OK,' she said, giving the mixture a final stir. Lifting Captain's hoof, she pasted on the green ointment and held it in place with a piece of clean linen. It was true, the ointment was already starting to look a little darker than usual.

Orla let down Captain's foot and wiped her hands on her breeches. 'Next time you escape, stay away from the village,' she told him. 'Too much glass and nails and trouble up there. Can't have you getting lost.'

Captain lowered his head to sniff his foot, and snorted.

Orla raised an eyebrow. 'The ointment looks fine to me. You'll feel better in no time.'

The plants whispered behind her, like a shiver in the wind.

'I *can* hear you, you know,' she said.

Pine tar, said the plants in chorus.

Pine and ash, cook it till it sticks! said the ivy.

Orla shot them a scornful look. 'I said *no*,' she repeated, wiping the mist from her nose and putting her knife back in her pocket. 'Captain's going to be fine,' she said. 'Coffee's half-burnt already, then I gotta pick carrots for dinner. I'm not going hunting for pine. I know what I'm doing.'

But in the back of her mind, she knew the ivy was right. It had watched over her garden for many years; its roots twisted thick and secure into the foundations of the woodshed.

Comfrey's not enough, said the ivy. *Pine, or he'll die of infection. Pine, out beyond the village. Pine, from the Borderwoods.*

Orla squinted in the direction of Thorn Creek. A twisting path ran up from the river to a cluster of dark houses, wooden and rain-soaked, along cobbled streets. Lamps were already lit, and shadows gathered around the tavern and the chapel, drifting in the fog. Beyond, a line of dark pine trees watched over the village. The hairs on the back of Orla's arms prickled and her legs felt heavy.

You're scared, said the bitter wormwood.

'I'm not *scared*,' mumbled Orla, but her stomach was twisting like ropes. Nothing good ever happened when she went up to the village.

Orla stomped inside the woodshed and bolted the door behind her. Then she poured herself a cup of acorn coffee and sat on her home-made chair to warm her feet by the fire. Her boots let off curls of steam into the damp air. Now and again, she peered outside. Captain stood with his foot held pitifully in the air. The ointment was slowly dripping through the linen. Orla thought of the speckled comfrey leaves and groaned. Her eyes darted to the wooden box beside the fire – the box that held Ma's book. But the time had long passed for checking recipes. She could do this by herself.

Dusk's falling, whispered the grass outside. *Birds are roosting.*

Can't wait another day – can't wait, called the dog rose.

Time to go, said the sage. *Time to go.*

Orla was fond of Captain, fond of his dark eyes and snuffling breath, though she would never tell anyone that. To other people, he was just a horse – good for keeping the grass short by the apple trees and for fertilizing the vegetable patches. But for Orla, he was a friend. Her only friend, apart from the plants. And she couldn't afford to lose him.

'Fine,' she said, eying the trees. 'Pine tar it is.'

2

Forest Pine *Pinus sylvestris*

Sap: for use as a disinfectant on shallow cuts and an insect repellent. Needles: a tea to reduce fever.

Orla followed a narrow trail towards the Borderwoods. It was little more than a deer path, winding alongside the creek. It was a longer route into the woods, but it kept her out of sight of the village. The marsh grasses were tall and straggling here, laced with cobwebs that caught the fog in little jewelled lines. The plants watched Orla, and they said little. They were not like the plants in the garden. They kept their secrets close, talking in gossiping whispers.

All alone, they muttered. *Where's your horse?*
Why not take the village path?
Trampling through marsh and mire.

Orla marched onwards. 'Anyone going to point me in the direction of a nice sappy pine?' she said aloud.

Autumn's here, replied the marsh grass.

'I know that,' said Orla with a huff, adjusting her pack and peering towards the gloomy woods ahead. 'What's got into you all? You could at least move out the way.'

As Orla rounded the bend, a blackbird swooped out of the scrubby grass, shouting as it went. Here, the creek wound towards the wood, skirting around the base of the hill that rose towards the village. Houses crept up the hillside, dimly lit with candles. At the top of the slope was the imposing figure of Hind House, three storeys tall, separated from the village by a wall and a gate flanked by two stone deer. The grounds of the house ran down to the creek in a wide, grassy lawn, which Orla approached with trepidation. Her secret path to the woods disappeared here, blocked first by the stone wall and then by the featureless lawn, interrupted only by a jetty sticking out into the dark water. Orla clambered over the wall and waited a moment, looking first at the pine trees beyond the lawn, and then at the house itself.

The curtains had not been drawn and, inside, Orla could see figures moving about in the lamplight. Looking in on the warm house made Orla feel suddenly cold out there in the fog. Hind House belonged to Inishowen Atlas, the Warden of Thorn Creek. He was the richest man in the village and that, Ma had said, was why the

Marshall of Westharbour trusted him to uphold the rules of the land. Ma had scoffed and rolled her eyes and told Orla it was the same in all the villages – men from the city *thinking they know what's best*. Atlas barely even visited; he spent so much time in Westharbour, but the house was grand nevertheless. It was home to Atlas's sister, Josephine Claw, and her daughter, a girl named Ariana. Orla knew for certain that up there, they dined on goose and cranberries and wine. She could almost smell it.

For a brief moment, Josephine Claw appeared at the window, her dress long and white. She gazed out at the river. With a faint shake of her head, she drew the curtains closed.

With one eye on the house, Orla darted across the lawn towards the woods.

Run quick!

Quiet, quiet!

Into the trees, into the dark.

The woods swallowed her like a calm ocean, full of gentle rustles and creaks and the *drip drip* of dew falling from leaves. Orla scanned the darkening trees for a pine among the ash, beech and oak. Then she closed her eyes to listen.

Deeper and deeper, they said.

Long time, wise girl, whispered a wild rose.

'See, you do remember me,' she said. 'It's not been that long.'

She felt her pulse rise, imagining herself as a bright-eyed hunter, as she had always done when she came to forage in the woods with Ma. While Ma collected morels and tinder fungus, Orla would run and run, waving a stick and wearing a Hauler-blue scarf round her neck. She'd never told Ma she'd played at being free like the Haulers, who came from every corner of the country to work on the riverboats in exchange for a scrap of gold. The Haulers, who'd called Ma 'mad-woman' and 'witch'. The Haulers, who'd buried her somewhere in the woods . . .

Watch your step, hissed the honeysuckle that curled between the trees.

Ahead, the pine trees stood thin and silent. Now and again they creaked in the wind, a steady groan running right down to their roots. In one of the pines, she spotted a knot of pale sap where an old limb had fallen. The sap had oozed out from the wound, clotting like amber blood.

'Right,' said Orla, stepping up and placing her hand gently on the trunk. 'I'm going to take a little sap, if you please. It's for my horse's foot. It's gone gammy and he might die. Thank you.'

Orla swung herself up and scrambled through the branches. At the knot she unhooked her saw. It was a little rusty and the blade wobbled, but it would do. The pine did not object in any way that she could hear, so she sawed away at a fist-sized lump of hardened sap, the blade slipping easily into it. She continued until her sack was filled with sweet-smelling chunks.

Then she wiped her forehead and tucked the saw back over her shoulder.

'There,' she said, patting the trunk. 'Got what I need.'

She paused. As her hand came away from the tree, she noticed a faint, blackish stain on the bark, as if someone had marked it with ink. Orla shook her head. It was getting dark and the shadows were playing tricks on her eyes.

The wind had risen a little now, and the fog curled away with it – replaced by dark shadows of night falling. The tree creaked and groaned and cautiously, Orla lowered herself, letting her feet swing to feel for the branches below. It was only as she looked down that she saw the distinctive blue coat moving beneath her.

A Hauler.

Instinctively, she pressed her face close to the trunk and held tight to a stem of ivy.

'What's he doing?' she whispered.

Searching, said the ivy. *Lost*.

Orla peered down into the gloom. The Hauler moved here and there, his eyes fixed on the ground. He was moving cautiously, as though something was wrong with his legs, and he looked young for a Hauler – no more than a teenager. His hair twisted in soft curls, with no hint of grey like most of the men. Orla thought that his face looked familiar – but it was hard to see in the dim light. He stumbled towards her tree and she caught the scent of woodsmoke on his coat, river mud, too. And something else – something that smelt like damp and decay and fever.

The Hauler did not see the root across his path. He tripped, steadying himself against the trunk of Orla's pine. His breath was ragged, and she could see beads of sweat beneath his curls. His eyes glistened in the damp air, looking up into the branches.

Orla froze, her heart pounding. She could feel her palms wet against the tree as she struggled to hold still. She closed her eyes slowly, trying her best to blend in with the darkening woods. The Hauler sighed, cursed and then – finally, stumbled away.

Orla waited, then eased herself down through the branches. 'You shoulda warned me,' she said to the ivy, crouching down to examine the root which had tripped up the Hauler. It was soft and black, like the bark where she had cut the sap.

She gritted her teeth, feeling suddenly cold in the darkening woods. She could hear the sound of the creek flowing through the marshes, the trees murmuring.

'There's something you're not telling me,' she said to the plants.

The forest did not reply. Orla clenched her fists

around her saw. Her hands were shaking.

'You gotta let me know what's going on,' she said, as sparks of anger began to flit and flicker through her. But she knew it was no good. The plants could only tell her what they saw, not how they felt.

'Fine,' she said. '*Keep your secrets*. I'll work it out by myself.' Her cheeks were burning. The branches reached out like hands in front of her face and Orla swatted them out of the way as she strode through the trees. Nothing was going right. The plants in her garden had told her to come here, but they couldn't tell her what was going on either. Were the black marks on the pine tree the same as the marks on the comfrey leaves?

Emerging from the undergrowth, Orla found herself below Hind House once more. Hurrying across the lawn, she saw that a lamp swung from the jetty now, lit with a dancing orange flame. A Hauler boat was tied up, drifting among the reeds. She looked back towards the woods, wondering how far the Hauler had wandered from his boat.

Not right, whispered the river weeds at Orla's feet. *Not right at all . . .*

Eyes wide, she scrambled down to the water's edge and ran her hands through the long sharp stems of the river grass.

Not right at all, it echoed.

Orla took a sharp breath. It wasn't just the comfrey in

her garden, or the pine in the forest, that was affected. Here, the plants were so covered in marks that their stems had turned entirely black.

The Hauler boat gave a heavy *thunk* against the jetty, and Orla realized her heart was racing. There was something wrong with the plants in Thorn Creek, and she had no idea what to do about it.

3

Sage Salvia officinalis
Steep leaves in hot water to soothe the throat.

Plants get sick, Ma had told her. *Just like people.*

Orla knew that. The earth in Thorn Creek was damp, and it was not strange for crops to struggle. There was fireblight and leaf rust, and potato rot too. Plum blossom could wilt, apples could canker. But Ma had known what to do. She and Orla had taken care of the garden like birds weaving their nests. They'd spent afternoons cutting back old apple branches so that new ones could grow; plucking fallen herbs to dry by the fire; carefully collecting seeds from old flowers to spread around the village on their walks, so that bright flowers popped up in spring. Ma could spot a single leaf that didn't look right, and she'd prune it away so the plant could grow strong. But this was nothing like anything that Orla had ever seen. No sickness had ever touched the plants in her garden *and* those in the Borderwoods beyond.

She'd make the pine tar; that'd take her mind off the sick plants. Captain was snoozing against the woodshed, trying to keep his weight off his bad foot. Orla gave him a scratch on the neck and went inside to search for a pot. Dust and spiders coated the ground floor of her home, where she kept a stack of seasoned logs and Ma's chair by the stove. Above, a small room was reached by a ladder, where Orla had a straw mattress beneath the roof. The mattress had been big enough for her and Ma together, piled comfortably with woollen blankets. There was even a little window, made from glass Ma had brought back from one of her trips. From there Orla could watch over the garden, and keep an eye on nosy neighbours – Ariana Claw peering through the hedges with her wide eyes and neat blond curls; old Elias Dawson traipsing over to offer her things that she didn't need.

Orla unearthed an old pot from beneath a pile of blankets. It was too big for her little stove, so she dragged it outside and put it on top of the metal stand she used for fires. She lit a fire beneath the pot, tipped in the pine sap and hoped for the best.

It was starting to rain, fat warm drops, and Orla took shelter beneath the porch beside Captain's warm shoulders, watching the fire spit and spark.

'Pine tar, indeed,' she said to the plants. 'All very well saying pine tar, but you could've told me how to make it.' It didn't look right. She was struggling to keep the fire stoked in the rain without scorching the tar on the bottom of the pot. 'How do I know when it's ready?' she said, poking it with a stick. But there was no response.

'Fine. You're sulking,' she said. 'How was I supposed to know?'

Ma would have known, said the wormwood.

Orla pulled her knife out of her pocket and jabbed it towards the wormwood.

'You be quiet about Ma,' she said. 'Why can't you be more like the ivy?'

The wormwood fell silent. Orla knew that all the plants had their purpose. The ivy was wise, the comfrey was faithful, and the wormwood – well. The wormwood always told her the things she didn't want to hear, even if she knew that she should.

Her eyes flickered indoors to the box that held Ma's book.

'Just needs ash, that's all,' she said, scooping up a handful from the pail by the door, and stirring it into the sticky tar.

'That foot don't look right,' said a gruff voice from the hedgerow.

It was Elias Dawson, hunched in the gateway, where the honeysuckle and ivy grew in an arch between two

19

hawthorn trees. He had thick sideburns that joined up with his eyebrows, and he looked weathered like he'd been in the water too long – the damp air of Thorn Creek did this to most people who lived there all their lives. He was holding a hessian sack. Orla sighed. Elias was a chandler, making candles from beeswax for the villagers, and oil lamps for Hauler boats. Ma had left her with him and his wife Agnes when she'd taken trips to Fleetwater and Westharbour. Orla had had enough of Elias's help for a lifetime.

'What do you want?' she said, giving the pine tar another stir.

'Maybe you should try what they been using on the coach horses up at Hind House,' said Elias, rain dripping from his eyebrows. 'Black pitch, or something like that. Heard it works wonders.'

'I'm not using *anything* they think is good up at Hind House,' said Orla, pulling her hood over her head and turning back to the fire. The tar was bubbling into a dark, sticky glue. She pulled the pot away from the flame so that the pine tar could cool.

'Brought you oats from Marianne Reed,' said Elias, waving the sack.

'I told you we don't need 'em,' Orla replied. 'We've got enough food in the garden.'

Elias unlatched the wooden gate and ducked beneath the thorns.

'I'll just leave it here,' he said, putting the bag on Orla's chopping log.

'We don't need 'em,' mumbled Orla again, pulling up Captain's hoof between her knees and scraping the tar on to it. Captain sniffed it and wrinkled his nose.

'Yes, you do,' said Elias. 'Your ma asked—'

Orla let down Captain's hoof with a *clunk* and swung round to face Elias.

'She didn't ask you to interfere,' she said. 'We're *fine*.'

'We're just keeping an eye out,' said Elias. 'Like we told Elizabeth we would.'

'And we all know how well that worked out,' said Orla, pursing her lips. She folded her arms and waited for Elias to leave.

But he didn't move.

'You should heed my words, Orla,' he said at last. 'Haven't you heard what they're saying?'

'About Ma?' snapped Orla. 'Saying she didn't know what she was doing? Saying she's a fraud? I hear that every day, no thanks to you.'

A shadow passed over Elias's face. 'They're saying there's a sickness with the plants,' he said. 'I heard it from Callahan Reed up at the White Hart, no word of a lie. They're saying the plants—'

'Gossip,' interrupted Orla. 'Just like it always is. The plants are fine.'

'No sick plants? Well, you're lucky, then.'

21

'Ma knew what she was doing. I know what I'm doing. I can handle it.'

Elias sighed. 'Perhaps you gotta admit your ma didn't know everything, Orla. After what happened at Hind House . . .'

Orla felt her eyes prickle unexpectedly. Everyone always thought they knew what had happened with Ma. After Ma had left her with Elias and Agnes, in their too-small house up in the village. Before it had all gone wrong. She tossed the bag of oats under the porch and marched over to the gate. Elias shook the water from his cap and opened his mouth, as though he wanted to say something comforting.

'I don't need your opinions,' said Orla, pushing the gate closed behind him so quickly that her hands caught in the brambly hedge. 'And I don't need no more oats!' she called after Elias as he disappeared down the dark lane. 'The garden's fine. *We're* fine.'

Sharp thorns, said the brambles, as Orla untangled herself.

'Tell me about it,' she said, licking a scratch on the back of her hand and turning back to Captain, who had his nose in the oat bag.

'*Don't* eat those,' she warned. 'They gotta last.' As she pulled the sack away from him, it caught under his foot and tore in two. Orla kicked the pot and watched as the flames sparked and spat. The smell of burnt pine filled the air.

Autumn's here, said the ivy.

Rain's coming, said the daisies, closing their flowers tight.

No food, no leaves, no medicine, said the wormwood.

Orla crouched down to look at the stem of the wormwood. It was speckled and dark like the rest. Elias was right. The plants were right. Without the plants, she would have no food or medicine for herself, or Captain.

And no friends, said the wormwood sharply.

The rain was coming down hard when Orla went out to check on Captain's foot. The fire had burnt low, and the garden was dark save for the glowing orange coals. Captain was chewing peacefully below the porch. The plants murmured in a steady rhythm among the raindrops, murmuring and muttering about the wind and the rain and the dark, dark river. The blackthorn hedge piped up as Orla came out into the garden.

Someone here, it said.

Orla tensed. She couldn't *see* anyone.

The plants rustled in the wind.

Someone here, said the brambles, readying their thorns.

Someone here, said the nettles, their needles glistening.

Orla seized the stick that she kept by the door, and lifted her lamp to light the garden.

There was a boy standing next to Captain. He was stocky and brown-haired, and his eyes shone in the lamplight.

It was Idris Romero, a Hauler's son.

He patted Captain calmly, but did not say hello.

'Get away from my horse,' said Orla fiercely. 'I don't know how you got in here, but get out. This is private property.'

'I'm not after your stupid horse,' he said.

'I don't need no Hauler coming on to my property, telling me what to do.'

'I'm not a Hauler,' he said.

'You got the coat,' she said. 'And your legs are soaked to hell, too. You creep in by the river, toad?'

Orla felt something acid rise in her throat. He looked like one of them, with his blue coat and his weather-worn face. The men that rode the river, trading skins and grain and anything else they could find – taking boats up the river and into the mountains, or out across the sea. Idris and his brother Castor had been in Thorn Creek as long as Orla – perhaps longer. Their Hauler pa worked out in Westharbour and sent them gold once a month, or so Orla had overheard in the village. She curled her fists and looked him dead in the eye.

'Get outta my garden,' she said.

Idris glared back at her. He was fierce, that was for sure. But there was something else in his expression that

Orla could not read. Was it fear? His brow crinkled slightly. Then he shook his head.

'You gotta come with me,' he said. 'Honest to God.'

'Why should I go with a *Hauler*?' Orla growled.

Idris leant into the lamplight.

'My brother, Castor. He knows why your plants are sick. And if you come with me, he'll tell you.'

4

Bog Myrtle *Myrica gale*
Keeps the midges away; tea for arthritis.

They came to a house on the creek bank, half a mile away from the village. It was almost as small as Orla's woodshed, low to the ground, as though it were made from the bank itself. Orla and Idris ducked through the door. A lamp lit the floor of woven reed mats, where a body lay, hair curling softly. With a jolt, Orla recognized the Hauler she'd seen in the woods. She had not seen Castor in a year, perhaps longer, and now – he looked like a different person. His face was gaunt, his eyes cloudy. She recoiled at the sight of him, quick as though she'd touched hot iron.

'He's sick,' she said furiously. 'You didn't tell me he was sick.'

'I seen you with the plants,' said Idris, suddenly sounding desperate. 'You know what they do – you know their medicine. I seen you – medicining those birds and animals you found. I seen you with the horse. Now you're gonna use that wit and make my brother better. No one else can do that.'

'Whatever you think I can do, you got it wrong,' said Orla, looking around the room. She had expected furs and gems and strings of salt fish, but Idris's house was dark and sombre, a single room with walls thick with soot, filled with nets and hooks and oilskins tidily arranged on the walls. There was no sign that an adult lived there. A fishing net lay on a small wooden table, mid-repair – and Orla wondered if Idris had made it himself.

Idris knelt beside his brother.

'Please,' he said. 'I found him in the creek.'

Orla swallowed. Everything was telling her to run. But she had to know the truth. If Castor could explain why the plants were sick, then she had to find out what he knew. But he did not look like he could say a word. He was drenched in sweat and silent as grave bones. His face was an ashy grey, his lips dry and cracked.

'He shouldn't have gone,' said Idris, wrapping the blankets around his brother's shoulders. 'He shouldn't have.'

'He needs hot water,' said Orla. 'You can light a fire in

this hole, can't you?'

Idris nodded. Dragging his eyes away from his brother, he stooped over a stove in the corner. The hut was damp, as though all the heat had left with their pa, wherever he was.

In spite of herself, Orla knelt down beside Castor. He groaned, moving his lips, as though he was trying to say something. The veins on his temple stood out from his skin like the webbing on a dead leaf. He wasn't going to tell her anything.

'Ask someone else,' she said, getting to her feet. 'Ask your Hauler friends. I'm not the one you need. You know I don't make medicine for people, not without Ma. Animals only. That's the rule.'

Idris wrung his hands, his eyes darting around the little hut.

'He's my brother,' he said. 'I thought you'd understand.'

'Well, I don't,' said Orla.

'It's true what they say, then, is it?' said Idris. 'That your ma never really knew how to help those people, and neither do you. All that herb medicine, it's all pretending.'

'She didn't *pretend*,' growled Orla. 'You're the one that lied. You told me Castor knew why my plants were sick. But he can't say a word and you know it.'

Orla was shaking now. She shouldn't have come.

Castor reached out a bony hand and grabbed Orla by the ankle.

'*The river*,' he said in a hoarse whisper, as though his throat were made of bark.

Idris rushed to Castor, pulling his face towards him.

'What did you say?' he said desperately. 'Castor!'

'Leave him!' said Orla. 'Can't you see it hurts for him to talk?'

But Castor had opened his eyes. 'The river!' he insisted.

'He needs water,' said Orla.

'Tell me!' said Idris. 'Where did you go?'

'The river!' said Castor again. He was tossing and turning so much that Idris had to hold him still – he was trying to get up.

'The river!' he cried out. 'The mountains . . . pitch black . . .' He tried to get the words out, but his lips quaked and his limbs shook.

Idris was frantic. 'He says there's something—'

'Idris, it's the fever talking!'

'It's not – he's trying to tell me something important. I know my brother,' he said fiercely.

'I can't help you,' said Orla, fastening her oilskin.

'You can't leave!' said Idris.

'He's not gonna tell me anything about my plants. Can't you see how sick he is? People with fever like this don't get better,' said Orla, moving towards the door.

Idris darted after her. 'You have to help him.'

'You lied to get me here,' said Orla, as Idris tried to

block her exit. 'You told me he knew about my plants. But you knew I don't help people. You know that's my one rule. Everyone knows it. But you fooled me into coming here – typical Hauler. He's dying, and there's nothing I can do about it.'

Idris's face was a storm of fear and confusion and hate. The sympathy Orla had felt before now slipped away. He was just one of them, dressing up in his Hauler coat. He wanted to be like them. And Haulers deserved everything they got.

Idris called after her, his voice choked: 'I thought you'd know what it's like.'

Orla remembered the cold day when Ma had come back on a riverboat – from Fleetwater, or Westharbour, her arms filled with dried herbs. She'd scooped Orla up from Elias's house, and by the time they'd reached the woodshed Ma's skin was feverish and damp. *It's normally me who makes the tea, isn't it, Orla?* she'd said, as Orla mixed honey and feverfew and sage. She'd crumbled the herbs into balms and infusions and tinctures. But nothing Orla made took away Ma's fever. Nothing made her better. And before she knew it, Ma was gone – just a pale figure in the distance, carried out into the woods by the Haulers to be buried. Carried out there to keep the village safe.

'Just because we're the only kids on our own here, don't mean we have to be friends,' said Orla to Idris.

'You're still a Hauler. And it's because of you my ma's dead. It's because of you she's buried out there in the woods and not in the garden where she belongs. You're on your own.'

The words felt like steel on her tongue. Orla knew Ma would never have used those words. Ma had always said that the plants were for everyone. It wasn't Idris, or even his brother, who had taken Ma away from her. But they were Haulers, and that was enough.

Orla ran into the dark. Only the stars peeked down from above the trees, judging her. She scowled up at them, tears spilling hot and heavy down her face. They knew the truth: even if she wanted to help Idris, she couldn't. Ma had travelled far and wide making medicine, from Fleetwater to Westharbour. She'd known how to help the sick. But Orla never could – not even when it mattered the most.

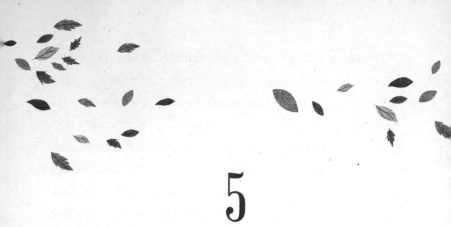

5

Foxglove *Digitalis purpurea*
Highly toxic. For conditions of the heart.

The next morning Orla hurried through the crowd towards the wooden chapel, ducking between people with yellowed teeth and hair as thin as thistle-down. Gnarled faces and weather-worn clothes blocked her view. Mules laden with sacks of grey linen stood in her path. Every person in Thorn Creek had joined the current of people flowing towards the market. And on every street corner, Orla saw a Hauler in a dark-blue coat, watching and waiting. It made her bones feel cold. *They look like wolves,* she thought. *Lurking around like that.*

'Watch it!' snapped Eve, the tavern-maid, as Orla knocked against her.

Pay attention! said the scraps of dandelion between the cobbles.

'Stupid market,' said Orla. 'Shouldn't have come.'

She set her hands into the thick ivy that grew up the side of the chapel, and climbed. Perching on the roof, she surveyed the market. In the drizzle, the stalls looked like slaughtered beasts: fur upon fur lay on the wooden tables, while men and women in heavy coats prowled around sizing up the value of a bundle or a skin. Each pelt was threadbare and torn – covered in scorch marks and brands. Sometimes there was otter or marten, but mostly Orla saw moth-eaten scraps of squirrel and beaver. The best were taken to Westharbour for real money. Orla checked her pack. With her hood over her head, she'd skirted round the market stalls, swapping a coin here and there for dried venison and salt beef without saying a word.

Needed food, said the ivy kindly.

Orla grunted. Since Elias had brought her the bag of oats, she'd found her potatoes at the bottom of the garden had rotted in the ground. The summer corn beside them had blackened too, and the pumpkin flowers had withered away to nothing. Huddling on the rooftop, she bit into a salty strip of deer meat and surveyed the market. Even up here, she could still make out the sound of the villagers gossiping, their voices scurrying around the market like chattering rats.

'It ain't right,' said a woman with hair like cobwebs. 'Reminds me of what happened at Hind House that time.'

'Where she let those people die, you mean?' said another, as she shook moths from a scrap of pelt she'd just bought. One landed in her hair.

'She was supposed to be helping them, so they say,' said the cobwebby woman. 'But I think she never did know what she was doing.'

'Nor I,' said the moth lady. 'Women shouldn't meddle in such affairs.'

Orla blocked her ears and chewed furiously on the tough venison. Raindrops began to fall, thick and heavy, and the sky rumbled.

Season's changing, said the rowan tree that stood next to Dawson & Reed, the small shop where Elias sold his candles.

From her position on the roof, Orla could see a string of boats ploughing along the dark river beyond the village. Haulers, coming from the east. It made her shiver to think of them travelling up and down the river, turning up in places they shouldn't. She wondered where Castor had truly been. Her stomach twisted when she thought of his gaunt face. Is that what Ma had looked like when she was sick, all alone?

Thunder rumbled again, and the market folk looked uncertainly at the sky. Orla's skin prickled. She saw

Callahan Reed, long-haired and bearded, talking with Elias, passing a candlestick to a customer. She saw Josephine Claw, wrapped in an ornate shawl, hovering at the edge of the market, faint as a ghost, watching the world passing by. Something caught Josephine's attention and she turned to look out towards the bridge beyond the marketplace – the Westharbour road.

Someone's coming, said the ivy on the wall. *Dark coat, dark horses. Out towards the road. Over the great bridge.*

Orla heard the clatter of a coach and horses in the distance, sharp and loud as a blacksmith's hammer, ringing out over the river. It was not a good sound. Most people came to Thorn Creek by boat, for it was cheaper and you could hitch a ride with a Hauler taking his load down to Westharbour. There were not many who could afford a coach and horses to travel the rough and winding road, where forest beasts roamed, picking off anyone who thought that walking was an option. You needed money to travel by road and survive.

The whole village held its breath, listening to the rattle of the coach approaching, the snort of the horses and the shouts of the coachman.

It was as though a wild animal had entered the square: men leapt aside, their hats flying as they dodged the stamping hooves of the horses. One man's leg became trapped beneath a wheel. Another cried out, for the coachman had hit him with his whip to stop him peering into the coach. It ground to a halt beneath the looming bell tower. The horses steamed and tossed their heads.

From Westharbour, said the hawthorn around the square.

Orla felt a rush of foreboding. The sky seemed to press so low on Thorn Creek that she thought the whole village might be swallowed up into the clouds. A warm breeze tossed the rowan trees and ruffled the feathers of the rooks that gathered in the bell tower. There was a Hauler standing by the coach now. He had hulking, broad shoulders and a creased brow that reminded Orla of a bull. A little way behind him, she saw Idris, leaning against the ironmonger's stall. He caught her eye, and then quickly looked at the ground.

The leaves in the hedge behind the chapel began to whisper.

Best not be seen, they said. *Best hide away.*

Orla flattened herself against the roof, edging forward to peer over the gutter. She had to know.

The crowd parted as a man stepped out of the coach, and Orla recognized him with a jolt. It was the Warden, Inishowen Atlas of Hind House, come back to Thorn Creek. He strode over to the steps of the chapel.

He was thin, and younger than most of the Haulers, though he had lines around his eyes and his brown hair was streaked with grey. Beneath his wool coat he wore a fine suit. He was not a Hauler, but he paid them, and that was just as bad. Why had the coach brought him here to the market square and not taken him straight to Hind House? Josephine Claw watched her brother from the steps, a thin frown creasing her forehead.

Atlas whispered something to the bullish man. Then he raised his head, and addressed the village.

'This market is to be closed,' he announced.

A murmur ran through the crowd.

'There is a sickness coming,' he continued. 'It threatens to carry you shivering into death, if you do not heed these orders. It has been seen in Westharbour and it has been seen in Fleetwater, and before long it will reach Thorn Creek. We must take precautions – starting with the closure of this market. The Marshall of Westharbour has ordered it.'

Orla felt a cold sensation running down her spine. Did Atlas know about Castor? Had others in the village fallen sick as he had?

'But it's my livelihood!' cried a woman from behind her stall.

'What about our money?' called the butcher.

Orla felt a surge of hatred, as though it were in her very blood. Atlas only ever came back to Thorn Creek to interfere with the lives of the villagers, or to find a new way to make money.

He raised his hand to calm the crowd.

'Wherever there is sickness, there is rumour,' he said. 'But I am here to tell you the scientific truth of the matter. This sickness is not brought about by witchcraft or sin. No. This sickness has come from a place of disease and pestilence. It has come from the *wild*.'

He spat the word out as though he couldn't stand it in his mouth. His lip curled.

The villagers looked towards the woods and the wilderness around Thorn Creek. Some were whispering, some were nodding.

'We must be rid of it,' said Atlas. 'The plants, the weeds, the swamp, the forest, the *wild gardens*. Disease lurks among the plants and the wild things, breeding mosquitoes and poisons.'

Orla scowled. Where had he got this 'scientific truth' from? No one had ever got sick from living near the wild. People got sick from eating rotten meat, or drinking from a bad well. Perhaps a poisonous plant in the wrong hands, or grains afflicted with rye rot. But to say every plant was a danger – that was not right at all.

'The Marshall of Westharbour has advised that the sickness will be here within the week. Protect your families and protect your children,' Atlas went on. 'If we clear the village, we will live longer and healthier lives. We will not succumb to this disease. Start with those weeds! Cut them down and burn them, so they do not spread! Silas – proceed!'

The bull-like Hauler beside him drew a hatchet from his belt, and began hacking at the ivy stem that grew thick against the chapel wall. Orla flinched as she heard the screeching cry of a plant cut without good reason.

Atlas gazed across the marketplace. 'We cannot afford to let this sickness destroy our village,' he said. 'We must *all* clear our land. It is a necessary precaution.'

Orla's heart thudded. He meant the plants: all of them. He meant *her* garden. The garden she'd grown with Ma. A ripple of fear ran through each and every leaf around her. Orla snapped her eyes away from Atlas and climbed down from the roof. She needed to get back to the garden. Hurrying through the crowd, she pushed past market stalls and baskets of firewood and Haulers at every corner.

'Pull it all up,' she heard one say, pointing to a straggly patch of fleabane outside the tavern. 'Burn it.'

A rat-faced Hauler pulled a flask from his hip and emptied it on to the plants. With a flick of his fire-lighter, he set the plants alight. The flames licked into the air. He took out a saw and set about cutting into the trunk of the rowan tree outside Dawson & Reed. Orla felt a sharp pain in her chest as the tree toppled and the Hauler dragged it towards the fire.

They are destroying everything! cried the plants. *Fierce hands and fire!*

Mud flew in Orla's face as she ran downhill, past the

patchwork gardens and vegetable plots, where already the villagers were cutting down their plants. And her heart gave way as she heard the sharpening of axes and the slicing of blades.

When she reached the garden, she knew that it was too late.

The gate had been pushed down, ripped away from the bramble and the hawthorn trees. There was a Hauler in her garden, a scythe in his hand.

We're sorry, called the plants that had clung so tightly to the gateway. *We're so sorry, Orla.*

6

Rosemary *Rosmarinus officinalis*
Leaves: tea, for remembrance.

The Hauler grinned when he saw Orla. He was toothless and grey, and wore a flat woollen cap. The wooden handle of his scythe was worn smooth from use. Orla was so furious that, at first, she could not speak.

'Get on with it!' he called, his voice rough with smoke. Another man, skinny as a sapling, was standing a little way down the garden, beneath the apple trees. Next to him, Captain was chewing his way through the fallen apples. 'What's taking you so long?'

'He won't lift his head, Bouchard!' called the other man.

'Just do it, Leblanc!' called the toothless Hauler. 'Master Silas is waiting.'

The grass flickered at Orla's feet. *Stay calm*, it said.

Orla was not calm. 'Get your filthy hands off him!' she shouted, running towards Captain. But something snagged her sleeve, and she stumbled. The tip of the Hauler's scythe was caught in her oilskin.

'Get off me,' she said. 'And get out of my garden.'

Bouchard stepped towards her, placing his boot quite deliberately on a small buttercup.

Help us! it cried faintly.

Men and blades, called the wormwood.

Searching, searching, said the daisies.

'You're getting in the way of our work, young miss,' he said. Orla caught a whiff of his breath then, stinking of salted fish and ale.

She shrank away from him, unhooking the scythe from her coat.

'That's my horse,' she said.

The man called Leblanc was now striding up the garden, dragging Captain behind him. There was a sharp scent of herbs as they trampled through the rosemary.

'You ain't got the right!' cried Orla, jamming her fingers into her ears as Leblanc crushed the marigolds and honesty Ma had sown for cut flowers. The plants were screaming now, sending waves through every stem and root.

'Warden's orders,' said Bouchard. 'You can have him back once you've cleared the garden. After a period of *quarantine*. Do it by the end of the week, or we'll do it for you.'

Clear the garden? It was so ridiculous that Orla stifled a laugh. 'Is this a joke?' she said to the Hauler. 'I'm not clearing anything.'

Bouchard lowered his scythe. With the softest sweep, he let it slice through the grass.

The whole garden shivered.

'We'll be back,' he said. He smiled a thin, toothless smile and wiped the green stain from his scythe with his sleeve. 'Leblanc! Let's go.'

Captain had planted his feet firmly in the ground. Leblanc pulled a stick from Orla's runner beans, and with a *thwack* he hit him on the hindquarters. Orla winced. Captain took a reluctant step forward.

'I told you, you're not taking him,' said Orla through her teeth. She stepped in front of the fallen gate, blocking the exit to the garden, and folded her arms.

'Move,' said Bouchard.

'No,' said Orla, as Leblanc pulled Captain towards her.

Duck! warned the water mint. But it was too late. Bouchard's arms were around her. Orla tried to kick out, but he had lifted her clean off the ground. She scratched and bit at his coat, but it was tough cloth and he took no notice.

'It ain't polite for young girls to get in the way,' he grunted. 'You sort out your garden, like you been told.'

Captain was looking at Orla, his ears pricked, as though asking why she was letting this happen. She felt a tugging sensation beneath her ribs.

'No!' she groaned, as Leblanc led Captain straight over the broken gate. 'Let me go!'

Bouchard only tightened his grip. Orla kicked her feet hopelessly. She could feel Captain's warm breath as he passed and stretched out his nose to her, but she could not reach him.

Not fair, whispered the rosemary. *Not right.*

'Get the beast gone,' Bouchard said.

Once again Leblanc raised his stick and brought it down hard on Captain's flank. The horse gave Orla one last look, and slowly followed Leblanc.

Biting down on Bouchard's hand, Orla slipped free. 'I'm not letting you take him,' she cried, racing towards the gateway. But something large and solid blocked her way. Moving too quickly to stop, Orla collided hard with it and fell to the ground with a thud. Clutching her ribs, she looked up at an enormous figure. It was the bullish Hauler from the market. He spoke with a voice like gravel, barely more than a whisper.

'Trouble?' he said to Bouchard, as Orla wiped the dirt from her face and brushed the grass from her hair.

'No, Master Silas,' said Bouchard hastily, lifting his cap and wiping his own sweating brow.

Orla pulled herself to her feet. 'I'm just off to get my

horse back, if you don't mind.' She tried to slip past the enormous man, but he reached out a lazy hand and pulled her back. Up close, Orla could see the whites of Silas's eyes were stained yellow. He smelt strongly of stale sweat and pipe smoke and something metallic that Orla didn't recognize.

'I don't think so, poppet,' he said, squinting into the rain. Thick drops of water ran down his face, but he did not wipe them away. 'You're coming with me.'

7

Thorn Apple *Datura stramonium*

Approach cautiously, for it is highly toxic and may lead to death. For surgery; a sedative.

Hind House loomed over the garden. The lamps inside had already been lit and the windows of the house looked down on Orla like great glowing eyes. Silas led her along the winding path, through clusters of rose bushes that snickered and gossiped to each other as Orla brushed against them, sending out clouds of heady perfume into the gloom. Orla dragged her feet. She had never been inside Hind House, and she wanted to keep it that way. Ma had been here, of course, coming to tend the sick many years ago. Back when the rumours had started.

Little girl lost, snickered the roses.

All alone, they said.

'Move,' said Silas.

They were high enough on the hill that Orla could see the broad sweep of the river down below, its surface a glimmer in the dim afternoon light. A cluster of lanterns moved like fireflies along the bank, a steady stream of Haulers moving between the jetty and the road to Hind House. Orla could hear the men grunting and shouting.

'What are they doing?' she asked Silas.

'Get on with you,' he said in his quiet, gravelly tone, pushing her into the shadow of the house. The garden rustled, and Orla felt suddenly apprehensive. *This must be how a mouse feels*, she thought. *Chased into a corner.*

An enormous oak door stood before them.

'*In,*' grunted Silas, pushing open the door.

As he led her down the hallway, her eyes darted around the wood-panelled passage, searching for a way out. But there was none. After passing several closed doors and paintings of what looked to Orla like half-dead flowers, they arrived in a study. There was a fireplace, and a desk stacked with books, behind which sat Inishowen Atlas, still wearing his coat.

He did not look up as Orla tumbled into the room. He was scribbling so furiously with his pen that blots of blue ink flew into the air and landed like rain on the page. Orla wondered if Ma had been into this room when she came to Hind House. It seemed so polished and solid, nothing like their little windblown shed, where plants tried to find their way into every crack and corner.

'You said to bring anyone who resisted straight to you, Warden, sir,' said Silas.

Still Atlas did not look up. He merely carried on writing in the ledger in front of him.

Orla glanced around the room. It was filled with polished wooden cabinets, stacked with neatly tied piles of paper. Behind Atlas, Orla noticed a door, slightly ajar, and beyond that, the shimmer of light on glass. You hardly ever saw glass in Thorn Creek, for it was mighty expensive. Fleetwater was the place for glass, Ma had told her. But in that little room behind Atlas, Orla saw at least a hundred glass jars and vases, all arranged on wooden shelves in glittering lines. The Atlas family had made their fortune in ink, so Ma had said. And in that room Orla could see a dozen or more colours: from the blackest pitch to a brilliant rose pink.

'The horse has been quarantined,' said Silas, breaking the silence.

'For no reason!' interrupted Orla. 'Captain belongs to me and you got no right to take him.'

'The horse is diseased,' said Atlas mildly, without looking up. *Scratch, scratch*, went the pen. 'And anyway, didn't you steal him in the first place?'

'He's not diseased,' said Orla. 'He got an infected foot from stepping on something. And actually, I found him.

The farmers were going to shoot him.'

She didn't mention that she happened to take Captain before they'd technically said she could.

'Oh, and how would you know that?' said Atlas, now looking at Orla, his pen paused in mid-air. A drop of ink dripped ominously on to his paper. 'You are a child: ignorant, and unschooled.'

'I most certainly am not!' she said, lunging forward with every intention of seizing Atlas's ink pot and throwing it across the room. But Silas grabbed her by the shoulders and Orla felt herself pulled backwards with a jerk.

Atlas set down his pen with a sigh.

'You have spent too long in the wild,' he stated. 'You have been told to clear the garden and that you may have your horse back once that is complete, and only then after a certain period of quarantine to ensure that he is not diseased.'

Orla clenched her fists. 'My horse isn't diseased. My plants aren't either.'

'Oh, but they are,' said Atlas, rising from his chair. 'People touch the wild, then they touch each other. That's how it spreads, and I intend to stop it.'

'There's nothing wrong with my garden,' lied Orla, thinking of the dark spots on the comfrey leaves. If there was a problem with the plants, it certainly wasn't for Atlas to deal with.

'I am the Warden of this village,' said Atlas. 'My role is to inform the people of Thorn Creek about the dangers of the outside world, and to provide a solution.'

Orla felt the heat rise in her cheeks. This was wrong.

'You mean telling people to cut down their crops so that they starve over winter?'

'For their own good!' said Atlas, a vein in his temple beginning to pulse.

'I lived near the wild this whole time,' said Orla. 'And I never seen anyone get sick.'

Atlas looked at her with piercing eyes. 'Except for your mother,' he said sharply. 'And the people she failed to save. Two men died in this house because of her. I don't have time to argue the science of the matter with a child,' he said, closing his ledger with a snap. 'Silas, take her away.'

'She didn't get sick from the wild!' insisted Orla. 'She got sick from your stupid *men*. The people you forced her to help.'

'And who made them sick in the first place?' said Atlas. 'Who came out of the wild into our village, messing about with plants and medicines and things they shouldn't?'

Perhaps, in hindsight, Orla should have known that it is sometimes better to keep your knowledge a secret than to prove that you are right. But injustice burnt through her, and in that moment she would have breathed fire on Atlas if she could. He had always been so wrong about Ma.

'Ma knew what she was doing,' said Orla fiercely. 'Ma knew her plants and her herbs, and she'd never have let this happen. If she wasn't buried in those woods, I bet she'd know how to fix this. It's all there, in her book. She had it all written down. It's *science*.'

Atlas's expression changed then, just for a moment. His eyes sharpened, like the eyes of a hawk. It was the look of a predator, Orla thought. The look of someone who would not stop until they had found what they were looking for.

'Is that so?' he said carefully. For a moment Orla thought he was going to ask her something more. But then he picked up his hat, placed it on his head and said, 'I think your mother had no idea what she was meddling with. I think she went too close to the wild, and the wild put an end to her. That's the *science* of it.'

Orla swallowed hard. It felt as though Atlas had slid something sharp and ice-cold into her heart. But she did not want him to know that. She bit her tongue, and tried to pull herself together, as if she were facing down a mountain lion.

'I'll prove it's not the plants,' she said. 'I'll prove Captain isn't diseased. Then you'll give him back, and you'll leave my garden alone.'

For a moment, Orla thought she saw a shadow pass behind Atlas's eyes. But he blinked, and turned to Silas, who gave the slightest nod. Orla felt the prickle of goose pimples on her arms.

'You will prove nothing,' he said, reverting to his mild tone. 'You will clear your garden, and you will not set foot in Hind House again. That will be all.' He wiped the nib of his ink pen on a piece of cloth and began buttoning his greatcoat. 'I assume the men are ready,' he murmured to Silas.

'Cargo's almost loaded,' said Silas.

Atlas sighed, and lifted his collar.

'Get rid of the girl,' he said. 'Then take me down to the boats.'

Silas shoved Orla out of the room.

'You clear that garden,' he said, as he tossed her out on to the doorstep.

'I'll do it,' she lied.

The door closed with a *thunk* behind her, and Orla was left alone. A row of rooks watched her sleepily from the trees around the house, sheltering from the rain. In the flowerbeds, she saw pale seed pods of honesty, round as silver coins.

Orla shuddered. It was Hind House that made her feel sick, not the plants or the forest. Atlas was wrong if he thought that his 'science' would prove anything. Ma had known more about science and sickness than Atlas ever would.

There was the click of an upstairs window opening, and Orla turned to see a girl looking sheepishly out into the garden. It was Ariana Claw, her hair wound in neat ringlets, held back from her face with a golden pin. She wore a fine fur cape, fluffy as dandelion seeds, which gave the distinct impression that a strong gust of wind might blow her away completely. She was holding a small glass container that appeared to be smoking. She coughed and wafted the smoke away, then, leaving the smouldering glass on the windowsill, pulled a crust of bread from a pocket of her dress and tossed it towards the rooks.

Orla stared at the glass. It reminded her of something Ma had used once, for heating delicate oils she'd got from the plants. What was Ariana doing with something like that? Perhaps she was trying to make perfumes, Orla thought. Or maybe ink, like her uncle. Whatever it was, Orla decided she wasn't interested. She had barely spoken to Ariana since Ma died, and she wasn't about to start now. They'd played together once or twice when they were very small, after Josephine had taught them maths in the little schoolhouse by the chapel. Orla had taken Ariana down to the creek to paddle, the crayfish nibbling their toes. But that was long ago. Now Orla only ever saw Ariana's mother floating around the market, dressed in white, and Ariana trotting along the lane by Orla's hedge in her silk shoes.

Long time past, said the honesty, rustling its silver-moon seed pods.

Orla was just about to turn away when Ariana noticed her. She brushed the breadcrumbs from her fingers and looked straight at Orla, her big eyes widening so much that they reminded Orla of the owls that swooped over the marshes.

'He won't give up, you know,' she called down matter-of-factly.

'What?' hissed Orla.

'My uncle – he won't give up,' said Ariana. 'He would cut down the whole forest if it might help his business. You'd do better to stay away. Coming up here is rather foolish.'

Orla narrowed her eyes. 'And what would you know about that?' she said. 'All you've got to worry about is tearing your dress on a rose thorn, or dropping the butter knife.'

Ariana twisted one of her curls between her fingers. She gave Orla a faint smile.

'I see,' she said. 'Well, it sounds like you have every-thing under control.'

Before Orla could reply, a voice came from some-where inside the room.

'Come away from the window, *ma chérie*. Quick, now. Mustn't catch a cold.'

Ariana sighed and pulled the window closed with a snap.

For a moment, Orla paused. When Josephine Claw

had guided Orla and Ariana through their times tables, her voice had been gentle, but now it sounded high and worried, like a bird calling to its lost children.

Orla shuddered, glad to put Hind House behind her as she set off down the lane. All around her the willowherb whispered, shaking its pink flowers. Looking back over her shoulder, Orla paused, staring at the enormous silhouette of Hind House, with the scent of roses curling up from the flowerbeds. If Atlas was so certain that the plants caused the sickness, then why hadn't he cut down his own garden?

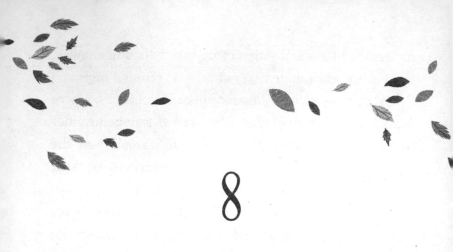

8

Willowherb *Chamaenerion angustifolium*
Known also as fireweed; for healing burns and sore skin.

The book was a little larger than Orla's hands. It was bound with soft leather, and stuffed with dried leaves and scraps of parchment. Orla breathed in the smell of the paper and ran her finger over the cover where Ma had painted the title of the book in gold. *Plants and their Medicinal Uses*, she'd called it. Each page had a delicate drawing of a plant, labelled in Ma's neat handwriting with how the plant should be used for medicine. Orla remembered Ma licking the nib of her pen to get the ink flowing.

She turned the pages carefully, holding the dried leaves up to the light to see their veins. It had been a long time since she'd looked at Ma's notebook. She knew all the remedies – she'd learnt them from Ma; and anyway, what good had it done her?

Orla stopped when she reached the final pages, where Ma's writing changed. Here, it looked as though a spider had taken up a pen and ink and walked all across the page. Orla swallowed, hard. These were the notes that Ma had made in the days before she'd died.

Hastily, she turned to the front of the book, where Ma's inky map spread over two pages. It showed the deep forests of the Borderwoods, following the river from Thorn Creek to Westharbour. In the north there were mountains, and in the south, the endless foggy landscape of the Long Moors. Right in the middle of it all was the river. In the flickering candlelight, Orla found Thorn Creek and the marshy river that ran through the village. Tracing her finger along the water, she followed the creek for an inch or so until it met the main river, labelled the *Inkwater*, which flowed towards Westharbour. But Orla's finger did not follow the Inkwater downstream. Instead, it turned *upriver*, against the flow of the water. Northwards.

Orla whispered the names of the places along the riverbank that Ma had labelled in delicate script. Dead Elm Strand. Roaring Weir. Fleetwater. Alder Carr. Inkenbrook. She'd drawn the plants that could be found in the forest, on the riverbank, in the meadows. Tiny ink portraits, all across the land – with each flower and plant carefully named: hawkbit, self-heal, catchfly, guelder rose, yellow iris, traveller's joy – and a hundred more.

'Something looks different,' she murmured, holding the book close to the candle to examine the village of Fleetwater, where Ma had often travelled with her medicines.

Wise girl, said the ivy which grew in through the window frame.

In one corner of the map, close to Fleetwater, Orla noticed a line, drawn around the plants like a loop of thread.

And beside it, in letters so small that a spider might have drawn them, Ma had written the word *here*.

Orla wasted no time in packing her bag. It was a ragged old thing, sewn back together more than once. It had a leather strap for each shoulder, and a buckle to keep it fastened. She wrapped a dark loaf of pumpernickel and placed it at the bottom of the bag, along with a handful of hazelnuts and three apples, one for each day that she planned to be away. She packed her smallest hatchet, a roll of twine, a woollen blanket and then stuffed a handful of fresh bulrush seed heads into her tinderbox. Her knife went in the pocket of her oilskin.

Beside Captain's bridle, she kept a stub of wax. She gave her boots an extra coat to keep out the rain, and looked longingly at the bridle, wanting more than anything to run back to Hind House to check on his foot and slip him a bundle of *proper* meadow hay. *It's only a few days*, she thought. *Then I'll be back for him.*

Finally, she covered Ma's book with a piece of oiled cloth to keep it safe from the rain, and tucked it into the top of the bag. She hadn't wanted to look at it before, but now she couldn't bear the thought of leaving it behind. A chill drifted through the walls of the woodshed. She thought of Captain, who should be grazing the garden. She worried about the plants, and the Haulers who would come with their axes and scythes. And she thought of Ma, who had been here, once, and was not any more.

The plants were anxious, too, fluttering their leaves against the shed walls. Memories were strong in Thorn Creek. Like Atlas, most people still thought that Ma had brought the sickness back to the village during her travels. They would pounce on the garden the moment Orla left it unprotected, glad of an opportunity to take their revenge.

Keep it safe, said the ivy. *Keep it all safe.*

'What do you think I'm trying to do?' said Orla, tossing water on the fire. The wood hissed and steamed as she pulled on her oilskin.

Outside, a stem of honesty waved its green leaves. Pale moths danced between the silver seed pods.

Hurry home, it said.

The hedges had grown tall and straggly that summer, leaving gaps where a determined Hauler might squeeze their way in. Collecting dead branches from beneath the hedges, Orla used her blade to sharpen each branch into a spike, before jamming it into the soil wherever she found a gap. She then pulled out long strands of bramble from the hedge and wove them through the branches.

Grow and grow, said the blackthorn.

Nice and hidden, said the bindweed.

'You'd better,' said Orla, hoping that it would be enough.

The next problem was the gate that the Haulers had broken when they'd come to take Captain. With a great effort, Orla hauled the gate upright between the hawthorn trees that stood guard at either side. Sweating, she drove two sharpened hazel stakes deep into the ground behind the gate so that it would not open.

Safe as trees, said the hawthorns.

Orla cleaned her hatchet on her sleeve and then wiped her brow. In the dark distance, she heard the clang of Haulers down by the jetty. All she had to do was make her way along the creek. There she would wait until the Haulers stumbled up to the tavern. If she was going to get upriver, then a Hauler boat was what she needed. It shouldn't be hard to steal one in the dark of night.

'It's time to go, isn't it?' she whispered.

The garden moved around her in a breath of night wind.

Up the running river, said the herbs.

Into the winding woods, they echoed.

Off through the marshes, the woods and the fields.

Then home again, they whispered. *Hurry home.*

Orla's throat tightened as she picked up her pack and fastened her oilskin. The plants were encouraging her to leave, but as she pulled up her hood and made sure the woodshed was shut fast, her heart felt heavy. She bit her lip and took a deep breath. This was her chance to prove that the plants had not caused the sickness. If she could find out what was really killing the plants, Atlas would have to leave her alone. He would have to give Captain back. He would have to say he was wrong about Ma.

Fleetwater and Ma. Castor and the river. The answer was there, somewhere.

Time to go now, said the sage.

Orla nodded as firmly as she could. With one last look at the woodshed, she waded through the long grass of the garden and crawled beneath the blackthorn hedge, emerging on to a hidden path that ran alongside the creek. As she stood up, the thorny branches clung to her coat, as though reluctant to let her go.

'You'll be all right, won't you?' she asked the garden, unhooking the thorns from her coat.

Make haste, said a scraggly stem of thyme in the

garden behind her.

The scent of the herbs followed her all the way along the river path. Reaching the grounds of Hind House, Orla climbed the wall and kept to the shadows. Now, a whole row of boats swayed against the jetty. Her heart quickened and her ears tuned in to every tiny noise: the slap of the water against the wooden jetty, the creaking of the boats and the flapping of canvas in the breeze. And in the darkness, footsteps.

Edging closer, Orla saw a figure with a lamp, walking away from the boats. Silas. He lifted the lamp to reveal Leblanc and Bouchard, and, beside them, Elias Dawson. He was clutching a sack of grain. Orla's eyes widened as Elias placed it on the ground beside the Hauler. Silas gave him nothing in return.

'Atlas's orders,' said Silas. 'It's all to be burnt. You're keeping this village safe, Mr Dawson.'

Orla swore under her breath. 'No, he's not!' she whispered to the willowherb beside the path. 'He's a fool. That's our winter oats – Captain's too.'

Elias disappeared into the darkness, shaking his head.

'This whole village believes Atlas's lies,' she muttered. 'They deserve to starve, if they're burning perfectly good grain.'

But the Haulers did not look like they were going to burn the grain. The moment Elias was out of sight, Silas lifted the sack with one hand and carried it down the jetty. Bouchard and Leblanc followed, each picking up another sack from somewhere in the darkness. Orla crept between the willowherb and the reeds until the jetty was almost within reach. The Haulers were loading the sacks into a small boat. It was made from light-coloured wood and had a canvas cover stretched over the stern, like a tent. In the lamplight, Orla glimpsed the words written on the prow: INKENBROOK TRADING CO.

Secrets, secrets, whispered the reeds.

'Fetch the crates,' she heard Silas say. 'And be quick about it.'

Keeping to the shadows, Orla darted under the jetty. Through the gaps in the wooden planks, she saw the lamps flickering. A moment later, she heard Bouchard and Leblanc return, their feet sliding on the wood.

'Careful!' said Silas. 'Watch it, I said!'

But it was too late. Orla heard a crash as a crate hit the jetty, followed by the sound of shattering glass.

'You *fool*, Leblanc!' growled Silas.

Orla looked up through a gap in the planks. A dozen glass bottles lay smashed on the jetty, shards of glass glittering in a pool of dark liquid. *Ink*. Atlas's ink. Orla shrank back as it began to drip down into the water. Leblanc bent to pick up a broken bottle.

'Don't touch it!' said Silas, kicking the bottle away. It tumbled into the river with a *plunk*. 'Clean up this mess before the Warden sees,' he said, striding off towards the village. 'But keep your hands off the stuff – got it?'

Bouchard stepped over the shards with a *tsk*. 'I hate delicate cargo,' he muttered.

He and Leblanc sat down to light their pipes, their legs dangling over the side of the jetty in front of Orla.

'At least he's not sending us upriver,' said Leblanc darkly. 'Short trip to Westharbour and half our pay in advance suits me just fine.'

Orla pictured Ma's map. The Haulers were taking their supplies downstream towards the coast, and along the way would pass a fork in the river, where another branch of the river led *upstream*, towards Fleetwater. It was too good an opportunity to miss.

Leblanc coughed, and tossed his tobacco into the water. Then the men stood up and kicked the other broken bottles into the river.

'If you catch the sickness before we leave, I'm taking your share,' laughed Bouchard, his boots thudding back down the jetty.

When she was certain that the men were gone, Orla swung her pack on to the jetty and climbed up after it. The moored boat swayed like a beast in the moonlight. Her skin shivered. She felt as though she were about to step willingly into the belly of a whale. She did not want to hide so close to the Haulers, but this was her best option.

She tiptoed along the jetty, avoiding the broken glass, and climbed into the boat, creeping beneath the canvas. She sat among cases of lantern oil, rolls of canvas and netting, boxes of ink bottles and several bags of the villagers' grain. Orla shook her head at the villagers' foolishness, and made her way to the stern on all fours, squeezing between tightly packed parcels of tobacco, rolls of cured leather and piles of furs. At the very back of the boat, she found what she was looking for: a small, empty space. With a sigh, she pulled her pack alongside her, ready to settle down for the journey ahead.

But as she reached out into the void, Orla felt something stirring in the shadows.

Suddenly, a hand grabbed her wrist. Another clamped tightly around her mouth. And before she could resist, she was pulled down into the darkness.

9

Sweet Violet *Viola odorata*
Gather the whole plant in summer; soak for a morning, boil, infuse for ten minutes. For insomnia, coughs and head colds.

'Don't talk!' said a voice.

Orla grabbed at the hand around her mouth and dug her nails in. With a small yelp, it let go.

'Idris?'

'Quiet!'

Orla squinted into the dark. As her eyes adjusted, she could just make out a hunched figure in a Hauler coat. Anger prickled her skin. This was her hiding place – not his.

'You gotta leave,' she announced. 'There isn't room for both of us.'

'I was here first,' hissed Idris. The river slapped and

the boat knocked against the wooden mooring post with a heavy *dunk*. Orla steadied herself on her hands and knees.

'Well, you can't stay here,' she said.

'What are you going to do, drag me out?'

Orla pulled her pack in and sat down with a huff.

'You said Castor was a fool,' said Idris. 'And now you're suddenly interested in a Hauler boat on its way to Westharbour. Thinking of running to the city? Telling them Atlas is selling stolen grain? No one will believe you. No one will care.'

'I don't care 'bout the city,' said Orla. 'I'm not going to Westharbour.'

'So you're going up the Inkwater, then?'

Orla narrowed her eyes.

'Keep your voice down,' she said. 'You'll get us both thrown in the river if you don't watch it.'

The water lapped against the wooden boat. It reminded her of the river beside Idris's house – and the image of Castor, lying sick in the little shack. It was clear why Idris was hiding in the boat. He was going upriver too.

'You gotta let me handle this,' she whispered. 'I know what I'm doing. More than you or your Hauler brother.'

'Why do you say Hauler like it's a bad thing? They're just men, doing their job, hauling furs from one place to another.'

Orla didn't reply. Idris must know what had happened to Ma, even if he hadn't been there four years ago.

'Anyway,' he went on. 'If it weren't for Castor, you wouldn't have known where to start looking.'

'It's not because of Castor that I'm here. I got other sources. Better sources than his feverish ramblings. You should go back to him, while you still got the chance.'

There was a silence.

'I didn't want to leave him,' muttered Idris at last. 'But he's not getting any better. The only way to find answers is to go looking for them. Just as you're doing, I reckon. So why don't you just be *quiet* and—'

There was a thud on the deck. Both Orla and Idris instinctively pulled themselves back into the shadows. Orla held her breath. It would be much harder to keep *two* stowaways hidden from the Haulers. She cradled her pack, feeling the solid shape of Ma's book wrapped safely inside.

Just because we're both going upriver don't mean we gotta follow the same path, she thought. *It don't mean we gotta be friends. I'll be rid of him soon.*

But the sound of the water murmuring so close beneath her made her feel uneasy. The tips of the willows rustled like birds settling their feathers. And the reeds along the riverbank whispered.

Hush, they said. *Hush, wise girl.*

Orla bit her tongue.

There would be answers upriver, she told herself. It would not be long. The wind winnowed through the reeds, soft and calming.

Suddenly, Orla heard the rumble of footsteps. Two – no, *four* – pairs of boots now came thundering along the jetty.

'That's the last one,' said Bouchard's rough voice. 'Ready the paddles!'

'Get her unmoored, before the Warden can add any more cargo,' said Leblanc.

A rope was untied, then another. She had not expected the Haulers to leave at night. It was a good thing that she'd come aboard when she did.

From a little way inland, Orla heard a faint cry.

'Speak of the devil,' muttered Leblanc.

'Blast it,' said Bouchard. 'Too late. He's bringing her down.'

Carefully, Orla peeled back the canvas just a sliver. Several pairs of boots clomped along the jetty.

'Move,' said Silas, in his quiet whisper. 'Or I'll toss you in the water and leave you for the fishes.'

Orla heard a faint, pitiful sob, and then the boat rocked as the Haulers and their cargo climbed aboard.

There was a clunk as the Haulers arranged their paddles, and a moment later Orla felt the swoop of the boat moving through the water. Down in the dark of the hull, it was a strange feeling, like floating and flying at once. Through the gap in the canvas, Orla saw the lights of Thorn Creek fading into the distance. She thought of Captain, alone up at Hind House with his bad hoof, and her heart ached. She couldn't help feeling that she was abandoning him.

It's only a few days, she told herself. *Then you'll be back for him. And the garden.*

They moved out on to the river, passing the myrtle marshes and the willows that draped their boughs mournfully in the water. A beaver watched from between the branches, disappearing with a splash as the boat passed – and then the world was dark and still. It made Orla feel cold and empty. What if, when she came back, there was no garden left to return to? What if all the plants turned black and died? She let the canvas fall, and curled herself up into the pile of furs stacked in the stern of the boat. It felt as if there were a thread running from her heart to the garden, and now it was pulling and pulling, so hard that it would surely break. She hugged Ma's book, and told herself that she was doing the right thing. Beside her, Idris sat in silence, his coat collar folded up to hide his face.

Along the creek, the willows watched, their branches twisted and curled with old age and wisdom. They saw the children hidden away in the boat, drifting like seeds in the current, out into the world they did not know, and they sighed, relieved that finally someone was looking for answers.

Back on the jetty, Inishowen Atlas did not immediately return to Hind House. Instead, he took the lamp and strode down the narrow path along the creek, until he reached a tall gate, surrounded by hawthorns. He pushed the gate with one hand. It did not move.

Holding the lamp aloft, he peered at the little woodshed in the garden beyond. There was no light from inside. He pushed the gate again. He did not hear the plants whispering and muttering. He did not hear their voices rise into a howl as he summoned the men that waited in the lane. He did not hear them calling for Orla as the men hacked at the garden gate, taking the hawthorn with it. He heard nothing as he carelessly trampled the gate, the hawthorn, and all the other plants along the path that led to the door of the little woodshed.

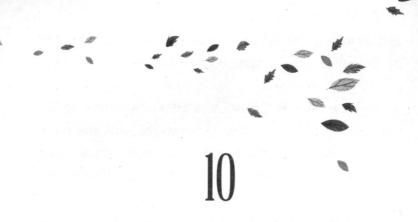

10

Wormwood *Artemisia absinthium*
To kill parasites in an animal, worms in particular.
Mixed into ink, it will stop mice eating letters and books.

Rain thundered down, and the Haulers, cold and wet, sang: a low, chanting rhythm like the thud of a drum.

> Heave-ho, ya Hauler lads,
> *Prenez donc le portage,*
> Heave-ho, past woods in the dark,
> *Chassez comme un loup en hiver.*

Orla peered through the canvas. A blur of arms and legs – grey hair, blue coats. Rain running in rivers from the Haulers' arms as they thrust long paddles into the water.

She was cold, aching and her stomach rumbled. She'd eaten some bread and an apple while Idris slept – how had he managed to sleep? – and now that daylight was dawning, she was starting to feel cramped and miserable. Rain drummed on the canvas roof and trickled through the gaps on to her hair. The Haulers were bailing water out from between their feet, swearing and groaning.

'You seen how many are out there?' asked Idris when he woke. Even as day broke, it was dark in their hiding place, but his eyes caught the light like glass.

Orla shrugged, trying to stretch out a crick in her neck. 'Does it matter?' she said. 'They're Haulers on Westharbour business. Nothing to do with me.'

'You're on a boat to Westharbour,' said Idris. 'When it reaches the Inkwater, it'll turn right, *towards the sea*. You want to turn left, *up* the Inkwater, but it sounds like you haven't thought about how you're going to get off this boat in time to do that.'

The boat jolted in the wind and Orla felt an uneasy feeling in her stomach. She didn't need Idris to tell her which way to go. She'd spent the whole night as wide awake as a badger in a trap, expecting the Haulers to pull back the canvas at any moment. She'd watched for every movement, every flicker of lamplight. And she'd worried that the boat had long since passed the fork in the river, and was rushing towards Westharbour, with no chance for her to slip ashore and take the turning upstream. Now she stared out for any sign of the river changing, desperate to be closer to the banks, to hear the trees whispering once again.

'Stop fretting,' said Idris. 'We're not there yet. But we will be, before nightfall.'

'Where?'

'Dead Elm Strand,' he said darkly. 'The fork in the river. It's a sandbank, right where the creek joins the river Inkwater. The Haulers always stop to camp in the woods there – Castor told me. If we're going to continue on foot, that's our only chance to leave them behind.'

Orla chewed on an apple core, trying to squeeze out as much juice as she could.

'Stop saying *we*,' she said. 'I been this way before, I don't need your help.' It was partly true. She remembered travelling to Fleetwater with Ma – holding Ma's hand in the village of meadow flowers, and the sun sparkling on a row of glass bottles. 'I got my own plan.'

All she knew was that she needed to get away from the boat, and away from the Haulers.

'What're you going to do, ask the trees for directions?'

Orla narrowed her eyes at him. That was *exactly* what she'd been planning to do.

Idris pulled a stick of liquorice from his pocket and began to chew. He did not offer any to Orla.

'You don't like helping people,' he said. 'Don't think anything's going to change there. But there's no reason not to listen to someone who's got good advice. I know what I'm doing.'

Orla pursed her lips. 'I got my own plan,' she said again, more firmly.

Idris shrugged and took another bite of liquorice, then pulled a needle and thread from the pocket of his coat. He hummed quietly along to the Haulers' songs as he sewed, stitching a rip in his sleeve. He looped the needle expertly through the fabric, his brow creased. Orla could tell he was trying to take his mind off Castor. She, too, was trying not to think about him. She knew she'd been harsh to Idris the other day, but that didn't mean she'd feel sorry for him now.

Orla leant towards the light and took out Ma's book.

Idris looked up from his sewing. 'Is that a map?' he asked, leaning closer.

Orla pulled the book away from him. 'It's private,' she said, tucking it into her lap. Settling back in the pile of furs, she examined Ma's map in the dim light. She found the place where the creek and the river joined: labelled Dead Elm Strand, like Idris had said. There the river curled up towards Fleetwater – '*here*' – and up to the mountains. Orla swallowed. On the map, everything looked small and neat. But out here the world was enormous and wild. And, in spite of what she'd just said to Idris, she didn't have a plan.

A little before dusk, Orla was woken by something small and hard hitting her on the head.

'Ouch!'

With a grunt, she pulled herself out of her blanket to find a dried plum on the floor beside her.

'Wake up,' he whispered, spitting out his own plum stone. He'd tucked his sewing away and was pulling his bootlaces tight.

Orla dusted off the plum and chewed it apprehensively. The noises of the river had changed; the rhythm of the Haulers' paddling had slowed.

'Almost there,' whispered Idris.

A moment later, the boat slid on to a gravel shore and the Haulers dragged the boat out of the river. Orla heard the *thunk* of a post being driven into the ground, then the scrape and slide of wooden paddles pulled ashore and the clomp of Hauler boots fading into the distance. Now, they were alone in an abandoned Hauler boat, its tail still bobbing in the shallows. Orla peeled back the canvas ever so slightly. She could see the flicker of light between the trees, and smell the sticky scent of a fire lit with pine branches. As the Haulers busied themselves with the fire, an idea stirred in her mind. It was dangerous, but it would beat walking ten miles upriver.

'I've got an idea,' she said to Idris. 'But it's risky.' She swallowed hard. The next words seemed to catch in her throat. 'I'll need your help.'

'Risky?' said Idris, with the faintest grin. 'Sounds like a Hauler plan to me.'

11

Valerian *Valeriana officinalis*
Gather the roots in the autumn and dry in the dark.
For insomnia; and some say, to tame a wildcat.

Orla and Idris slipped out from beneath the canvas and dropped down silently over the side of the boat. Orla felt an icy chill as she entered the ankle-deep water. The sun had set completely now, and the Haulers' fire was close enough that it cast an orange light on the water. Beyond, the crack willows reached up their straggling arms, and the forest was in shadow. The darkness would work to their advantage.

They crept through the shallows towards the bank.

Who is that? whispered the willows. *Out all alone?*

Orla winced as the gravel crunched beneath her feet, but the men were busy around the fire, roasting meat and drinking ale, and they did not hear or see the children clamber up the bank and into the trees. Bouchard, toothless and stocky, broke twig after twig and tossed them into the fire. Silas, twice the size of the others, sharpened his knife and held it up to the firelight to check his work. Leblanc was the only Hauler who did not sit down. He clutched his ale and paced around the fire, never turning his back on the forest.

Orla saw the paddles – three of them – lying against a log. She needed to think of a better plan than simply running into the camp and snatching them from beneath the Haulers' noses.

Branches snap and fall, said the crack willows threateningly.

Wildcats stalking, owls a-hunting, said the bulrushes.

Strangers in the shadows, said the willows.

'What's the matter, Leblanc?' said Silas. 'Afraid of the woods?'

Leblanc took a sip of ale, then spat into the embers. 'You ain't been upriver,' he said in a low voice. 'You don't know what it's like. Gives me the shivers just knowing we're near.'

'We ain't going back there,' said Bouchard calmly. 'And we ain't that near. That place is thirty miles from here, and we ain't going that way.'

'It's a godforsaken place, that's what it is,' continued

Leblanc. 'Nothing but stone and rot and, once in a while, a scrap of gold. Atlas is a fool for—'

'Keep it down, Leblanc,' growled Silas. Orla squinted. She'd counted three Haulers, but there was another figure behind the fire, obscured by the smoke and flames.

'Anyway,' said Bouchard. 'Atlas ain't thinking about that. He's got much more *academic* concerns, now.'

'Books, you mean,' tutted Silas.

Bouchard and Silas laughed, but Leblanc shook his head.

'If he hadn't paid us half already, I wouldn't trust him as far as I could throw him,' he said.

'But he has,' said Silas. 'And a good thing, too. You couldn't throw a stick for a dog.'

A chill swept in from the river, rippling the leaves high above. Orla eyed the willow branches. She knew they were prone to falling without a moment's notice. Beside her Idris pulled his coat tight.

'Tell me you've got a plan,' he said. 'I'm not getting stuck out here all night.'

Watching the men sitting nervously around the fire had given Orla an idea. The forest out here was different. It had a fierce breath, sighing and swaying, as though it could not settle. It was a warning, she thought. That this was not a good place to be. And she could use that to her advantage. The Haulers might stride around Thorn

Creek like autumn bucks with their fine coats, but out here they were unsettled. They did not like resting at Dead Elm Strand.

'Did your pa ever hunt deer? Back when he was in Thorn Creek?' whispered Orla.

Idris nodded. 'Me and Castor went with him. He preferred fishing, sure. But he knew how to catch a deer, good as the rest. Once, he—'

'I don't need your life story,' interrupted Orla. 'You know what a wounded deer sounds like?'

Idris nodded again.

'Follow me.'

Orla led the way into the woods, circling the Haulers' camp until the fire was between them and the boat.

'When I give the signal,' she said, 'you're gonna call out like a deer that's had its leg broke.'

'What?' hissed Idris, his eyes widening.

'Just listen, OK?' said Orla. 'They'll come running – thinking there's wolves and wild things out here. They'll want to find whatever got the deer, and they won't sleep easy till they do. They'll come running, right here.'

'Right at me, you mean!' said Idris.

Orla ignored him.

'Meanwhile, I'll be down there, ready to grab the paddles.' She pointed back the way they'd come. 'Once the Haulers start moving, you give one more cry, maybe two, and then run back down this path.'

Idris shook his head in disbelief.

'I think I'd rather get back in the boat,' he said.

'No chance,' Orla replied. 'You're definitely a faster runner than me.'

Idris sighed heavily. But he did not try to leave, which Orla took as a sign of agreement.

'Great,' she said. 'You'll hear me do an owl call, and then you go.'

She set off back around the camp, leaving Idris standing alone in the dark. Suddenly the world felt a little colder. She felt like the willows were watching her, judging her every step.

Drawing level with the fire, Orla crouched low to the ground. Then she cupped her hands together and blew, sending the gentle *whuuuu* of an owl out into the night. The Haulers had heard many an owl, and they did not even blink. They were stretching out beside the fire now, readying themselves for sleep. It was the perfect time.

But where was Idris? Orla could hear nothing but the wind in the trees, the crackle of the fire and the thud of her own heartbeat. She bit her lip and began to wonder if it had been a mistake to put her trust in the son of a Hauler.

When she couldn't bear it any longer, Orla clasped her hands together, this time sending a shrill *hwwweeeee* out into the woods. Idris didn't reply, and Orla stared helplessly at the fire. What was to say Idris hadn't run off to steal the boat, even without its paddles, leaving her stuck on a sandbank with the Haulers?

Suddenly there was a terrible, blood-chilling screech from the forest. Orla froze. That was no wounded deer. It was a raw, animal shriek, so horrifying that, for a moment, Orla could not move. Out there, somewhere, was a *real* wild beast. What if it caught Idris? What if it came for her next?

The commotion by the fire brought her to her senses. The Haulers leapt to their feet, drawing knives and pistols. Bouchard pulled a rifle from among the blankets, and loaded it. All four men stood still as startled deer: frozen, listening. Silas signalled for them to move forward, and they crept towards the trees, Bouchard leading the way with his rifle raised.

Run, Idris, Orla found herself thinking. *Run now.*

It was only then that she remembered what she was supposed to be doing. She ran to the fire and lifted two paddles. They were as tall as she was, and swung awkwardly as she hoisted them on to her shoulder.

She was about to make for the boat when the figure beyond the fire moved. It was thin as an autumn leaf, dressed in lace as pale as cobwebs.

Ariana Claw.

Orla froze. What was she doing here with the Haulers, deep in the forest?

Ariana's eyes widened. She opened her mouth, and

for a horrible second Orla thought she was going to scream in terror. But then she looked at the forest, where the Haulers were thundering through the undergrowth. She took a shuddering breath, and stared at Orla.

Orla swallowed and adjusted the paddles on her shoulder. Shocked as she was to see Ariana, she had to get back to the boat. Turning away from the fire, she struggled back towards the water. But when she glanced back, she saw Ariana on her feet, glowing in the firelight. Then, to Orla's astonishment, Ariana came running right towards her, the third paddle in hand.

'No chance,' said Orla. Reaching the water's edge, she dropped the paddles into the boat and then gave the boat a shove. It drifted away from the gravel bank, pulling the mooring rope tight. Orla looked back at the trees. Where was Idris?

'They're taking me to Westharbour,' came a breathless voice. Ariana, pale and panting, was standing ankle-deep in the water in her silk dress. 'I don't want to go to Westharbour! Wherever you're going, I'm coming too.'

'You gotta be kidding!' Orla looked at the mooring ropes. There was no sign of Idris. Perhaps it wasn't too late to leave him behind – leave him *and* Ariana behind – and carry on upriver alone.

She clambered to the front of the boat and began pulling at the ropes. Ariana stumbled towards her, splashing through the shallow water.

'Help me in,' she said, tossing her paddle into the boat.

'No,' said Orla sharply, tugging at the rope so hard it burnt her hands. Swearing, she pulled Ma's knife from her pocket and started hacking at it, one eye on the forest. The wind tossed the willows, which shuddered their branches together threateningly. Orla could hear the shouts of the Haulers now, and they were getting closer. She couldn't bring herself to wait for Idris any longer – fear prickled up her spine at the thought of what might happen if the Haulers reached her first.

She sawed at the rope, but it was thick and twisted and her knife was designed for plant stems, not tough fibres like this.

'*Pull* it,' said Ariana.

'What?'

'Pull it, there, at the base.' She pointed to the short end of the rope.

Orla tugged at the tail of the rope, and at once the knot came undone. The boat came loose and began drifting away from the shore.

'Quick!' said Ariana, clinging feebly to the boat.

Orla jabbed at Ariana's hands with the paddle.

'Ouch! No,' said Ariana. 'Help me on—'

CRACK.

Orla thought for a second that it was a willow branch breaking – and then froze.

CRACK. The gunshot rang out among the trees.

Idris.

Orla stared into the woods. The Haulers were shouting in the dark now.

'There's summit out there all right!' one yelled.

'Show yourself, beast!' growled another.

A moment later, Orla saw Bouchard stumble out of the shadows, aiming his rifle into the trees.

Orla's stomach swooped. The Haulers were shooting at Idris and it was her fault.

To stop the boat drifting, Orla flung out her arms and grabbed handfuls of leaves and branches, rooting her feet hard into the deck.

Let go! growled the willows as her hands pulled and broke the branches.

But Orla held on. 'Sorry, I'm sorry—'

There was a ripping noise as her sleeve caught on a jagged branch.

'Argh, no!' she said to the willow. 'I said I was sorry.'

'There!' shouted a Hauler. 'It's getting away! Kill the beast!'

Idris came bounding out of the woods, over the willow trunks and down on to the gravel shore. In one great leap, he cleared the water between the bank and the boat, landing with a thud on the deck. Orla thrust a paddle at him before he had a chance to catch his breath. But Idris didn't take it. He was staring, in shock, at

Ariana, who was wading knee-deep in the water, still clinging to the side of the boat. At once, he bent down and pulled Ariana on board. She collapsed in a heap at Orla's feet.

Orla shook her head and jammed her paddle into the water, pushing the boat away from the shore until they were out of range of the Haulers' guns. 'What were you *thinking*, bringing her with us?'

Idris swallowed and mopped the sweat from his brow. 'Couldn't leave her with the Haulers,' he said, still breathless. 'Though it seems like *you* didn't have a problem leaving her. Or me, for that matter.'

Orla looked back at the shore, her heart pounding. The Haulers were gathering at the water's edge, three shadows silhouetted against the light of the fire, watching them. All that mattered now was being as far from them as possible. Idris eyed her carefully.

'You've torn your sleeve,' he said.

'I know,' snapped Orla. 'And what was that noise, anyway? That wasn't a wounded deer!'

'A wounded deer wouldn't frighten Haulers,' said Idris, staring at Ariana, who had picked up a paddle and was working it ferociously. 'That was a lynx. *And* they believed it.'

12

Self-Heal *Prunella vulgaris*

A compress with rose oil will soothe a headache; infuse with boiled water to cleanse cuts and discourage bruising.

The stars sparkled overhead. Idris lit the lamp at the bow of the boat so that they could see the way before them. No longer were they heading downstream towards Westharbour. With their lamp dangling ahead of them like the light of a great undersea fish, they steered the boat up the channel that the Haulers called the Inkwater. Now they were heading north, paddling upstream away from the sea, and against the flow of the river.

It was Orla's turn to keep watch as Idris and Ariana paddled, ready to spot rocks or fallen trees that could gut the belly of the boat. But she couldn't help peering back towards the Haulers' camp, expecting the men to somehow appear out of the blackness to take back their boat. The trees shrouded the riverbank, shaking their heads in the wind. The plants between their trunks hid themselves in the shadows. They did not call to Orla.

'Watch the water,' whispered Idris, when he saw Orla looking distracted.

The river was deep and dark, and the boat slipped quietly through the inky water. Orla was surprised to find how light the boat was, how easily it moved against the current.

'No trees,' said Orla, still thinking of the crack willows that threw their branches down into the river. 'No rocks.'

'Rivers are living things,' said Idris. 'What you see now – that can change in a moment. Keep watch.'

'I think we should stop,' said a faint voice from behind him. It was the first time Ariana had spoken since they'd stolen the boat.

'Stop?' said Orla. 'You're not even paddling any more. You can't say you want to come with us and then not even bother to help.'

'I just don't think we should go any further if we can't see what's ahead,' said Ariana calmly.

'You want to go back, don't you?' said Orla. 'Back to Thorn Creek. Well, there'll be a road at the next village. We can let you off there.'

'Actually—' Ariana began.

'Let me finish,' said Orla. 'If we keep on upriver

tonight, we'll pass the Westharbour road in the morning, won't we, Idris?' she added. She didn't want to hear Ariana's opinion. What did she know about travelling on the river?

Idris grimaced. 'Actually, I agree with Ariana. We need to drop anchor.'

'We haven't come far enough!' said Orla. 'They'll catch up!'

'Even if they manage to crawl their way through that scrabbly bank,' said Idris, 'we're in the middle of the river. They're not gonna swim out here.'

'They're Haulers. You don't know that.'

'I do. I know they're cowards. They won't swim and risk their lives. They'll go running back to Thorn Creek to rat on us. We're safer here than heading upriver at night.'

'Since when did Haulers have plans?' muttered Orla, pulling at a loose thread on her torn sleeve.

'Since they didn't want to get swept out to sea on a riptide, or get their boat cut in half by a wandering log,' Idris said.

Ariana scrabbled around in the dim lamplight. A reel of rope, bundles of nets – and a rusty anchor, curved like a boar's tooth. She and Idris heaved it into the water. It vanished with an ominous noise, but the boat stopped moving.

Still, the trees on the riverbank watched in silence.

They did not let on what creatures – or which men – were lurking between their trunks.

'We should put out the lamp,' said Orla, thinking about the best place to spend the night, away from the others.

'There's no one coming,' said Ariana. 'Idris is right.'

'I'm going to see what supplies we got,' said Orla in a huff, suddenly realizing that Idris and Ariana were not on her side.

She pushed past the tangle of legs and paddles towards the rear of the boat. Under the canvas Atlas's glass bottles glowed eerily in the lamplight, among strings of kippers and rolls of tobacco leaves. Idris and Ariana squeezed in behind her. Idris tucked the canvas closed, turning the boat into a small, lamplit cave. Orla sighed. Wherever she went, Idris and Ariana always seemed to follow, like burdock burrs caught on her boots.

From beneath the pile of furs, Ariana pulled out a woollen blanket, which she wrapped around herself like a shawl. Her mouth formed into a small *o* as something fell from the folds of the blanket. She held up a leather coin purse.

'It's my uncle's payment to the Haulers,' she said, opening the pouch. Orla saw silver coins glitter in the light. 'For the ink, and for taking me to Westharbour.'

'They're gonna want that back,' said Orla warily, still

uneasy at the thought of spending the night afloat on the river. She felt like she'd been swallowed up into the belly of a dark river creature. She wanted to be out in the garden and the Borderwoods, with the plants whispering around her, not here with the smell of painted wood and river mud.

It was Idris who broke the silence first.

'Why're they taking you to Westharbour?'

Ariana hesitated for a moment, pulling at her sleeves.

'My uncle . . . doesn't think Thorn Creek is a suitable place for a young lady,' she said. 'He must think that Westharbour is better.'

Orla rolled her eyes. Ma had told her that the schools in Westharbour taught women nothing but dancing and sewing. It would suit Ariana perfectly.

'But I'm not going to Westharbour,' announced Ariana. 'And I'm not going back to Thorn Creek, either. I'm coming with you.'

'What?' said Idris, wide-eyed.

Orla was shocked. 'No chance,' she said. 'As soon as we find a road, you're going back to your ma.'

'No,' said Ariana firmly.

'We're not doing this for *fun*, Ariana,' said Orla. 'You can't just come along because you fancy a taste of adventure.' She thought of Ariana peering into her garden after Ma had died, asking Orla the best way to make rose perfume.

'I *know*,' said Ariana. 'But you know as well as I do that Westharbour has the sickness too. It's not safe, and neither is Thorn Creek. And I'm certainly not walking along *that* road on my own on the off-chance of finding a passing carriage. Wherever you're going, I'm coming too.'

Orla bit her lip. 'I don't think so,' she said firmly. 'I'm going alone.'

'With Idris,' Ariana reminded her.

'That's just a coincidence!' said Orla, giving Idris a scathing look. 'We both just happen to be going in the same direction, in the same boat.'

'So you're not both going upriver to find where the sickness is coming from? To find a way to stop it?'

Orla paused. 'How do you know that?' she said. 'You've been eavesdropping again, haven't you? Wait – you knew we were here!'

'It was rather obvious,' said Ariana. 'The Haulers were too noisy to notice, but I could hear you arguing like scrapping foxes. It's clear why you're both here.'

'You're a sneak, Ariana Claw,' Orla spat.

Ariana looked at her fiercely.

'I don't sneak,' said Ariana. 'I *listen*. Castor came back sick from a journey upriver – you can't ignore that. Perhaps if you let other people have a look at that book of yours, they might actually be able to help.'

'*Spy*,' said Orla bitterly.

Ariana folded her hands carefully in front of her. 'This

isn't being nosy, Orla. It's called *caring*. I've never understood how people can live in such a small village and ignore each other so easily. You know how long Idris and Castor have been alone in that shack? *Four years.* You know how long you've been alone without your ma? *Four years.* And all that time, you barely talked to each other. I don't understand it.'

Idris looked down. But Orla did not feel ashamed. How dare Ariana criticize the way that she did things? Ariana had been waited on, hand and foot, at Hind House. She had no idea what it was like to survive on her own. Just because they'd played together once or twice when they were small didn't mean that she owed Ariana anything at all.

'And you spent all that time sneaking around, watching us,' said Orla bitterly.

'That's not true,' said Ariana, fiddling with the torn hem of her skirt. 'After my father died, Atlas . . .' She paused and did not finish the sentence. 'Anyway. I understand, that's all. I wanted to help, but how could I? I could barely walk five minutes from Hind House without Mother coming after me to "keep me safe". I couldn't exactly set off into the Borderwoods to try and work out where this sickness was coming from. But now I *am* away from them. I want to help. I *can* help. I've been doing some research and—'

'I'm sure we'll need lots of help sewing skirts and

folding lace,' interrupted Orla.

'That's not kind,' said Idris sharply. 'And sewing is more useful than you'd think, on a boat.' He patted the canvas cover and Orla saw the neat row of stitches holding it together.

'Why would someone like *her* want to help *us*? She don't really want to help. She just wants to tag along, like this is some kind of game!' said Orla. 'This isn't a game. Unless I find a way to stop that sickness, I'll never get my horse and garden back.' She didn't want to mention Ma, but the thought was there, as it always was, clinging to her like ivy.

Idris stiffened. 'Your horse?' he said angrily. 'Your garden? Unless I find a way to stop the sickness, my brother will die!'

Orla felt her cheeks turn hot, but she couldn't say sorry.

Idris stared at her, as though daring her to say that she *did* care. But she didn't. She didn't want any of this. She wanted to carry on alone, without having to think about Idris or Castor or Ariana.

'Well, I'm sure you'll make a great team,' said Orla. 'I'm going to sleep.' She snatched a blanket from the pile behind Ariana, and then clambered over Atlas's crates of ink into the very back of the boat. She arranged the blanket on the cold deck, then pulled her own from her pack and curled up inside it. She was glad to be away from

94

Ariana's poking elbows and Idris's restless legs. They were whispering together now, their shadows flickering in the lamplight.

Orla burnt with rage and shame all at once. If she'd taken the boat alone, she'd be halfway up the river by now.

She could hear Ariana asking Idris about his brother, her voice calm and gentle.

'Once, he even built me a boat,' said Idris. 'Did I say he builds boats? This one was round, like a dish. I helped him stitch deer hide over the hull and we took it out fishing for crayfish. You shoulda seen me spinning away in the current without a paddle! Castor couldn't stop laughing, but he swam behind me the whole time, holding on.'

Orla pulled the blanket over her head. She could still hear snatches of Idris talking. 'But then the crayfish started dying off and we needed the gold. I didn't think he'd come back sick. Elias and Agnes said they'd take care of him while I'm gone, but with Pa away, working . . .'

Orla jammed her fingers in her ears. Everything out here felt wrong. Not like being in the Borderwoods back home, looking for bilberries with Ma . . . Captain's rope in her hand . . . She didn't want Idris's memories – they filled her mind with too many thoughts.

But Ariana was talking now too.

'I can help,' she said. 'I really can. I've been monitoring the water back home. Something really isn't right and I want to find out what.'

Orla groaned. Just like the villagers, Ariana thought the wild had caused the sickness.

Orla closed her eyes and tried to listen to the plants instead. Somewhere beneath the boat, waterweed looped and swirled in the current. She could hear it murmuring – but the words were mumbled and indistinct, as though it were talking to someone else – not her.

She thought about the plants in her own garden, and by the creek. They had never stopped talking to her before. Pulling Ma's book on to her lap, she ran her fingers through the dried leaves and stems that poked out between the pages. The plants at home had never abandoned her. But out here, she realized, as the reeds mumbled and drummed against the hull, the plants did not trust her one bit.

13

White Water Crowfoot *Ranunculus aquatilis*
Water buttercups. Acrid juice; may cause skin to blister.

Orla woke with a start. It was dark beneath the canvas and she could hear the wooden planks groaning and creaking. *Something* was scraping along the side of the hull. Orla imagined the claws of an enormous river creature ready to slice into the belly of the boat, and felt the hairs on her arms prickle like nettle stings. *Thud*, it went. *Thud, thud.*

Orla threw off her blanket and scrabbled to the side of the boat.

Thud.

Right beneath her.

Thud, thud.

'There's something in the water,' she said. There was a

rattle and a click. Idris had woken too and he was fumbling with the oil lamp. Orla lifted the canvas and peered out at the river. Cloud now covered the moon and stars, and she could not see the trees or the riverbank.

'Blasted lamp,' said Idris.

'Here,' said Ariana in the darkness. Orla heard her crawl out on to the deck and followed, clambering over the furs and stacks of oats.

Thud, went the noise again. *Thud, thud.*

The waterweed whispered beneath them. It sounded uneasy, but Orla couldn't make out the words.

Ariana lit the lamp and leant over the side of the boat, holding the light towards the water.

An orange glow passed over the surface, rippling with strands of waterweed swaying in the current.

There was a solid shape there, too. Knocking again and again against the side of the boat.

Orla glimpsed a swirl of dark hair, the blue sleeve of a Hauler coat, before Idris snatched the lamp from Ariana and held it up to illuminate . . .

The body of a man, caught in the weeds. His long hair swirled in the current and his white shirt bloomed out like the sail of a sunken ship. He did not move. His eyes were closed, his face to the sky.

'Is he dead?' whispered Orla.

'He'll go under if we don't do something,' said Idris. 'It's a heavy coat.'

Orla could see that the man's coat was wet through. How long had he been in the water? She looked at the sky. It was turning deep blue. Dawn was coming, and soon any Hauler on the riverbank would see them there.

'No chance,' she said. 'Pulling him up here? We'd capsize. Leave him. He's dead.'

'We can't just leave him,' said Ariana.

'Get ready to paddle us ashore,' said Idris, grabbing a hook from under the gunwales and attaching it to a length of rope. He leant over the side of the boat and slowly let out the rope until the hook caught in the collar of the Hauler's coat. Then, he rushed to the bow and started hauling up the anchor chain. Ariana already had her paddle in the water, but as soon as the anchor was up, the current tugged the boat, pulling it downstream, away from the shore.

'Orla, help!' cried Ariana.

Orla stared at her. 'He's a *Hauler*,' she said.

Idris grabbed the paddle Orla was holding and pushed them hard towards the shore, towing the man behind them.

Orla folded her arms. The boat slid into the sandy bank beneath a strip of feathery trees. Idris jumped out and pulled the boat into land. Then he waded into the water and tried to grab hold of the man, but Orla could see that the Hauler's coat was dragging him beneath the surface. Ariana climbed out of the boat, then stepped cautiously towards Idris. When the water reached her knees she looked round at Orla, her face stricken with panic.

'I can't swim,' she said quietly, the water buttercups curling around her skirts.

Down to the depths, they said threateningly, shimmering their white flowers in the twilight.

'Fine,' said Orla, kicking off her boots. 'If I drown . . .'

She jumped into the icy river and helped Idris seize the man by his shoulders and pull him towards the narrow beach. His face was bearded, his hair long. His forehead was bruised and his mouth bloody. As they dragged him on to land, he did not move.

Idris pulled his coat aside and opened the man's mouth, leaning close to him. Ariana watched over his shoulder, clasping and unclasping her hands.

'I think he's breathing,' said Idris.

Orla surveyed the shoreline. The raggedy band of trees was coming into focus in the dawn light. They did not have much time.

'We saved him,' she said. 'Let's go. If those Haulers catch us up, they'll take us back to Thorn Creek and we'll never find answers.'

'Your ma would never give up on someone,' said Idris. 'We have to do what we can. He's still alive – feel that. Can't have been in the water long. He's burning hot.'

Orla's cheeks flushed, and she was glad Idris could

not see them in the dark. He was right, Ma helped anyone who needed it.

Idris grabbed her hand and touched it to the Hauler's brow. The Hauler's damp skin was hot as embers, when it should have been dead and cold as river rocks. Orla snatched her hand away, her heart pounding.

'He's sick,' she said. 'We should never have touched him.'

'This could've been Castor,' said Idris, marching to the boat and pulling out a blanket.

'We can't be here,' said Orla. 'What if *we* get sick?'

'Idris spent all night with Castor,' said Ariana, her voice shaking. 'He's not sick.'

'We don't know what this is,' said Orla. 'It might not be the same.'

She could feel her heart racing now, and a sharp pain in her gut – a feeling that had been with her all along. The truth. Everything was telling her to leave.

'Do you believe that?' said Ariana, as Idris tossed the blanket to them and returned to rummage inside the boat. 'Come on, help me.'

Orla helped Ariana spread the blanket over the man. As she tucked it around him, something caught her eye. The Hauler's hand. It did not look right at all. Perhaps it was just the strange dawn light, throwing a bluish tint over the grey landscape . . .

Orla cautiously peeled back the man's sleeve.

Suddenly, a wave of nausea hit her. The Hauler's arms were streaked with thin purple lines that showed like dye through his skin, as though his veins had been drawn in ink.

'No,' said Orla faintly, as the world began to spin around her.

Ariana's face loomed pale in the twilight.

'What is it?' she said.

Orla swallowed, trying not to remember. The words scratched her throat as she spoke them.

'It *is* the same sickness – and I've seen it before.'

14

Bittersweet *Solanum dulcamara*
Also known as Woody Nightshade. Poisonous: do not use.

'Castor's arms – they looked just like this,' said Idris, his voice shaking. 'When I left, they—'

He stopped suddenly. Orla heard the thunder of footsteps among the trees.

'Hide the boat,' said Idris, putting out the lamp at once.

Orla blinked. Her world was still spinning. Voices carried through the dawn-lit trees, but it was not the plants that spoke.

'This way!' called a hoarse voice. 'They can't have got far!'

Somewhere behind her, Orla heard Idris drag the boat across the sand. But Orla couldn't move, though

Ariana was tugging at her oilskin. She stared at the Hauler's purple-blue arms.

'Come *on*, Orla. They're coming,' hissed Ariana.

Stumbling to her feet, Orla scrabbled across the sandy shore to a thick cluster of pine trees, where Idris was hiding with the boat, crouched low among a patch of rushes.

'We can't leave yet,' said Idris. 'They'll see us pull out into the channel. Keep your head down.'

Can't leave, murmured the pines.

Stay hidden, said the rushes.

Peering between the knotted trunks, Orla could make out the flaming torches of the Haulers, like fireflies in the early morning light. At first, their chatter was loud and obnoxious. But it soon turned fearful as their torchlight found the body. Their words echoed across the little beach.

'God have mercy,' said Bouchard, holding the torch high, casting a golden halo on the man.

'Where'd he come from, half-dead as that?' said Leblanc, trembling.

'You know blasted well where he come from,' said Bouchard.

'What do we do with him?' said Leblanc.

'Leave him,' answered Silas, nudging the man with his foot.

'No medicine? No healers?' said Leblanc.

Bouchard shook his head. 'You know what they called it up at Fleetwater?' he said. '*Mapafoglia*: the Map of Leaves.'

Orla saw a small glimmer as he lit a pipe.

'Day by day, it draws a map over your body. Once it reaches your heart, you're done for.' He peeled back the blanket with a stick and shook his head. 'You saw what happened at Fleetwater. Best place for him now is a hole in the ground.'

'Once those marks appear, you don't last long.'

The sick Hauler drew a long, rattling breath.

Bouchard shook his head. 'He's a goner, if you ask me.'

Orla leant against the pine for support. Her legs felt suddenly weak. Scrunching her eyes closed, she could still see the lines like an inky map on Ma's skin, thin as the veins on a leaf. And it brought back the smell of the woodshed, Ma lying by the fire, burning lavender to hide the smell of sickness and sweat until Elias and Agnes came to take Orla away . . .

The Hauler's words echoed in her mind.

What happened at Fleetwater . . .

Fleetwater, echoed the pines.

Ma, with those spidery marks on her arms.

Let me go to Fleetwater, she'd said.

The Haulers had stopped her.

Orla caught her breath as the memory came back stronger. Not just the Haulers.

Atlas standing by the garden gate, his large-brimmed hat shadowing his face.

'*You're sick, Elizabeth,*' he'd said. Orla remembered him calling Ma by her first name. '*You cannot go eighteen miles up the river.*'

Ma had argued with him, her brown eyes shimmering with rage, her hair twisted and tangled like vines – and her arms stained purple-blue. Orla remembered the scent of thyme fading as Elias and Agnes led her away to Dawson & Reed.

Something fierce bubbled up inside Orla now. She glared at the Haulers, holding back the urge to rush at them and tear at them with her bare hands. They'd stopped Ma from leaving Thorn Creek. Ma had wanted to go to Fleetwater when she was sick – and Ma always had a reason.

On the beach, the sick Hauler gave one last rattling breath and then fell silent.

Silas snorted and spat on the ground.

'He's dead,' he said. 'Bury him, and then find the boat, before the boss finds out. They won't have got far.'

15

Liquorice *Glycyrrhiza glabra*
For maladies of the voice. Among other uses, the root has a sweet
and aromatic flavour.

'We have to go to Fleetwater,' said Orla fiercely.

'Those Haulers said there was nothing left,' said
Idris. His face was stony as he paddled the boat north up
the river. They'd slipped silently though the reeds while
the Haulers buried the dead man. Orla hoped they
hadn't been noticed.

'The Haulers don't know what they're looking for,'
she said.

'And we do?' replied Idris, raising an eyebrow.

'Are you all right, Orla?' asked Ariana cautiously.
She'd spent the last few minutes dipping a metal cup into
the river and examining the water.

'Why wouldn't I be all right?' said Orla, putting down her paddle and squeezing the river water from her breeches. She could not stop her teeth from chattering.

'Because of your mother,' said Ariana, watching Orla with her enormous eyes. 'She died of the same sickness, didn't she? The same as that Hauler – the very same that Castor has.'

Idris lowered his gaze.

'It's all connected,' said Ariana.

For a moment, it felt to Orla as though a stem of bindweed had twisted around her throat. She thought of Ma scribbling day and night in her book, examining the plants, holding their leaves up to the light, scattering their seeds on her wooden table.

With shaking hands, she reached into her pack. She hesitated for a moment. Ariana busied herself pouring the river water from the cup into an empty ink bottle. She held it up to the light and Orla saw that it was grey and unpleasant-looking: much darker than the water in Thorn Creek, which flowed clear down from the marshes. Idris pushed on determinedly, but Orla saw he was struggling against the current.

'Pull in to the bank, for a moment,' she said. 'I need to show you something.'

Idris and Ariana turned to her then. Idris slowed his paddling, letting the boat drift gently into a patch of bulrushes at the edge of the river. Orla heard them murmuring reassuringly, their tall stems capped with seeds like cat tails.

She carefully unfolded the oilskin wrapped around Ma's book, trying her best not to drip river water on it. She opened the book and turned to Ma's map. Fleetwater was halfway between Thorn Creek and the northern mountains. Her mouth was suddenly dry. She felt like a tree, with its bark stripped away. She had never shown anyone Ma's book before.

'It *is* all connected,' she said, trying to sound certain. 'When I was small, we'd go to Westharbour, to the cottages up on the Long Moors – and to Fleetwater. Ma went to Fleetwater often. She'd make tinctures and balms and poultices and things, to sell, you know . . .' With a swoop in her stomach, Orla remembered Captain's rotten foot, and hoped that he was not wondering why she hadn't come to rescue him yet. She cleared her throat and carried on. 'I went with her to Fleetwater – but I was very small and I can't . . . really remember.'

She chewed her lip, thinking of a moment long ago, wrapped in a woollen cloak and tucked on to Ma's lap as Ma scooped a poultice from a wooden bowl, the sound of the river rumbling nearby. Was that at Fleetwater?

'And when my ma was sick,' she went on, 'she wanted to go back there. More than anything. Either she knew what was causing the sickness and thought she could stop it, *or* she thought that something there might be a way to fix it. My money's on the second one. She knew what she was doing. She knew medicine, she knew plants.'

'Why?' said Idris, his brow furrowed. 'What proof do you have?'

Atlas's words echoed in Orla's mind then. *You will prove nothing.* She tugged at the hem of her sodden coat. No one believed Orla, that the plants didn't cause the sickness. No one had believed Ma knew what she was doing when it came to medicine.

'If your ma had those marks on her arms, she'd have known it was too late for her,' said Ariana. 'You're right, Orla – she must have hoped that there would be a cure in Fleetwater.'

Idris's eyes lit up. 'A cure?'

Orla clutched Ma's book, trying not to think about how life would be different if Ma had found a way to make herself better. But if there was a cure for the sickness, Atlas would no longer be able to blame *her* plants for causing it. He would leave the garden alone. And people wouldn't be able to say those things about Ma any more. Determination coursed through Orla's veins. So she was surprised to see Idris looking back at her, his brow furrowed in concern.

'Are there mountains at Fleetwater?' he asked.

Orla looked at the map and shook her head. 'It seems to be surrounded by meadowland and forest.'

The lines on Idris's forehead deepened, but Orla felt

like her mind was bursting with spring shoots. That moment, sitting on Ma's lap as she scooped up the poultice. A woman had given Orla a glass flower, in thanks for Ma's help. It had felt cold and heavy in her palm.

'It's a glassmaking town,' said Ariana, as though she were reading from a book. 'The glass is made from the sand in the river there. It's heated in furnaces at over a thousand degrees. In fact, quite a number of scientific instruments . . .'

Orla stopped listening. Her mind could think of only one thing. Glass! Ma had kept her best medicine in glass. She used wooden pots for balms and clay jars for dried herbs, but glass for the remedies that would otherwise go bad. She'd always come back from her trips with bottles – hexagonal in shape, not much larger than an ink bottle – filled with liquids. Orla remembered the smell of lavender; the deep smoky scent of pine; the sweet nectar of rose oil. All in glass. What if there was something *stored* in Fleetwater – something that Ma needed. Something *hidden* from the Haulers.

A burst of excitement ran through her. In Fleetwater she'd find people who had known Ma. She'd find out what they knew. And, perhaps, the plants there would be kinder. Perhaps they too would remember Ma and the cures that she had made. They would surely want to help Orla save her garden.

Orla stared out at the river, the surface of the water

dancing in the morning sunlight. There would be answers in Fleetwater, but to get there she needed Idris and Ariana. She nodded, feeling certain now – and was surprised to see Ariana smiling at her. But Idris had pulled a bulrush leaf from the river and was absent-mindedly tearing it to pieces.

'You just learnt that this was the same sickness your ma had,' he said, 'and now you're jumping to conclusions . . .'

He let out a long sigh. Orla noticed that he was twisting the fibres from the leaf until they formed a thread. She was silently impressed.

'Castor's not got a lot of time,' he said, winding the strands around his fingers. 'Are you *sure* about this?'

Orla pulled her hair back from her face. 'Yes,' she said firmly. She didn't like to admit it, but three pairs of hands would be a lot quicker for paddling. Idris and Ariana might be her only hope of getting to Fleetwater, finding the cure, and coming back to save her garden. Two nights had already passed since the Haulers had threatened it. How long would it be before they took up their axes and scythes once more? And what about Castor – how long did he have?

'If you're right,' said Ariana, 'this could be the answer to all of our problems.'

'I'm right,' said Orla. 'The sooner we get to Fleetwater, the sooner we get back home.'

Idris swallowed, and then nodded. 'All right, then,' he said quietly, winding the thread around a bulrush stem and tucking it away in his trouser pocket. Then he rummaged around inside his blue coat and pulled out a bundle of liquorice sticks. He handed one to Orla and one to Ariana, holding his own piece of liquorice between his teeth. 'We'll stop at Fleetwater. On our *way* to the mountains,' he added. 'But only on one condition.'

'What?' said Orla.

'Let me fix the tear in your coat sleeve while you and Ariana paddle,' he said. 'It's annoying me like nobody's business.'

He held out his hand and motioned for Orla to pass him the coat.

Orla chewed her liquorice for a moment, sighed, and wriggled out of the old oilskin.

'Fine,' she said, emptying out her pockets full of string and bulrush fluff, and placing the contents neatly in her lap. 'But mind you do it properly,' she added, taking up her paddle. 'And fast, it's not warm out here.'

'You'll be pleased, just you see,' he said.

On the riverbanks, the plants and the trees found their voices and urged the little boat onwards.

On and on, they called. *Wild river, wild woods.*

Old as oak, they said. *Dark as stone.*

Secrets in the woods, secrets in the water.

Four days, they echoed. *Not long, not long.*

At Hind House the roses shivered and shuffled in the breeze. They watched as the tall man ran his hands through his hair and then pulled on his gloves. He mounted a bay stallion, who snorted and tossed his head in the damp evening air. The plants closest to the horse's hooves winced as Atlas turned the stallion around, crushing their leaves. As they turned, Atlas caught sight of a plant growing in his rose beds. Its silver seed pods put him in mind of silver coins. When he returned, he must tell his staff to cut the weeds down. They reminded him too much of that *woman*, trailing everywhere with her seeds tumbling out of her pockets, as though to taunt him. With his eyes firmly set on the forest, he kicked the horse into the night, and rode northwards along the river path.

16

Lady's Mantle *Alchemilla vulgaris*
Found on higher ground. Leaf: to stem bleeding. A sprig under the pillow aids sleep.

Fleetwater approached, and with it the thundering roar of the weir. It reached them a mile before the town, rumbling beneath the surface of the water and shuddering against the hull of the boat like the sound of a deep, echoing drum. The hairs on Orla's arms prickled. She had not forgotten the ominous roar of the weir, and as it came into view her fingers gripped the paddle tight. Like a great, grey mouth, it stretched across the river Inkwater. It was a solid wall, three feet high from end to end. The water rushed over the wall, churning into white froth and spilling out dark, swirling eddies that rattled towards the boat.

But it was not the weir that filled Orla with apprehension. All along the river Inkwater she had tried to remember what it was like, visiting Fleetwater with Ma. But it was as though the village was hidden behind a haze of river mist. Her memories came in glimpses that vanished as quick as a blink.

She remembered holding Ma's hand as they walked down a cobbled street in the bright sunshine, the light sparkling on a row of glass windows; the scrawk of jackdaws flapping around the chimneys of a white house, where honeysuckle grew around a sage-coloured door. And the small wooden bed that had rolled out from underneath Ma's. But she remembered no people, no places. Just the smell of warm milk in the morning, and the endless rush of the weir. She swallowed, trying to hide the butterflies rising up into her throat. How would she begin to explain to the people of Fleetwater why she was there, or what she was looking for? As the town came into view, she felt uncommonly sick.

Perched above the weir was a strip of thin white houses and alleyways twisted with climbing plants. Half the buildings tumbled out over the water, their foundations built on stilts or balanced on wooden jetties. Behind the cluster of houses, there was a broad stretch of meadowland swathed in mist and dotted with the occasional farmhouse. Beyond that, Orla saw the ever-present shadow of the forest.

Careful, said the willows on the bank. *Watch the roots, watch the weir.*

'Watch the roots,' said Orla. 'They'll drag you under.'

'It's the weir I'm worried about,' said Idris, as they drew closer to the churning stream. 'No getting out of that spill if you fall in.'

He held the paddle with white knuckles and steered them into a narrow channel that branched away from the main river. A little way ahead Orla was startled to see a great wooden gate, like two enormous wooden wings in the water. It completely blocked the channel.

'It's a lock,' said Idris. 'I've seen this before, in West-harbour.'

'But we don't have a key!' said Orla, looking at the jumble of buildings above them as Idris steered them into the enormous stone chamber. He scrambled up a ladder and Orla watched as, a moment later, another set of gates swung closed behind them. Suddenly, the boat felt very small indeed.

'I thought you said you'd been here before, Orla,' said Ariana. Orla ignored her.

'Throw me the line and then hold tight,' said Idris, who was now high above them. The stone sides of the chamber were dripping with water, and clusters of bright- green ferns hid among the cracks. Orla tossed the rope to Idris, who looped it around the bollard and threw it back. Orla held it firmly as instructed, while Ariana watched Idris nervously. He was now at the top gate, where he'd found a huge iron wheel. He turned it cautiously and there was a deep gurgling noise from somewhere beneath them.

'Oh, that's *fascinating*,' said Ariana. 'The water's rising. I assume that's supposed to happen?'

'That means it's working!' Idris gave the wheel another turn and suddenly a cascade of water shot out from somewhere between the top gates. Orla felt the boat swing forward and winced as it scraped the stone, pulling them towards the torrent of water. She concentrated on tightening the rope as the water rushed the lock, bringing them up and up until they were level with the houses. When the raging water calmed to a gentle gurgle, Idris was able to open the lock gates and hop aboard.

Orla wiped her sweating hands on her breeches and looked up at the crumbling houses beyond the lock. No one had come out to greet the new arrivals, or to chase them away. As Idris steered the boat out of the lock, they heard nothing but the gentle slap of their paddles in the water. There was no glimmer of lamplight from the windows, no hint of smoke from the chimneys.

'There's no one here,' said Ariana, as Idris guided them towards a wooden jetty, sticking out into the water like a bony finger. There were droplets of mist clinging to his eyelashes now, and to the lace of Ariana's dress. Orla pulled her own mist-dampened hair back from her face, and cautiously watched the riverside as they drew alongside the jetty, quiet as a fish in the water. It was not unusual for the mist to swallow every sound on the river; but the alleyways that led between the houses were also ghostly quiet, and the shutters on the buildings were drawn closed. There were no shouts of welcome, no fishermen smoking on the waterside. Fleetwater was a ghost town.

'I think the sickness mighta got here before us,' said Idris. Orla nodded.

Nervously, she slung her pack over her shoulder and hopped on to the jetty. Ariana passed her a rope, which she looped around the mooring post. Her footsteps echoed on the wooden planks as she secured the other end of the boat. This silence was not right at all.

'Blasted cold town,' she muttered, trying to explain why her fingers refused to tie the knot she'd done a hundred times. But the others were not listening. They had climbed out of the boat and were peering up at the ramshackle houses, where plants grew between broken roof tiles and plaster cracked and crumbled before their eyes.

'You know where we're going?' said Idris, buttoning his coat against the cold.

Orla nodded, but inside she already felt lost. If it weren't for the rumbling weir, she would have wondered if this was even the right village. But behind her on the jetty, Idris and Ariana waited expectantly for her to lead the way.

'It's rather quiet,' said Ariana. Her ringlets hung sadly around her face, and she trotted after Orla like an eager puppy.

Wishing that she were on her own, Orla bit her tongue and focused on the path ahead – a narrow alleyway between two houses that leant together so dramatically their roofs touched at the top. At the end of the alley was a cobbled street and a terrace of faded white buildings. They each had glass windows, watching sadly over the empty street. A string of gas lamps stood in a skeletal row, draped in dense cobwebs. Turning left on to the street, Orla tried to look as though she knew where she was going. She led the way between the crumbling buildings, hoping to find a doorway or a window that looked familiar – but with every twist and turn, she felt her heart sink. Fleetwater was a maze, and the mist did not help at all. It swirled through the streets and played tricks on her eyes, making ghosts and Haulers appeared at every corner.

'Are we lost?' asked Ariana.

'No,' said Orla with a sigh.

Ariana kept pace beside her, eyes wide, taking in the gloomy streets.

'Fleetwater lies very low in the land,' she said. 'That's why there's so much mist.'

'Very useful,' said Orla. 'Can you look for green doors, rather than commenting on the weather?' she added, hurrying ahead to a little side street, while Ariana peered down a narrow alleyway.

Between the houses, she was relieved to see a thick parade of foxgloves, their soft leaves soaked in beads of dew. She marched ahead so that she could talk to the plants without Idris and Ariana hearing her.

'Which way do I go?' she asked the foxgloves, without looking down.

Cold town, they said, only echoing Orla's words. *Ghost town*.

'That's not helpful,' she hissed. 'I'm looking for a house with a sage-coloured door – with honeysuckle growing all around it.'

The foxgloves swayed their pink flowers dimly in the mist. Perhaps, like the plants on the river, they didn't trust strangers. Orla held out a cold hand and turned over one of the downy leaves. The underside was speckled with black marks.

Footsteps behind her broke her concentration.

'Where are we *going*?' asked Idris.

'We're going to find the *cure*, Idris,' said Orla.

Desperate, she marched to the next alleyway, where a jumble of buildings fought for space, their glass windows cracked and cobwebbed and dotted with silent clusters of ferns and toadflax. Each building bore a metal sign, sticking out into the mist like lifeless flags. And each door was painted sage-green.

'Aha,' said Orla. 'This is it.'

'Glassmaker Row,' said Ariana, reading one of the signs.

'There're no glassmakers here,' said Idris, pressing his nose to a dusty window, peering inside.

'That don't mean there's no cure,' said Orla. 'We're gonna find it. Ma wanted to come back here for a reason. House with a green door. Well, here we are.'

There was no honeysuckle around the first door that she came to. Orla bit her lip. Many years had passed, perhaps the honeysuckle was long gone . . .

She pulled out her knife. If she had to search every house with a green door, then she would. She rattled the blade between the door and the frame until the latch clicked open, and then stepped into the dark and dusty room.

Gone like ghosts, called the toadflax behind her. *Nothing left but seeds and stone.*

Idris and Ariana hovered on the threshold.

'I don't know about this, Orla,' whispered Ariana. 'Are you sure it's safe?'

As her eyes adjusted to the darkness, Orla saw that the room was lined with bare shelves and cupboards. There was a small fireplace, draped with cobwebs thick as shrouds, and a small table set for tea.

'We're looking for small glass bottles,' she told Idris and Ariana. 'No bigger than an ink bottle. Hexagonal.' Kneeling down, she used her finger to draw the shape in the dust. 'Come on. They could be anywhere – somewhere the Haulers wouldn't have seen. Look *everywhere.*'

They opened cupboards and pulled out drawers, lifted loose floorboards and rummaged through bookshelves. They searched in every dust-covered box and cobwebbed alcove. Idris found a small door leading to a yard, laid out with metal tools and a strange stone dome that Ariana said was a *furnace* for glassmaking. But there was no glass – not even a broken shard. It was as though every speck of glass had been swept away by the river, save for the windows of the houses.

The Haulers' words echoed in her mind. *There's nothing left*, they'd said.

Nothing left, echoed the toadflax on the doorstep.

'We'll try next door,' said Orla, wiping the dust from her face and hurrying out into the street. The second house leant out over the river. Its door was not locked, and the floorboards creaked and groaned as they stepped inside, threatening to drop them down into the swirling water below. The bedrooms were mildewed, the hallways dripping with river mist. When Ariana asked Orla if she was *sure* they were looking in the right place, Orla snapped and ordered her to rummage through an enormous trunk of forgotten keys and candlesticks. But it did not take much looking to find that there was no trace of glass in this house either.

'Let's move on,' said Orla, pulling a dead spider from her hair and marching out into the cobbled street.

'There's nothing here,' said Idris, as they left. 'You're just leading us round in circles and it's almost dark. We should be getting back to the boat.'

Dusk had fallen over the buildings, making their flaking white paint look dim. Tall stems of honesty grew in the cracks of the cobbles, and it echoed Idris's words.

Nothing here, they said. *Nothing here.*

'Is there any more information in your ma's book?' asked Ariana.

'No,' said Orla sharply. 'There's nothing else.' She felt a flush of shame then. She did not want to show Ariana Ma's feverish scribbles. Whatever Ma had written about this place – it was indecipherable. Ma had been so clever: it was not fair to show Ariana her writing when she was sick.

Orla rubbed her eyes. She was just about to open the door of the fourth building when a scent came to her on the evening air: a familiar, warm, honey smell.

Honeysuckle, she whispered to herself, and raced ahead.

When the plants couldn't speak, they had other ways of telling her things. She knew that scent well. It led her towards the water – and towards a tall white building right on the bank of the river. Hurrying up a set of stone steps, Orla found herself at a fading green door. Honeysuckle grew in a twisting vine right to the roof. Its stem was speckled black, but a dozen or so flowers remained – damp with mist, but spinning their honey scent into the evening. Orla felt a sudden glow of familiarity. The plants had called her here. *This* must be the house. A flicker of a smile crossed her lips.

The door opened to reveal an empty workshop. Orla saw the remains of a fire – charred wood in a stone chimney, surrounded by metal instruments that she did not recognize. It was a furnace, like the one she had seen in the first house. A glassmaker had lived here, she was sure of that – but there was no sign of any glass bottles. To her left, there was a wooden spiral staircase.

She climbed creakily upwards and found herself in an attic room, with windows that looked out across the village in each direction. Night was falling, and the sky was deep blue. Orla could see the great swoop of the river, winding like a ribbon between the trees and the rocks, out into the never-ending expanse of the Untold Forest. She felt suddenly very far away from home. She missed Captain, and she missed her garden. The plants in Fleetwater were not the same. Even the honesty seed pods were a different colour. Instead of the silver Orla knew in Thorn Creek, these seeds had a purplish hue, like a shadow cast over a bright moon.

There was a desk beside the window, with a candle and a box of matches. Orla lit the candle, and discovered that the room was lined with wooden shelves. They were empty, but a trail of fingerprints ran through the dust. They looked new. Her skin prickled. Who else had come to Fleetwater recently? Who else was *here*? Holding the candle aloft, Orla searched the attic. A small wooden door led to a bedroom, and a great brass bed, but it had not been slept in.

She waited – but no memory came back to her at the sight of the bed. Ducking underneath, she saw no wooden trundle bed. She kicked the bedpost in frustration, then bit her tongue to stop herself crying out as her toe throbbed furiously.

'Orla?' called Idris from the stairs. He appeared in the doorway, with Ariana behind him. 'This isn't right,' he said. 'We shoulda found your medicine by now. I thought you said you'd been here before?'

'I *did*,' said Orla. 'I came with Ma.'

'Then why haven't we found it?' replied Idris.

Orla gripped the candle so hard that the wax began to bend. 'Because I don't remember, all right? I don't remember anything about this stupid place.' Her breath sent the flame of the candle dancing back and forth, casting angry shadows around the room.

'You seen those empty shelves?' said Idris. 'There's

nothing here. Haulers looted the place – sold it all in Westharbour, I bet.'

'Idris is right,' said Ariana. 'It's the same in every house.'

Orla felt her cheeks flush.

'But I'm not *done*,' she said fiercely, staring out at the darkening meadows beyond the town.

'We can't stay here in the dark,' said Idris. 'It's too—'

'Are you scared?' said Orla. 'We got candles. We can carry on all night. There's no ghosts here,' she said, trying to convince herself. She looked at the fingerprints. Not ghosts, no. But she was starting to think that they were not the only people in Fleetwater. Perhaps she was imagining it, but over the scent of the dust and the burning candle, she thought she could smell the faint and familiar scent of a wood fire, rising up and up towards the open sky.

'We gotta get back to the boat,' said Idris.

'The cure is here!' shouted Orla. 'If you *really* want to help your brother—'

'Don't you *dare*—' said Idris. But before he could finish, Ariana had grabbed him by the sleeve. She was staring out of the window with a look of panic on her face.

'*Stop!*' she hissed. 'Look – there's a light outside.'

She pointed down towards the forest. At once, Idris licked his finger and pinched out Orla's candle. Orla

127

heard the *hiss* of the wick, and they were plunged into darkness.

'You won't get much chance to find it if Haulers get us first,' said Idris.

'That's not Haulers,' said Orla firmly, squinting into the evening mist. 'That light's in the east.' She pressed her face against the window of the house and felt the rumble of the weir coming through the walls. Down in the darkness, she could see the scraggly outline of the forest. And just below it, inland, the flicker of firelight.

'There's people still in Fleetwater. And I'm going to find them.'

17

<u>Oak</u> *Quercus robur*
Bark: to tan leather and dye yarn. Galls: for ink.

Orla scrambled over roots and bumps and nettles tall as her head, half-tripping, half-running. Around her, the plants called out, rustling their leaves. Orla's heart skipped to hear them again. Away from the river, their voices grew louder and louder.

Out by the woods, called the nettles.

Hidden and safe, said the dogwood.

Firelight; dry earth, sang the wild roses.

'Keep up!' called Orla. 'Whoever's out there, they'll know everything. I'll make 'em tell us where to find it.'

She followed the path out into the open fields, up towards the forest. There were no houses here, and the roaring of the weir was no more than a faint purr, muffled by the whispering grass and the rattling seed pods in the fields. Whoever was out here had hidden themselves far away from the village. Orla's heart hammered as she ran through the grass. Ahead, the fire stood out like a beacon among the trees. It was calling her closer.

Like a wildcat, she slipped into the forest, with Ariana and Idris on her tail. The trees swallowed the starlight, and Orla heard the deep murmur of the oldest trees, their roots running into the earth below. There was no sickness out here, Orla thought. The oaks, the chestnut, the beech: they all rumbled contentedly, preparing to drop their leaves for winter. A deer gave a bark, and Orla heard a dozen feet scattering across the damp forest floor.

A little way into the woods, she held up her hand, signalling for Idris and Ariana to stop. The orange fire-light flickered on their faces.

'I don't see anyone,' she whispered. 'But that fire's been going a while. Let's go and look around.'

'Maybe *you* should go and look around,' muttered Idris, as Ariana leant against a tree, catching her breath. 'Seeing as this was your idea.'

Orla rolled her eyes and crept towards the fire.

Welcome stranger, said the oaks. *Safe in the woods, safe from the wind and the cold.*

Reassured, Orla strode into the light. A little way beyond the fire, she saw a tent stretched between two

130

trees. Leaves had already begun to fall, scattering the tent with garlands of red and orange. Beside it stood a large wooden cart, its wheels as big as the trunk of an oak. It had a canvas roof, held up by bowed wood, and a set of wooden steps led down from a canvas door, holding milk churns and baskets. There was a stack of chopped wood, a water trough and, Orla noticed, at the edge of the firelight, a long-haired cow, dozing beneath the trees. A pot stood on a stone beside the fire, and Orla caught the scent of turnip greens, coffee – and something that smelt like mushrooms. After the chill of Fleetwater, this place felt warm and deep and wise. The musky scent of the cow reminded her of Captain. This was not a Hauler camp. She turned her back to the fire and whispered to Idris and Ariana.

'Someone's living out here,' she said.

'Why wouldn't they stay in the empty houses?' said Ariana.

'Because they're scared,' said Idris. 'Scared of the sickness. Scared of the Haulers. They're the only ones left alive . . .'

Orla dipped her finger into the stew. It was still hot.

'We should hide here,' she said. 'Wait for them to return and catch them—'

She stopped. There was a rustle of leaves and canvas behind her.

'Hey!' came a shout. 'You get away from there!'

Orla turned to see a girl with straw-blond hair rushing towards her wielding a broom. She thrust it at Orla, nostrils flaring.

'I said, get away!' she cried, swinging the broom so wildly that Orla stumbled backwards.

Orla grabbed the broom handle with one hand and held it still.

'Don't you do that,' she warned, curling her free hand into a fist.

The girl's hair was tied in two neat braids, her cheeks were flushed, and as Orla came closer she pushed her hard.

'You bring the sickness here!' said the girl.

'No, I don't,' said Orla, holding her hands in the air and taking a step backwards.

'Magda!' said a voice from the tent. A boy emerged. As he stepped into the firelight, Orla saw that he, too, had hair like straw, and both of them had the same streak of freckles across their faces. They must have been brother and sister – a couple of years older than she was. The boy wore a neckerchief the colour of autumn, and a serious face.

'We just come to ask questions,' said Idris.

'Come from where?' said the girl called Magda, holding the broom towards them.

'From Thorn Creek.'

The girl's eyes widened.

'You had the sickness here,' said Orla. 'That's what we

come to ask about.'

The boy peered at Orla, his face puzzled.

'I know you,' he said, stepping closer.

'Get back, Matteas. They could be sick!'

'We're not sick,' said Orla.

'You look it,' said the girl, nodding at Ariana.

Ariana pulled nervously at her sleeves. 'We've travelled a long way,' she said. 'We're *tired*.'

'We don't welcome strangers here,' said Magda.

'That's no stranger,' said Matteas. 'That's Orla. Orla Carson.'

Magda stared in disbelief. 'That's not possible,' she said, lowering the broom. 'She and her ma died of the sickness. The *mapafoglia*,' she hissed.

'The sickness took my ma,' said Orla. 'But I'm not dead.'

'I can see that,' Matteas said calmly.

Orla swallowed. Beside her, Ariana shuffled closer. Idris watched from the shadows.

'Why's he think you died, Orla?' he asked.

Orla drew her eyes away from Matteas, and turned to Idris. He looked tense. Orla stayed silent. She was asking herself the same question.

'Because there's no cure for the sickness,' said Magda. 'And she had it, *bad*.'

18

Witch Hazel *Hamamelis virginiana*
For cholera and dysentery.

The shock hit Orla like a wave. Four pairs of eyes stared at her, flickering in the firelight. She could not move. The world had turned to thick pine tar around her.

Ariana was shaking her shoulder. 'Is it true?' she said, her eyes wide. 'You had the sickness?'

Orla couldn't answer. She was still reeling from Magda's words: *She had it, bad.*

In the meadow behind them, Orla heard the grasses murmuring.

Fever, they said. *Sickness.*

'No,' said Orla, her mouth dry. 'You're wrong.' *Ma* was the one who had been sick; *Ma* was the one who fought the fever, her arms stained dark as purple ink.

How could she, Orla, have had the sickness without knowing? How could she have got better from it, when Ma had not?

The world spun around her. She felt suddenly wobbly.

'She doesn't remember,' said Magda, looking at Orla in disbelief.

Matteas moved closer, his brow wrinkled in concern. 'You should sit by the fire,' he said. 'You need to rest.'

Shelter, said the ancient oaks. *Safe home.*

But Orla did not move. The fire crackled and the cow let out a deep sigh.

'I don't want to sit down, I want answers,' she said. Beside her, Ariana shivered.

'Sit down,' said Matteas, pointing to the wooden benches beside the fire. 'Your friends are cold and hungry even if you're not. I'll tell you what I can, once you've eaten. There's no use fighting an empty stomach – you will lose.'

'Go on,' said Ariana, nudging Orla forward.

Go on, echoed the oaks, their voices deep and kind.

Orla took off her pack and sat on the bench. Ariana sat beside her, while Idris pulled off his coat and sat on the ground beside the fire. But even in the welcome heat of the flames, she did not feel comforted. Her mind swirled, and when Matteas handed her a bowl of mushroom stew, she could not eat.

'It'll warm you up,' said Magda sternly.

Orla looked down at her bowl. On top of the mush-rooms, Matteas had placed three round dumplings filled with cheese, and a steaming portion of turnip greens. She took a spoonful of the hot stew. It tasted deep and earthy, like the woods, and as she ate Orla felt the world slide back into focus. Hours had passed since the liquorice that morning, and she had not realized how much she needed a proper meal.

Magda nodded with approval when Orla handed back the bowl for seconds. Orla watched as she spooned the stew from the pot over the fire. Magda showed no sign of the sickness; neither did Matteas. Their whole village had died, but *somehow*, they had not.

'You survived,' said Orla. 'How is that possible?'

Idris looked up from his bowl, listening intently.

'We were going to ask *you* the same thing,' said Matteas, looking at Orla. He was not much older than Castor, Orla thought, but he spoke like a grown-up.

'She don't know,' said Idris. 'That's why we're here. You're the only ones left alive in this cursed place. Tell us how you did it.'

'By the skin of our teeth, that's how,' said Magda, looking out towards the village. 'You seen it – there's nothing left of the village now. No glassmakers, no flower meadows. Nothing. First the plants died, and then the people. Then the Haulers came and took all the glass. We came up here, where things still grow.' She turned to

Orla, as though she wanted to say something more, but instead fell silent.

Orla was certain that she knew what Magda was thinking: Ma had not saved this village.

'It weren't Ma's fault!' she said. 'She travelled round the villages *helping* people – she tried her best – just because she couldn't save everyone don't mean . . .'

Matteas stoked the fire, sending a rain of sparks into the eaves of the trees.

'It's thanks to your ma that we're still alive,' he said.

'She told us to move into the forest,' explained Magda. 'She told us to drink water from the spring, and to wash our hands. And just before she left, she gave us—'

'The cure,' said Idris, with certainty.

Magda looked sad. 'No,' she said. 'She gave us *seeds*, seeds so we could grow pumpkins and corn and turnips. Without her, we would've starved. There's only so much we could take from the forest.'

'That's all?' asked Idris.

'I don't understand,' said Orla. 'She was trying to find a cure. She tried to come back here when she was sick. She was scribbling away in her book, working it all out – she knew she had to come to Fleetwater.'

'It happened little by little,' said Matteas. 'Your ma visited when she could, staying for a week or so, caring for villagers who were unwell, showing them how to treat their colds and fevers. Bringing seeds to help the gardens grow. At first, the sickness wasn't too bad – a few plants here and there. One or two people falling sick.'

Just like Thorn Creek, thought Orla, looking at Idris and Ariana.

'Wait – the plants and the people,' said Idris. 'It's the same sickness?'

Matteas nodded. 'Your ma took it seriously, straight away,' he said to Orla. 'She was *looking* for a cure. The trouble was that, after a time, the villagers lost their faith. When people started to die, and your ma didn't know how to stop it, they convinced themselves that she was a fraud.'

'Some even thought *she'd* caused the sickness,' said Magda. 'They turned against her. They threw out her medicines and burnt the plants in the meadow. They called your ma all kinds of terrible things and they wouldn't listen to her advice no more. When you got sick – well, that was it. She went home to Thorn Creek at once, and told us that she'd bring the cure back to us when she found it . . .'

Matteas untied his neckerchief and twisted it in his hands.

'But she didn't,' said Ariana softly. 'She *couldn't*.'

Orla bowed her head. This couldn't be right.

'But the cure wasn't in Thorn Creek,' she said, dragging her pack towards her. 'It was *here*. She wanted to come back *here*.'

'Maybe that was the fever talking,' said Idris bitterly, glaring at Orla, echoing her words to him back in Thorn Creek.

'We don't have what you need,' said Magda. 'The Haulers took all the glass – goodness knows why. And you've seen what's happened to the plants.'

It was true, Orla thought – the plants down in the village were all but silent. But up here – out in the meadow, out in the forest, they were whispering again, calm as a warm September night. Orla couldn't shake the feeling that Magda was hiding something.

Safe out here, said the oaks. *Safe with the owls and the deer and the trees.*

'We're not lying to you, Orla,' Magda insisted. 'You had the sickness. Your ma took you to Thorn Creek, and that's where you got better. If there's a cure anywhere, it's there.'

Orla's stomach twisted. 'You're wrong,' she said fiercely. 'It's gotta be here somewhere, you just don't know it!'

'Why would we live on the edge of a dead village if we had a cure?' Magda demanded, her cheeks flushing. 'Why would we live all alone? Why would we be the only ones left alive?'

'There's gotta be something here,' said Orla. She saw Idris then, his head in his hands, and felt a burst of shame. She had promised him that they would find answers in Fleetwater. Beside him, Ariana simply watched, her brow wrinkled with concern.

Magda turned to her brother, her voice calmer now. 'What about the key?' she said.

19

Hawthorn *Crataegus monogyna*
A tonic for the heart.

'What key?' said Orla.

Matteas ran his hands through his hair. 'I wouldn't get your hopes up,' he said.

'Anything could help,' said Ariana.

Matteas reached into his pocket and pulled out a tiny object. He held it out towards Orla. It was a silver key.

Orla took it carefully. It was no bigger than her little finger, and the bow was cast in the shape of a leaf, inlaid with green glass. She ran her thumb over the smooth surface.

Bread and butter, whispered the oaks.

For a moment, Orla stared at the key. And then she realized what the oaks were saying.

'What kind of leaf is it?' asked Ariana.

'Hawthorn,' she whispered, thinking how she and Ma used to pick the first leaves in spring, and say they tasted just like bread and butter.

It was a common tree. It grew in Orla's garden in Thorn Creek. It grew everywhere. There was nothing special about it.

'We found the key after your ma left,' said Matteas. 'And we've tried every lock in Fleetwater, with no luck. It must be for a door in Thorn Creek.'

The leaf glowed with familiarity. But it wasn't just that Orla knew the plant.

Leaves and paper and flowers, said the grass.

Ink and water, said the ivy.

'Hold on,' she said, hurrying to pull out Ma's book. 'I've seen that shape before.'

'On a plant?' said Idris sharply.

'No,' said Orla, turning to Ma's map. Ma had drawn the hawthorn leaves in Thorn Creek, in their garden – but she'd also drawn them somewhere else. '*There*,' Orla said, jabbing her finger at the paper. A little way upriver from Fleetwater, the river split into a *y* shape. To the left, it curled towards the mountains; on the right, it twisted into the trees. And there, on the branch to the right, Ma had drawn a single leaf, right beside the place she had written '*here*' in tiny letters.

Matteas peered at the map. 'That's just swampy

woodland,' he said. 'There's nothing else up that way.'

Orla ran her finger along the narrower stream. In tiny letters Ma had written *Alder Carr*.

'It's no coincidence Ma used a symbol that looks *just* like this key,' said Orla. 'All on its own out there.' She held the key against the paper, holding it up so that everyone could see. 'I think we should go there. If people here were burning the plants Ma used for medicine –' with a twist in her gut Orla thought of her own garden – 'if there's any chance of finding the cure there . . .'

Idris, who had been quiet all this time, turned to Orla with a thunderous look on his face.

'Any chance?' he said bitterly. 'We don't have time for *any chance*. We can't wander into the woods looking for a *chance*. You said there would be a cure! You said we would find it here, in Fleetwater! Now we've lost so much time – time we don't have! Why did you do this?' He glared at Orla and, when she could not reply, he threw his mug to the ground. 'I gotta go. Back to the boat. I gotta find some real answers.'

He pulled himself to his feet, his face set like stone.

'You can't leave!' said Orla, standing now too.

'Why should I listen to you?' said Idris. 'They said you had the sickness. If they're telling the truth, that means, somehow, you got better from it. And you don't even remember how. That plant? It's all over Thorn Creek. It's nothing but a hedge plant.'

143

Orla breathed deeply, anger surging through her. She'd got them this far, hadn't she? She'd brought them to Fleetwater, and she'd found people who *knew* Ma and had a key to a place that only Ma knew about. Why couldn't Idris see how close they were to finding answers?

'We're trying to help, Idris,' said Ariana tearfully, trying to pull herself to her feet and getting caught in her skirt. 'Don't be angry.'

'You didn't help that much,' said Orla under her breath. 'I'm the one that found this place, found the *key*.'

'Actually, Magda found the key . . .' said Matteas.

'My brother's dying!' said Idris. 'And all anyone can do is sit around remembering how great your ma was and how her special key is going to fix all this. Well, you know what? It isn't.'

'We all want to find a cure, as much as you do!' said Magda.

Hush, said the oaks softly, as though they were trying to comfort Orla. *Hush, there, wise girl.*

Idris looked at Matteas. 'My brother Castor went up the river. And now he's dying of the sickness. You must know something more than just that *key*.'

In the firelight, Orla could see that Idris had tears in his eyes. He wiped his face with his sleeve. She clutched the key. It didn't matter where the sickness was coming from. All that mattered was finding a way to stop it.

'He went up towards the mountains,' Idris went on. 'I gotta go find out where. I'm running outta time – *he's* running outta time!'

Magda shook her head. 'We don't go upriver,' she said. 'No one does. It's too dangerous to take a boat any further.'

'I can handle the boat,' said Idris. 'We gotta go on. It's the only way.'

'No,' said Ariana firmly. 'We have to rest. Can we stay here, by the fire?' she asked, looking at Matteas and Magda. 'Then in the morning we can work through this logically. We'll check everywhere in Fleetwater – in case something has been missed, and then we can work our way *methodically* upriver.'

Magda nodded. 'I'll bring you some blankets,' she said.

Idris scowled as he returned to the fire. He looked exhausted, Orla thought. They sat in silence as Magda reappeared with blankets and sheepskins, which they made into three small nests beside the fire.

Soft sleep, said the mistletoe, high in the trees.

As Matteas disappeared inside the tent and Magda climbed into the wagon, Orla wrapped herself in blankets and curled into a ball, listening to the *pat pat* of oak leaves drifting on to the forest floor. The leaves were falling early this year. How long before the sickness reached this part of the forest too?

Autumn's here, they murmured. *Everything's changing.*

'Tell me about it,' whispered Orla, watching the oaks' ancient branches swaying in the firelight. Summer was fading away, and it felt as though she – and perhaps the whole world – was running out of time. She shivered, thinking of her garden and Captain. Of Castor. It felt as though there were a hundred miles of mist and forest between her and home. Pressing the key into her palm, Orla tried to imagine the kind of door it might unlock.

20

Dog Rose *Rosa canina*
Hips: peel flesh away from inner seeds (irritant); boil and strain to make rosehip syrup. For colds and influenza.

Watch out, watch out! cried the plants.

Orla woke with a start. The fire had burnt low and the dawn light was just starting to illuminate the trees.

'What is it?' mumbled Ariana, as Orla shed her blankets and pulled on her oilskin.

Strangers, whispered the oaks.

Creeping between the trunks of the trees, Orla saw the misty expanse of the meadows beyond, and below them, the river. A dimly lit lamp was weaving its way from the bank, held by two shadowy figures.

Orla felt her blood run cold. She sprinted back to the camp, heaved on her pack, and prodded Idris in the ribs.

He stirred, and then scrabbled to his feet when he saw Orla's face.

'We gotta go,' she said. 'Haulers.'

She hurried to Matteas's tent and called quietly. 'Haulers,' she repeated, when Matteas appeared, his hair sticking up. 'You'll want to put out your fire.'

Matteas nodded. He watched the trees intently, and did not take his eyes from the forest as he spoke to Orla. 'Take the path round the edge of the village,' he said. 'You can cut back to your boat that way. Hold on.'

He dipped his head inside the tent and handed her some smoked fish wrapped in cloth, along with sticky dried plums and a handful of red rosehips. Orla took them gratefully, and was suddenly reminded of Elias back in Thorn Creek, always turning up with useful things, just as she needed them. And she was surprised to find herself wishing she hadn't been so grumpy towards him.

The children skirted the edge of the woods, weaving between the trees – where every shadow looked like a Hauler. When they came within sight of the river, they dropped down into the village, passing between the legs of the buildings on stilts, and back towards the tall white house. The plants had fallen silent once more, and all that Orla heard were footsteps echoing through the mist.

'There were only two of 'em,' said Orla to the others,

looking over her shoulder. 'Where are they, and where's the rest?'

'Right here,' said a voice from the shadows.

Ariana screamed.

Like a ghost from the mist, the face of a Hauler appeared. It was Bouchard. He grabbed Orla by the shoulder.

'Got you, river rat!' he said gleefully.

Orla scratched at his hands and kicked him hard in the shin.

'Get off me, you hound!' she spat, pulling herself free. She managed two steps then felt the Hauler grab hold of the pack on her back. 'Run!' she yelled to Ariana and Idris. Without hesitating, they fled between the houses.

'Come here, girl!' Bouchard growled, pulling her back. Orla caught a whiff of his stinking fish breath, but before he could tighten his grip, she let her whole weight drop to the ground, as though she were fainting. Both she and the bag slipped from his grasp. She quickly rolled over in the mud, out of reach, and sprinted through the winding streets towards the river.

'Get back here!' yelled Bouchard. But Orla did not look back. She turned on to a narrow flight of stone stairs and ran down into the cobbled street below. Ahead, she saw Idris and Ariana making for the jetty.

Voices carried through the mist like the howls of wild dogs.

'We can hear your footsteps!' they laughed.

'You bring back that silver, missy!' called Leblanc.

'We'll find you!'

'We seen your boat!'

Orla could hear the foxgloves calling her towards the river.

This way, this way! they called.

Finally, thought Orla. *Knew you'd remember me!*

Orla caught up with Idris and Ariana in the alleyway that led to the jetty, shrouded in mist. The roar of the weir almost drowned the Haulers' cries, but behind them, quite close, Orla heard Silas's gravelly voice.

'Forget the silver,' he said. 'Bring me her book.'

Orla felt suddenly dizzy. *The book?* She clutched the straps of her pack. *How does Silas know about Ma's book?*

'Find her!' he called. 'Or I'll have your guts for ribbons.'

Orla couldn't move her feet. *Why does he want the book?*

'Orla, come on!' said Ariana, pulling Orla's oilskin until she stumbled forward. Idris was ahead, racing towards the boat. For a moment Orla had the dreadful feeling that he was going to leave her there with Silas – just as she had almost left him back at Dead Elm Strand. She urged herself onwards, sprinting down the jetty with Ariana at her side.

There, at the end, Idris was waiting.

Orla's stomach swooped. Idris was not like she was. He would never abandon someone in danger.

He held the boat steady as she and Ariana climbed aboard. Then he slipped the lines free and Orla tumbled on to the deck, just in time to see Silas looming out of the mist. He fixed them with a yellow stare, his chest heaving, looking as though, if it weren't for the water, he would come charging at them like a bull on the loose – charging after the book hidden in her pack.

Panting, Orla scrabbled around for her paddle. This was not how it was supposed to be. The Haulers were supposed to go to Westharbour. They were supposed to want gold and silver and ale – not a book.

21

Hart's Tongue Fern *Asplenium scolopendrium*
Harvest fronds in the summer. Ointment: for burns and scalds;
infusion: for the spleen.

Leaving Fleetwater, the river twisted sharply. At once,
the trees bowed their heads together like a tunnel and
the water was dappled in the early morning light. Beyond
the rocky banks Orla saw enormous feathers of bracken
curling out from between their trunks, gemmed with drops
of mist. The children whispered cautiously, and made
their course northwards, out into the true wild. It would
not be long before they reached the fork in the river.

Untold Forest, said the ferns, their fronds shining
emerald in the mist.

Footsteps follow, said the hemlock that grew beside
the bank.

Keep on, keep on, said the moss. *Away from the men, away from the beasts.*

Orla muttered under her breath as she paddled. 'That's what we're trying to do,' she said. But inside, she was glad that the plants out here were beginning to trust her. She could tell that they wanted to help – even though their stems were blackened, their leaves speckled with black marks. The sickness did not end at Fleetwater – it was everywhere on the river.

Ariana was peering through the mist behind them, her white hands gripping the gunwales of the boat. Orla could tell that she was thinking about the Haulers too. How long would it be before they were back on the water, hunting them like a whale in the ocean?

'How'd they get to Fleetwater so *fast*?' said Ariana.

'They musta stowed a boat,' said Idris, hitting his forehead. 'Haulers do it all the time. Keep a boat hidden now and again along the river – in case your own gets pinched. Shoulda suspected.'

'*Sneaking toads*,' muttered Orla, watching over her shoulder as they moved upriver. She had the feeling Silas was still there but just out of reach, the smell of his breath hanging in the air.

'They want Ma's book,' she said quietly. 'And they came all this way for it. Why?'

Ariana shuffled uneasily in her seat.

Orla tucked her pack carefully under the canvas to

keep Ma's book away from the water and picked up her paddle again.

'We gotta move as fast as we can,' she said, pushing hard against the current. A fierce wind twisted through the trees, tossing the water into waves.

'River's getting rough, Orla,' said Idris.

'Then we push harder!' she said firmly, blinking the mist from her eyes.

Rising water, said the plants.

Root-ripper, tree-devourer, said the willows.

Sickness spreads, said a fern.

You can help us, wise girl. You can do it.

Ahead, the river snapped and thundered against the banks. Orla pushed on, all the more determined, glad that the plants were on her side – even if no one else was.

But after an hour, they had barely covered half a mile. Orla's shoulders ached and her sleeves were soaked to the elbows. The wind blustered and taunted the little boat, like a cat tossing them backwards with its paw, throwing them back just as far as they had come.

'They'll catch us,' said Ariana, starting to shiver again. 'They know we came this way. There's three of them: they'll paddle faster and harder and . . .'

Exhausted, she dropped her head into her hands and stifled a sob. Orla looked away. She couldn't decide if she felt sorry for Ariana, or annoyed at her sniffling.

'I can't go back,' said Ariana. 'Not yet.'

'I say we pull in,' said Idris. 'Hide. The Haulers will slip right past us.'

'We can't stop!' said Orla. 'We need to keep going – we need to get to Alder Carr. We need to see why Ma wanted to—'

'I told you, we don't have time for that,' said Idris. 'We need to head to the mountains – like Castor. That's the *other* side of the fork. And if we've got any chance of doing that, we gotta pull in here and *hide*.'

'But what if Castor went to Alder Carr?'

'You heard Matteas. It's nothing but trees and swamps. Castor followed the river into the *mountains*.'

Idris pushed the boat towards a small inlet at the edge of the river, where a large willow tree stretched its roots out into the water, making a natural dock for the boat.

'Why aren't you pleased?' said Orla, as Idris looped the bow line around a willow root and tied it, yanking it tight.

'Because there's something going on up that river – something more than your plants and your key: Magda as good as said so. The Haulers have been heading this way for years. I gotta know *why*. Castor weren't talking about the river and the mountains being pitch black for nothing.'

'But you can't ignore Ma's key – a key she left for a reason.'

'You've got no idea what you're doing!' he said. 'We can't just wait for you work it all out.'

Orla felt as though her skin had been stung by nettles. Just when everything was slotting into place, Idris wanted to carry on up the river like Ma's map didn't even exist. Scowling at Idris, Orla seized her pack and climbed ashore.

'Can we please stop arguing?' said Ariana. 'This is ridiculous. We need to rest.'

'I'm staying aboard,' said Idris.

'You should be grateful,' Orla muttered. Why couldn't they see that going to Fleetwater had been a good idea? Without Fleetwater, she would never have found the key.

'You coming?' he said to Ariana as he crawled beneath the canvas. Ariana squeezed the mist from her hair and shook her head. Instead, she pulled out a small gas lamp from the bow, along with a metal kettle.

Orla huddled beneath a silvery willow, keeping one eye on the river while Ariana lit the lamp and filled the kettle with rainwater that had collected on the boat's canvas.

Half-memories swirled through Orla's mind like a winter storm. Ma returning from Fleetwater, the marks on her arms.

'Tea will help,' said Ariana, pulling a handful of red berries from a pocket of her dress. She dropped them into the kettle and waited. Orla saw that her hands were red and raw from paddling the boat, and there were dark circles under her eyes. Orla wondered for a moment what life was like at Hind House, with her mother wandering silently through the halls, alone save for when Atlas visited from Westharbour. She thought of Ariana with her glass beaker at the window, and wondered if she was still trying to make perfumes; wondered if she still drew diagrams in her school books – of telescopes and waterwheels, clockwork . . .

It was as though Ariana knew what Orla was thinking.

'It's not like you think, at Hind House,' she said. 'My uncle fell into debt three years ago and since then – well, we don't have much at all.'

Orla thought of the roast goose she'd smelt on one of her trips past the kitchens. Perhaps Ariana's idea of *not much* was very different from hers.

'He convinced the Marshall of Westharbour to let him charter a ship to sell his ink over the sea,' Ariana continued. 'But he wanted to tighten his purse strings, so he didn't hire a full crew. The ship sank. He owes the Marshall a *lot* of money.'

'Why are you telling me this?' said Orla, irritated. She just wanted to sit with the willow tree in peace. 'I don't want to hear about Atlas. I don't want to hear about Hind House, or any of it. I gotta job to do . . .'

'I just want you to know that it isn't like you think it is,' said Ariana, checking the kettle. 'Being the niece of the Warden. After my father died, everything changed—'

'I don't care what happened, all right?' said Orla, feeling annoyed now. She wanted to climb up into the willow, rather than talk to Ariana Claw about Ma.

Ariana looked down at the ground, running her fingers through the earth between the willow roots. She looked as though she were examining every fine particle of dust and dirt.

'Orla, I saw your ma try to help my father,' she said, looking Orla in the eye. 'And I know she tried her best to save him.'

Orla looked away. She watched the willow leaves dropping one by one into the river.

'I don't need you to be nice to me,' she said. 'I just want to find the cure.'

'That's what we all want, Orla,' said Ariana, pouring the tea into a wooden cup and passing it to Orla. The rosehips swirled like red rubies in the water. Orla breathed in the sharp, woody scent. She had travelled so far since she left Thorn Creek that the world was a blur. She felt like a leaf caught in a breeze. For a moment, sitting there with Ariana, everything seemed stiller.

Until the sharp taste of the rosehips hit her tongue. At once Orla felt as though she had fallen back in time. She was lying by a fire, with Ma at her side, gently wiping the sweat from her brow. She'd pressed a wooden cup to

Orla's shivering lips. *For the fever*, Ma had said. *You must drink it, Orla.*

Orla gasped. The memory came so suddenly, like sunlight from beneath the darkest clouds. She remembered it vividly now. Ma had handed her a cup just like this. But the liquid inside it was not the rusty red of rosehip tea. It had been a shimmering, inky blue.

'*They were right,*' she whispered.

'What is it?' said Ariana, her brow wrinkling in concern.

Goose pimples prickled on Orla's arms. The world was spinning.

'Magda was right,' she said. 'I *did* have the sickness. And all this time, I couldn't remember it. But I remember now. Ma gave me a medicine, sure as you gave me that rosehip tea. She gave me a medicine, and it was *blue.*'

She remembered the room, dark and hot. Was it Fleetwater, or Thorn Creek? She could not remember. But she remembered the swirling liquid, the smoke from the fire, the smell of lavender oil to take away the smell of the sickness. Ma leaning over her, helping her drink. The shadow of someone else in the room, their face turned away from the fire, hidden in darkness.

'Magda was telling the truth,' she said. 'There's no medicine in Fleetwater. But now I know for sure that Ma had a cure. A cure that *worked.*' Saying it aloud, she could hardly believe it.

A cure from the leaves and the roots and the ground, said the plants.

Orla saw Ariana's eyes dart to her wrists, as though checking Orla for signs of the sickness, and then back to her face.

'Then *you're* the proof,' she said, looking intently at Orla, her eyes bright. 'Proof that the sickness can be cured. Your ma knew what she was doing.'

The warmth of the rosehip tea ran through her.

Medicine from the wild, said the plants.

Plants and leaves and roots and seeds.

Orla's heart swelled with hope. She opened her pack, unwrapped Ma's book and pulled out the silver key. Turning to the map, she held the key beside the hawthorn symbol that Ma had drawn. There was no doubting that they were identical. Orla felt a warm feeling in her fingertips. It felt like Ma had left this message, just for her. And it filled her with courage. She imagined Ma steeping flowers in hot water till it turned blue. She remembered the bitter, metallic taste of the medicine on her tongue. *What plant could make such a medicine?* wondered Orla. Was it the roots or the leaves or the seeds that Ma had used? There were plants that had blue dye, Orla thought. Dogwood bark, woad, bilberries . . . Ma knew all of this. And Alder Carr must have been the place where Ma had found the plant that made the cure. That's why she'd drawn the hawthorn leaf there, among the trees.

She'd kept it hidden: away from the world, away from the Haulers. And only the person with the key could find it. All Orla needed to do was follow the stream. It would be easy; Ma had even drawn the plants she would see along the way – guelder rose, iris, traveller's joy. They would be bright as flags at this time of year.

Orla twisted the key in her hand. The willows hummed gently. She blinked, and then looked up to meet Ariana's gaze.

'I know what I gotta do now,' she told her. 'I'm not gonna *find* the cure. I'm going to *make* it. Just like Ma did. Only . . .'

She paused, her heart thudding loudly in her ears.

'We don't have long at all,' she said, the enormity of the task suddenly dawning on her.

Ariana drained the last sip of her own tea, and tipped the rosehips into the undergrowth. She stood up carefully, brushed the dirt from her knees, and reached out her hand. Orla hesitated for a moment. Ariana was looking at her with a bright expression of hope and belief. It was an expression that Orla had not seen for a very long time.

'I think you can do it,' said Ariana, taking Orla's hand and helping her to her feet. 'In fact, I *know* you can do it. Now, let's get back on that river.'

22

Mullein *Verbascum thapsus*
Ointment of leaves and flowers for the skin; the dried stem for lighting fires.

The Untold Forest, Ma had called it on the map. *Why untold*, Orla wondered. Because those who had come this way had never quite reached its end? Because no one knew the stories that it held? The willow marsh had given way to trees that were giants, with trunks larger than the boat, larger even than Orla's woodshed. They swallowed the sky, reaching their arms up into the air and across the river as though they were trying to join hands across the stream, perching on rocky banks, a jumble of jagged boulders and trees. The whole forest was alive, and it was squeezing in on them. The water eddied and swirled, picking up speed as the river narrowed. Orla held her breath, and heard water rumble through the rocks.

Faster and faster into the woods, called the ferns in the trees.

Watch for the rocks and watch for the river.

On with the search, on with the voyage, they sang.

While there's still time, while there's still hope.

The children fought against the current, but the river pulled them back again and again. It was as though the water had turned to tar, tugging at the hull of the boat, sucking them back and back, no matter how hard they pushed against the flow. Before long, rocks rose from the swirling river, turning it into a maze of white water and deadly black rock.

'We need to paddle at the same time!' called Idris against the rising roar of the water. 'Stay away from the rocks.'

'Harder!' cried Orla. Her arms were soaked, her hair plastered against her face with river spray.

'It's too tough!' cried Ariana.

Over here! called the dock at the water's edge. *Calm water, safe passage.*

'That way!' shouted Idris, waving his arm towards the riverbank. They pushed the boat away from the churning central channel and into the shallows. Even here, the water flickered with white foam, dancing downstream like wildcats playing. They paused, panting.

'You still gotta paddle,' Idris said. 'Or we'll be heading back down into the rapids.'

But Ariana, distracted, had already let her paddle rest on the side of the boat. In a moment, the current grabbed it from her hands and sent it whirling towards the rocks. It shattered in two, and disappeared into the storm of water.

'You idiot!' shouted Orla, as the boat swung unevenly to one side.

'Don't call me an idiot,' cried Ariana, her face wet with river water. 'You wouldn't get half as far if I wasn't helping, and you know it.'

Orla stuck her paddle into the water, furious. It was all they could do to stop the boat spinning wildly back into the rapids. From the rocky bank above, she heard the whispers of the tangled creepers that overhung the river. *The river splits ahead*, they said.

According to Ma's map, this was where they needed to leave the main channel of the Inkwater, and take the narrower branch towards Alder Carr.

'Pull to the right!' called Orla, her teeth chattering.

'The main channel is on the left, Orla,' said Idris. 'We keep a straight course upriver.'

'No,' said Orla. 'We take the right fork to Alder Carr!'

Idris shook his head. 'I told you, we're not taking a side route,' he said. 'The mountains – that's where we need to go.'

'But Idris – I told *you*! Ma left instructions. She left a *key*.'

Idris simply pushed the boat onwards, as though Orla had said nothing at all.

Orla felt her cheeks burn hot. She didn't want to tell Idris about her memory, not after he'd dismissed the key so quickly. But she gritted her teeth – perhaps he would understand that it was the best hope of saving Castor.

'Idris – listen. *Magda was right*. I *did* have the sickness, four years ago. I remember now. Ma gave me a medicine – a blue medicine – and it *worked*.'

His paddling slowed then, just for a moment, as he thought about what Orla had said.

'So do you know how to make it?' he said coldly.

Orla blinked.

'So, no medicine?' said Idris. 'Orla, we're running out of time!'

Orla balled up her fists. 'I can do it, I can make a cure! Ariana believes me, don't you, Ariana?'

Ariana barely had the chance to nod before Idris cut in.

'Those Haulers almost caught us in Fleetwater – and whose idea was it to stop there?'

'Stopping in Fleetwater was *necessary*!' Orla snapped. 'It was worth our while. If we hadn't stopped, we wouldn't have found out that Ma saved Matteas and Magda – that she'd left me a key!'

'She didn't leave it for you,' said Idris. 'She lost it, or she left it there by mistake. There's a big difference. We haven't got time. We carry on *to the mountains*, like Castor said.'

Orla felt like a stone had dropped in her stomach. 'Ma marked it on the map.'

'She drew a leaf, Orla! Don't you know how ridiculous you sound? You want your ma's scribbles to mean something, but you know what? We're out on a godforsaken river, miles from home. You said it yourself. Those marks on his arms mean he's not gonna survive a week. We can't go after something on a whim because your ma decided to draw her favourite plant. We gotta go for *real* help. Up the river, to the mountains, like Castor said. We haven't got time for detours.'

Orla kicked the side of the boat. 'All the more reason to listen to me!' she said. 'I'm telling you, Ma hid something at Alder Carr. And we've got the key. You saw how those Haulers are after the book – it's important!'

'I don't care what the Haulers think,' said Idris. 'We're carrying on upstream.'

'You're not the captain!' yelled Orla, furious.

'And neither are you,' muttered Idris, paddling vigorously to keep the boat to the side of the river.

Make haste! called the dock. *Watch the water!*

'Then we vote!' said Orla, swinging round to look at Ariana.

'You can't make me decide,' Ariana said. 'That's not fair.'

'You're a fool, Idris!' said Orla. 'You'd rather ignore the truth and head off on a Hauler adventure. You just want to be a Hauler like Castor! You're the fool.'

Idris looked wounded. 'The same as your ma when she wrote in that book, then,' he said sharply.

Tears of anger bubbled up. Orla wanted to push Idris overboard. She wanted to throw him in, and every stupid piece of Hauler cargo in the boat. She wanted to tear up the book and send it streaming down the river.

'You don't care about anything,' said Idris, exhausted now. 'Other than yourself. You don't care about Castor, or a cure for the people in Thorn Creek. You just want to save your garden and your horse and your stories about your ma.'

Orla hesitated. Was it so wrong to want to save those things? They were all she had.

'They're not stories!' she said. 'It's science! Ma spent her whole life on this. I can prove she found the right plant! She marked it with a symbol . . . the same symbol that's on the key. It's clear as anything, I'll show you – she's drawn the plants along the way, guelder rose and irises and – it'll be easy to find – just let me . . .' She set her paddle down by her feet and pulled Ma's book out of her pack. She wrenched it open at the map.

'There!' she said. 'There – don't you see?'

'Don't you dare stop paddling, Orla Carson!' shouted Idris, as the boat swung back towards the swirling current. Orla scrabbled for her paddle, but it was too late. She felt a swoop as they were pulled out of the shallows and into the rapids, like a toy in the water.

'No!' she yelled, as Ma's book slid on to the deck. But the boat was already wildly out of control. The bow dipped violently towards the water and she was thrown backwards – losing her grip on the paddle, which disappeared into the blur of water and rocks.

There was nothing they could do. Idris yelled as the boat lurched sideways, dragged into the racing stream of the river, down and down until it swung into a rock with an almighty crash. The bow of the boat was caught against the jagged rock, but the river kept pulling, wrenching, crushing. In slow motion, Orla saw the boat tear in two. The wood screamed; splinters as big as her arm flew through the air. She saw Ariana's face, white with shock.

And then she was upside down – the boat flying through the air above her and the waves rising up to meet her, snatching, snarling and bitter cold. They swallowed her into blackness.

Deep under the water, the river was an endless, shapeless place. Orla's hair tangled around her face and it felt as though her clothes were made of lead. Shards of wood swept past her. The world was roaring – the world was moving. But breath did not come. Light did not come. Only the taste of water – sharp like metal . . .

She glimpsed Ma's book – the pages fanned open in the water like the fins of a fish.

Orla tried to move her arms, but they would not listen. She shouted for help – but all she heard was a roar.

And beneath it, voices.

We need you! cried the waterweed. *Don't give up!*

Air and light! it cried.

The waterweed whipped around her. *The plants. The garden. Captain.*

Wrenching herself free of the tangles underwater, Orla burst out on to the surface and found herself clinging to a rock at the water's edge.

Blinking the water from her eyes, she saw two figures huddled on the far bank. Idris and Ariana were alive – but they were on the other side of the river.

Orla flung out an arm and caught hold of a clump of dock.

Hold tight, it said, as she pulled herself from the freezing water. *Strong roots.*

She stood on the riverbank and tried to gather her breath. As her clothes dripped around her, Orla felt a surge of hot rage rising in her chest. She glared at Idris and Ariana. This was their fault. If they'd only followed her up the right side of the river, this would never have happened. It felt like a fishing spear twisting in her stomach. Now there was no way up the river. The boat was gone. And Ma's book had gone with it. Looking downstream, Orla saw the remnants of the boat's cargo – furs and oilskins and packages of tobacco, all swirling through the rapids like fallen leaves.

A shout came from across the river. Idris was waving, trying to get her attention. But Orla shook her head. She couldn't go with them. Idris did not think Alder Carr was important, and he was wrong. With a sniff, she unbuttoned her pocket. The key was still there.

Idris shouted again.

'There's a rope bridge a little way ahead – I can see it. You can climb over . . .'

'I don't need the stupid bridge, and I don't need you!' Orla shouted back.

She turned and marched away from the water's edge, leaving the swirling river behind her. The plants rose up to meet her, a tangle of weeds and thorns and curling stems that whispered and murmured, welcoming her into the forest.

You'll keep me safe, thought Orla. *I don't need anyone else. I'll be fine on my own. Just fine.*

23

Guelder Rose *Viburnum opulus*
Bark; for weary legs.

The alder trees grew tall and thin, their roots deep in the water. Alder Carr was not so much a stream, Orla soon realized, as a flooded, impenetrable forest. Where most forests had paths walked by deer and badgers, the trees here were submerged in a dark, glassy sheet, their trunks sticking up into the sky like the ribs of a giant creature. Now she understood why Ma had labelled this the *Untold Forest*. It did not look as though anyone else had ever walked this way.

A jay squawked in the canopy above. Orla waded knee-deep in the water, her feet sinking into the mud beneath. She could not make out the course of the stream marked on Ma's map, and the voices of the plants were nothing but faint, strangled whispers, and the water was as still as a mirror.

Stranger, said the jewelled strands of bryony berries winding through the trees.

Why's she all alone? whispered the ferns. *Where are her friends?*

Orla pictured Idris and Ariana alone by the river.

'I'm not thinking about that now,' she said. 'I'm not thinking about the book, or about Castor probably dying, or any of it. I'm going to find Ma's secret cure, and that's that.'

She tramped defiantly onwards, doing her best to head in what she thought was a north-easterly direction. The forest was dense and knotty. She climbed over fallen trees, tangling herself in the reeds and ferns that grew between the alders, stumbling into the water and the mud, sending startled crows storming into the sky. Her clothes weighed heavy, and her limbs were cold; but each step took her closer to finding the truth that would save her garden, the truth that would mean no one could ever say a bad word about Ma again, the truth that could – Orla shuddered to think of it – save Castor, if it wasn't too late.

Biting her lip, Orla felt a moment of panic. What if Idris was right – what if the cure really was up in the mountains?

No, she thought. *Ma knew what she was doing.*

And so do I.

Her heart skipped as she thought of the book, washed away with the boat.

She pushed the feeling down.

'No,' she said to the alders. 'I know how to find it.'

If you say so, said a patch of wormwood, just as doubtful as the plant in her garden.

The place Ma had labelled was in the north-east, a mound at the edge of the forest. All she needed to do was to follow the watercourse until she reached the edge of the woods, and she would be fine. She pictured the map in her mind, and the flowers that Ma had drawn there. Guelder rose, iris, traveller's joy.

She must have travelled a mile or so north-east along what she thought was the stream. Though she couldn't see the sun behind her, which would be setting in the west, she knew that the trees would stretch their branches more to the south.

Towards the sun, towards the light, said the alders.

'Right,' said Orla, feeling buoyant. After the sick plants along the Inkwater, this felt more like being at home in the garden. She took this as a sign she was heading in the right direction. 'And Ma drew a guelder rose among the alders – there!'

The bright-red berries stood out like glass beads in the dark woodland. She splashed ahead.

Wise girl, said the shrub brightly.

'OK,' said Orla, proud of herself. 'Next, there's yellow iris. That likes shallow water . . . but it's September, so it'll have seeds, not flowers. Green pods, copper-coloured seeds.'

She looked around, to where the trees showed their roots above the floodwater. And sure enough, there was a cluster of seed pods nestled among the waterlogged reeds and rushes. *Irises*. Orla's heart skipped. She was heading the right way.

'And finally, traveller's joy.'

Orla walked on. In summer, the plant would have creamy-white flowers scrambling up into the treetops. Now that it was September, they'd have turned into fluffy seeds. The plants would be reaching out into the sun – which meant finding the edge of the woodland – and . . .

Orla saw a gap in the trees. Daylight.

She ploughed her way onwards, and there it was: a clearing. She'd made it through Alder Carr.

Getting close, sang the traveller's joy.

Sunlight and sky-whispers! they sang.

Hidden place, wise girl! Hidden friends!

She hurried on. The trees gave way to a grassy mound, light and bright. The climbers and the brambles clambered out of the forest as though they too were trying to reach the sky. And when Orla reached the mound that rose from the forest like an island, she cried out in amazement.

There, tangled in the brambles and hawthorn, glistening in the sunlight, was a house made of glass.

24

Viper's Bugloss *Echium vulgare*
Expellant of poisons or venoms. Seeds: infusion to drive
away melancholy.

Like a glass chapel, it stood proudly on top of the little
hill, overlooking the water. The building was not
much taller than Orla, but it was three times as long. Its
walls and roof were made of glass panes, no bigger than
Ma's book, all held together by swirls of ironwork.

The brambles around her shivered in recognition.

Old friend, they said. *Long time*.

Orla's heart skipped. She imagined Ma climbing up
the same slope with her book, to sit on the hill and draw
the plants. She imagined Ma looking out at the same
flooded woodland below, to the great enormous trees of
the Untold Forest in the distance, and the ashy-grey

mountains beyond. And she knew then that Ma hadn't just wanted to go to Fleetwater when she was sick. She was trying to get back to the glasshouse.

Orla pressed her face to the misted glass door. There were plants inside, growing thick and fierce: some had broken the glass and were twisting out up to the sky. Taking the key from her pocket, she ran her thumb over the glass hawthorn leaf. Her heart thrummed like moth wings in her chest. Inside the glasshouse, she could hear the bright voices of a hundred plants, humming and chattering and trilling like birds in the spring.

Taking a deep breath, she pushed the key into the lock. At first it would not turn, but after she coaxed a tendril of ivy away from the keyhole, the bolt slid smoothly. Carefully, she pulled open the door and stepped inside.

At once, Orla could see that these plants had been kept safe from the sickness. Two long iron benches ran the length of the glasshouse, where dozens of plants had broken free from their pots, sending leaves and climbers spilling like waterfalls into the earth. Others hung from the rafters, trailing long green tendrils down to the ground. Every plant was different, Orla noticed. Some had leaves that curled and twisted against the glass. Others draped strings of red berries like jewels from hidden vines. Flowers like angels' trumpets gathered high in the rafters, while creeping roots ran down like claws into the earth. And between them, Orla saw a twisting system of pipes running down from the roof, where long gutters collected rainwater, guiding it down to the plants.

She had never seen these plants growing before, but now, walking into the glasshouse, they seemed strangely familiar. Orla wondered if, perhaps, she had been here before and had forgotten it, like she had forgotten falling sick. It took her a moment, watching the sunlight skim across the damp leaves, to realize that Ma had drawn many of these plants in her book: labelling the tiniest parts of their flowers to show where they made pollen and nectar and seeds. Some were flowers that Orla had never seen – flowers from far-off places. Ma had licked her pen to help the ink flow and set about drawing the stem, the petals and the stamen that held the pollen. She had told Orla about the plants that grew around the world; the people who had used them for centuries for medicine; the stories that she wanted to learn; the places she wanted to travel to.

Orla's heart fluttered as she watched the plants growing there, safe in the warm, humid glasshouse. It was like seeing a little glimpse into another world, away from the damp and dark of Thorn Creek. Would Ma have brought her here if she had lived? Would they have travelled to see the places these plants came from, and learnt about the medicines they could make?

Cautiously, Orla reached out to touch a spiny green-and-orange leaf. She jumped when it snapped closed on her fingers. Suddenly the plants stopped chattering and began to hum like a hive of furious insects.

Stranger, they whispered.

Who is she? they said.

A thief! A thief! chorused the plants.

Orla pulled her hand quickly back.

'I'm not a thief!' she said.

But every plant in the glasshouse seemed to bristle. They set their thorns on end. Orla smelt the scent of rotted flesh blooming from one of the trumpet flowers. The berries glistened brightly, deep purple and red. Among the flowers and the herbs Orla now recognized a dozen or more poisonous plants, some deadly even to the touch. Beside each plant, there was a label: written in Ma's careful looping script. Orla felt a flicker of fear, then. So many medicines were made from poisonous plants. Ma had known how to handle foxgloves and deadly nightshade; but Orla would never dare. She swallowed, her palms turning clammy at the thought of making a medicine from a plant that could kill.

'I can't do this on my own,' she whispered, wanting nothing more than to be sitting on Ma's lap, wrapped in a blanket, with Ma showing her how to read the names of the plants. She wanted help; she wanted Ma.

All around her, the plants watched, their spines glistening. She saw a flower, pale gold with red petals as though it had been dipped in blood, which had a label that read *Brugmansia sanguinea*. A plant with fruit like thorny apples read *Datura stramonium*. And another, its thin petals lined with purple veins, read *Hyoscyamus nox*: *deadly poisonous*. The plants crowded together, as though fighting for space. Orla saw that there had once been a path through the glasshouse, a trail of red bricks between the pots and flowerbeds, but the tangle of plants ahead was almost impenetrable. Looking up, Orla saw that the tallest stems had pressed so forcefully against the glass roof that a crack spread in a jagged line above her. Creepers twisted across the path, thick as an iron fence.

'I'm a *friend*,' said Orla. 'I promise.'

The plants seemed to whisper together, as though deciding whether she was to be trusted. Orla felt tears prickle in her eyes. The plants in the garden had never been like this. Why wouldn't they listen?

'I got the key, don't you see?' she said, waving it around. 'I'm not here to harm you, honest! I can help you – keep you all safe from the sickness that's spreading all around – you just gotta help me first.'

Orla heard the rustle of leaves, the drip of rain through the crack in the glass.

'You knew my ma,' she said, her throat feeling suddenly tight. 'I'm here to find a plant she used to make a medicine. A plant I *need* now. I just gotta find the right one. If you could just let me through so I could have a look around . . .'

She tried, cautiously, to step forward into the tangle

of vines and leaves. But at once she felt a sharp sting on her leg. She swore, loudly, reaching for her knife, before realizing that it was not in her pocket. Her heart sank – it must have fallen in the river with the book. Perhaps if she'd waited for Idris and Ariana, they could have helped her.

No, she thought. *You can do it without them. Me, the plants and Captain*, she found herself repeating, like an old rhyme.

'Is anyone listening?' she asked. 'My ma brought plants here to keep them safe; I don't know when, or how many, because she never told me.' Now that she'd started talking, the words spilt out easily. Much more easily than they had done with Idris and Ariana.

'She wrote about this place,' Orla continued. 'Maybe she even told me about it in real life. I don't remember, because I had a terrible fever that Ma made better – using a plant that's in here. A plant I need to find, because, if I don't, Atlas is going to destroy my garden and he'll *never* give my horse back. He told everyone that the sickness comes from the wild and they believed it. He told them it was Ma's fault – Ma's fault that people died at Hind House all those years ago – Ariana's pa too. And they believed that too. I gotta get back there and prove it – prove that Ma was right all along. That she really did know what she was doing.'

There was silence. The plants were listening intently.

'Go on, say something,' she said. Didn't they want her to save her garden? Orla couldn't help thinking that they were passing judgement on her. She remembered Castor lying in his house in Thorn Creek. Her stomach twisted with guilt. Idris was right. Castor did not have long. They'd be lucky to get back in time to save him.

'And so I can help other people, too,' she said quietly.

Orla was surprised to find that her eyes were wet. Had she really cried at the thought of Castor lying alone in his house? He was a Hauler; he didn't need her sympathy. She thought of Idris and Ariana, and, suddenly, she felt alone too.

Lots of plants, the vine said kindly. *Many friends.*

Orla sniffed and shuffled her boots in the dirt. A cloud passed over the sun, throwing the glasshouse into shadow. The plants shivered, and Orla heard the twist and rustle of leaves as they slowly, indiscernibly, turned their stems and flowers, trying to follow the light. She blinked, trying to focus. Perhaps her eyes were tired – or perhaps the river water had blurred her vision – but it seemed as though the plants had moved aside just a little to reveal a narrow gap that Orla had not noticed before.

And there, just ahead, a glimmer of sunlight fell through the whispering plants, illuminating a small hexagonal glass bottle: cracked and dusty, half-buried in the dirt.

25

Devil's Rope *Strychnos toxifera*

Potential medical use as an anaesthetic, but more commonly used in arrow poison. Very dangerous; fatal if it enters the bloodstream.

Orla scratched the bottle out of the ground and held it up to the light. It was made from dark-blue glass, so thick and heavy that she could not see from the outside whether the bottle was full.

She turned it over and found a label, the writing faded by sun and time. But it was not in Ma's hand, like the plant labels. The letters were spiky, like the prickles on a thorn bush.

Something about the writing made goose pimples creep up Orla's arms.

Again a cloud passed over the sun, casting the glasshouse into shade. Orla sighed and tipped the bottle, squinting to see if any liquid moved inside.

'Is this it?' Orla whispered. 'Is this the cure? Did Ma hide it here, after all?'

She shook the bottle and pulled at the stopper, but it was firmly stuck.

'Dammit,' she said, pulling at the cork with her teeth.

Another shadow moved outside.

Hush, said the plants suddenly.

It was not a cloud this time. There was someone out there.

Hide, said the plants.

The shadow moved to the door. Orla shoved the bottle into her pocket. Then she ducked and crawled under the nearest metal bench, disappearing behind vines and trailing roots. She peered out.

There were two shadows. One was short and scrawny. The other was broad as a bull, taller than the glasshouse.

The door rattled. The handle moved, but the door did not open. Orla held her breath. It must have locked itself behind her.

Then a third shadow joined them. Tall and thin, with a broad-brimmed hat.

A distant memory stirred in Orla's mind, but before she could place it, a voice rang out, sharp as glass.

'Break it open,' said Atlas.

An enormous hand thrust through the glass and pulled the door handle. Silas wrenched open the door and tossed it aside as though it were as light as a cobweb. The glass broke into a thousand pieces, scattering like raindrops across the ground. Atlas, Silas and Leblanc stepped into the glasshouse.

Run! whispered the plants as one. *Run, for we cannot!*

Orla scrunched her fingers into the dirt. She could not run – she could not even move. She was so afraid that if she even blinked, they would see her.

Atlas ran his hand through the tangle of plants and Orla's heart galloped against her ribs. He had come all this way from Thorn Creek. But why? How did he know the glasshouse was here?

'Still you hide your secrets,' he said, examining the leaves in his hand. 'Not for long. Find the girl,' he said to Silas. 'Take her north with the others. She has the book. Bring it to me.'

Silas pulled a knife from his pocket.

'And the plants?' he whispered, surveying the glasshouse with his yellowing eyes.

'Take them all,' said Atlas. 'I've waited long enough for this cure.'

Orla clapped her hand to her face to stifle a gasp. *No.* Atlas could not *also* be looking for the cure! He was not interested in making people better and he never had been. Back in Thorn Creek he had ordered the villagers to cut down their plants and burn their grain. He had sold it all to Westharbour, and didn't care one bit that they would all go hungry that winter. How could he possibly want a cure for the sickness? He liked to see other people suffer. He did not want to help them.

Orla was shaking now. Atlas had sent the Haulers to find her and ordered them to take Ma's book. Suddenly, she remembered the fire in his eyes at Hind House when she'd told him that Ma knew everything about the sickness. All this time, he'd been hunting her down. It was sheer luck that she'd left Thorn Creek on the Hauler boat before he could find her.

Don't hide, said the plants. *Run.*

Atlas's boots prowled closer, and Orla shrank further into the gloom. Leblanc trailed behind, running his fingers through a patch of blooming flowers.

'Leave nothing standing,' said Atlas. 'Elizabeth was a fool not to realize what could be done with all of this.'

Orla heard the shrieks of the plants as they tumbled into sacks, bruised and torn.

Knife and death, said the plants.

Danger, danger!

Orla had tears in her eyes now as she watched the plants fall.

'No!' she whispered.

Closer and closer the Haulers came, slicing through each and every stem. Soon there would be nowhere to hide. She could see Leblanc's arms were scratched and bleeding with thorns.

Get him! cried the nightshade.

Spine-scratch! cried the thorn apple. *Needle-sharp!*

Sting and blister, called the giant hogweed.

Orla crawled to the back of the glasshouse, between tall purple stems of wolfsbane, and crouched beneath a curtain of woody vines, without touching them. The label, she saw, written in Ma's hand, had a skull and crossbones drawn beside the plant's name: *Devil's Rope*.

Do not touch! cried the vines. *Death! Death!*

But Leblanc roared forwards, slicing into the Devil's Rope.

'Stop!' cried Orla.

Death! cried the plants.

For a moment, Leblanc's eyes met hers. Then he looked at his skin, stained with the green sap of the plant, seeping into the cuts on his hand. He took a sharp, rattling breath and fell to the ground, his eyes bloodshot and unmoving. He did not breathe.

Orla felt the vines around her rustle and shiver, as if spreading their stems to hide her from sight. But Atlas was striding forward – Atlas with his coat billowing behind him, his eyes unblinking. He stepped over Leblanc's lifeless body, his head turning here and there like a hawk, until his gaze locked with Orla's among the Devil's Rope. His pupils widened, his eyes so sharp that he would surely anticipate her every move – she was trapped like a hunted sparrow. There was no escape.

'The girl's here,' he said over his shoulder to Silas. 'Take her upriver to Inkenbrook with the others.'

Orla gasped. *The others*. Idris and Ariana.

Silas came crashing through the glasshouse. Orla felt as if she had been petrified. What could she do?

This way, called the vines.

Way out, way out! they cried.

She scrabbled along the wall, following the calls of the plants.

'Silas, do not touch that plant!' she heard Atlas say behind her.

Beneath a thick stem, she found a gap where the plant roots had broken the glass. But the gap was too small, and she could not squeeze through. Silas thundered closer, a bull on the charge. His face was blistered and raw from the touch of the hogweed. Orla kicked out, smashing the glass. Covering her face with her arms, she crawled through the narrow gap, wincing as the glass cut into her skin.

With one last look at Ma's beautiful glasshouse, she fled into the forest.

26

Giant Redwood *Sequoia sempervirens*
Leaves: a poultice, heated, for earaches. Sap: a tonic against fatigue.

Orla ran. She did not know where she was going. All she knew was that she wanted to be as far away from Atlas as possible. She let the plants lead the way, until the flooded woods and the glasshouse were far behind her. Exhausted, she found herself in a grove of giant redwood trees, their bark red as foxes, so tall that their crowns disappeared into the forest mist.

'I can't run any more!' she gasped, sliding to the ground. It felt like the world was spinning. The boat wreck, the shadowy glasshouse, Leblanc splayed glassy-eyed on the floor, the sound of breaking glass as Silas charged after her – and the race back through the flooded forest, until she lost him among the alder.

Orla threw her head back against the nearest redwood tree. She sniffed. The forest smelt softly of pine, reminding her of Captain's foot. But as the sound of blood rushing in her ears faded, she heard the drip of mist on branches, the distant rush of the rapids, and the occasional cry of a fox. But the plants here were silent once again.

'What's wrong with you?' she said bitterly, tears of frustration blurring her eyes. 'Why'd you leave me alone?'

She scraped her hands through the earth around her – soft pine needles. She needed to get to safety. If Atlas and the Haulers had tracked her from the river to the glasshouse, they would easily spot her footprints in the soft forest floor. Scrabbling back on to her feet, Orla stumbled through the trees, her legs heavy as lead, until she spied a tree with a gap in the roots. Her heart swelled as she heard the deep murmurs of the redwoods.

Friend, they said. *Safe home.*

Safe inside, they said.

'Thank you,' she whispered, crawling inside, wincing as the cut on her arm caught against the roots. The tree was hollow and the space inside the trunk was so large that it would have fitted the whole of her woodshed, with room to spare.

Rest, wise girl, said the redwoods, their deep voices echoing through the tangle of thoughts in Orla's mind. She rubbed her eyes. The cut on her arm was bleeding. She remembered Ma patching her up after she'd fallen while climbing a dead birch tree over the river, and wished that someone could do that for her now.

Forcing herself to move, she hauled herself back outside, gathered a fallen branch and began to break it up into small pieces. Rummaging through her pack, she found her tinderbox with the bulrush seed head, a lump of pine sap and her fire-lighting flint. The bulrush was a bit damp, but she pulled it apart to make fluffy tinder and scraped it into a pile in the middle of the huge tree.

'I need some hot water,' said Orla. 'So I'm gonna light a fire. Don't be scared.'

She struck the flint, wincing as the skin on her arm stretched the cut – and sparks jumped into life. Slowly, she placed the dry wood on the fire – whispering to the redwood. Out of all the trees, the redwoods were the least afraid of fire.

Wishing she had her knife, Orla pulled out her water-skin and filled it with rainwater that had collected in a hollow outside the tree. Among the pine needles she found a stone. She heated it in the fire and, when it was hot, used a stick to toss it into her waterskin. The water bubbled and steamed at once. She washed the cut and the scrapes on her hand, tossed a handful of pine needles into the water and then, exhausted, lay back against the soft wall of the tree and watched the fire sending curls of smoke up into the trunk as if it were a chimney.

But the hollow tree felt cold and empty, despite the

warmth of the fire and the calm rumblings of the forest. She was used to seeing Idris's glowering expression and his blue Hauler coat. She was used to Ariana's damp curls and big eyes, watching her like a curious puppy. The tree felt strangely empty without them.

Orla was cold now, too. Her feet ached painfully and, somehow, there was blood on her hands. She closed her eyes and leant against the tree. But all she could see was Atlas, his eyes on fire.

Elizabeth was a fool, he'd said.

She pushed the thought to the back of her mind, listening intently to the forest beyond.

He was not coming, not yet.

Carefully, she pulled out the blue glass bottle.

Could this be it? The blue medicine that Ma had given her?

Orla shook the opaque bottle gently and heard nothing. She managed to prise out the cork and peered inside.

The bottle was empty. A faint metallic smell remained.

Orla swore loudly.

This couldn't be what Ma had been looking for – it couldn't be the reason she'd wanted to go back to the glasshouse. It was nothing but a forgotten bottle, caked in dust and mud. It must have lain in the glasshouse for years. The label was peeling off and, holding it up to the light, Orla could see the letters now – in faded ink, not in Ma's writing.

PITCH BLACK, WATERPROOF INK.

Orla imagined Ma in the glasshouse, drawing her plants, dipping her pen in the ink.

She scrubbed the dirt from the bottle, revealing raised letters – letters stamped into the glass.

ATLAS INK LTD.

Disgusted, Orla punched the soft earth beside her. She hated the thought of Ma buying ink from Atlas. All he wanted was to sell that ink and make money. Finding the cure was just another way for him to do that. He'd taken Ma's plants. Ma had known what she was doing: she had grown all those plants in the glasshouse for a reason – and she'd wanted to keep them hidden. But Atlas had taken them: stem, root and seed. Orla stifled a sob. Everything Ma had worked towards was gone, everything Ma cared about. It was like Atlas was eating away at her memories of Ma. What would be left when he was done?

'A great big pile of gold,' muttered Orla. 'That's what.'

And now he'd taken Idris and Ariana, too. Just like he'd taken everything else from her.

Orla chewed the pine needles. She wanted to go home. She wanted to fall asleep in the woodshed with the garden singing around her and Captain grazing outside.

Friends, said the redwood.

'They're not my friends,' said Orla, leaning back against the tree trunk and closing her eyes.

Hmm, said the tree.

As night fell, Atlas rode northwards into the dark, with nothing but a lantern to dimly light the way. He hated the ride to the mountains; his coat whipped around him in the wind and the rain, and the trees reached out hooked branches as though they were trying to grab riders who dared to follow those narrow paths. But it suited him better than following the Haulers as they lifted their boat out of the river and carried it along the steep-sided banks to reach the calmer waters upstream. This was the proper way to do things: without their filthy blue coats and clumsy hands dropping his glass and ink at every opportunity.

Atlas passed an empty cottage, then another one, their gardens dead and rotten. He did not blink. Instead, his eyes were fixed on the stars above the mountains. A heavy thundercloud was swallowing the stars one by one. Rain was coming.

Good, thought Atlas. *The river will rise, and the Haulers shall make better time downriver.*

He felt pleased. Elizabeth had never thought to do this, but then, why would she have done? She thought the world's treasures should be for everyone. She didn't know the truth: that they were only for those brave enough to take them. The men in Westharbour would agree, he was sure of it.

27

Common Mallow *Malva sylvestris*
Roots: for a soothing poultice.

The next morning Orla perched on the rocky cliff high above the churning rapids, the hood of her oilskin pulled tight against the pouring rain. Below, she saw the scattered remnants of the Hauler boat: the canopy snagged in a fallen tree, waving like a drowning man in the current. She blinked back the memory of the churning channel beneath the surface. On the bank, she saw where Idris and Ariana had stood, their footprints now pooled with rainwater. She saw the remains of a little fire, now just a pile of wet ash; a broken strand of fishing net that Idris must have been repairing; and Ariana's metal cup, the one she'd used to scoop up river water. They had waited for her there. Waited until the Haulers had snatched them away.

Orla felt her lip tremble. She was exhausted and cold. She wanted to curl up against Captain's warm flank. The river below was rising steadily after the heavy rain, swallowing the rocks in the rapids. It flowed down towards Fleetwater and Dead Elm Strand and *home*.

Orla shook her head. Raindrops cascaded down her neck. Looking upriver, she could see the fork in the stream, where the river divided like a piece of cloth torn in two.

To her right, the stream seeped down from Alder Carr. And to her left, the Inkwater flowed dark and slick, down from the mountains, the banks lined with blackened bulrushes and ashy-grey gorse. And among the bushes Orla saw a trail of little half-moons filled with rainwater. Hoof prints.

They'd taken Idris and Ariana on horseback. And they'd taken them towards the mountains.

Orla wiped the rain from her face. Her legs ached and she wished that she had Captain with her now. With the plants so silent around her, she felt very alone.

'Cursing Haulers,' she muttered, scrambling down the rock. 'I'll get 'em, just you see,' she told the gorse along the river.

You get 'em, it said faintly, as Orla tramped onwards.

In the shadow of the mountain, Orla coughed. As she'd left the forest down below, the air had thickened to a greyish smog and now, following the trail of hoof prints out into a rocky grey expanse, she felt her eyes water and her throat clog with dust and smoke that lay upon the landscape like a heavy woollen cloak. It tasted like soot and hot metal. Focusing on her stride, Orla tried not to picture the Haulers hurrying this way, with Ariana shivering in her thin dress, and Idris, his leg scratched and bleeding.

Why north? she thought, winding through the angry thickets of gorse and broom. Atlas had planned to send Ariana to Westharbour – so why weren't they heading that way? Why into the mountains?

'Something's going on up here, isn't it?' she said to the silent gorse, which bristled and pricked against her oilskin. 'Castor knew it. Idris knew it. I shoulda—'

She spat, trying to get rid of the metallic taste that coated her tongue.

Ahead, the mountains rose up towards the clouds like silent grey giants. She had never seen so much sky – the sweeping arc of the hills, dotted with gorse and birch and mountain ash. But as Orla marched on, she saw the trees were nothing but ghosts, thin as Ma's ink drawings. The rowan should have been bright with red berries by now; the birch should have been turning golden like autumn sun. Instead the trees were leafless and withered, black-ened as though scorched by fire.

The echoing silence was broken only by the crunch of Orla's footsteps on the gritty rock and the gurgle of the river rising after the rain. Then, when she stopped to listen, the thudding sound of metal on rock.

The path before her curved out of sight. When Orla rounded the bend, her stomach turned.

It was as though a giant had taken a knife to the land, slicing away the mountain and leaving nothing but a sheer cliff of black rock, a hundred feet tall. Figures swarmed below like ants, hurling pickaxes into the black rock, carving it up like meat. Among them, she glimpsed a dozen blue coats.

Haulers.

Creeping closer, she saw a cluster of buildings at the foot of the cliff, camouflaged among the rocks. The river was a thin snaking line now, dark as tar. She saw Hauler boats, tied to a jetty. And as the smog shifted, Orla caught sight of a tall building right on the water's edge. It was at least four storeys tall, with a colossal chimney stack reaching up into the clouds, coughing out billows of acrid smoke and soot that stung Orla's nose and made her eyes water. On one side, a gigantic wheel churned the grey river water, sending it cascading down in white clouds. And from the belly of the building Orla could hear an ominous growling. It wouldn't have surprised her to see it come alive and devour the other buildings.

The sound of Haulers singing carried up through the fog, raucous and bold.

Du-hont, du-hont,
Sur la montagne vide,
Du-hont, du-hont,
Where the air is clear,
We toil and toil,
Till the land is empty,
On chant, on chant,
Till our souls are bare.

Among the quarried rock, Orla saw a line of carts emerging from a dark gap in the mountain, each filled with black earth. Not only were they carving away the mountainside, they were mining into its very core.

'Blasted Haulers!' she muttered, kicking a stone. It tumbled down the rocky slope, where Orla could just make out the trace of hoof prints leading to the river. She followed them and found that the horses had forded the river and climbed towards the buildings on the far side.

She hitched up her breeches, pulled off her boots and stuffed them into her pack. She was just about to step into the water when she saw that her feet were sinking into the blackest sand she had ever seen: so dark that it seemed to swallow the light around it.

'What's that?' she asked the gorse up on the bank.

Pulling back her hood, she hoped to hear the plants

whispering back at her. But the rain continued to hammer down. She bent and examined the coarse black sand. It was different to river sand – more like chippings of hard rock. Orla couldn't explain why, but it looked like it did not belong there. As she ran a handful through her fingers, the water around it instantly turned black, as though it had been dyed.

Castor's words echoed in her memory.

Pitch black, he'd said.

A feeling of dread swept through her as Orla stepped into the icy water and waded across the ford. Up on the mountain the stream looked like a thin slick of tar running down between the purple-grey slopes. It was clear to her now: the closer she came to the source of the river, the quieter the plants were. And the darker the river, the darker the stems of the plants.

This was Atlas's doing; she knew that much. This was his mine.

And not a living thing survived here.

28

Bulrush *Typha latifolia*
Pound the roots for flour, and as a poultice for burns and sores.
Use the fibres for weaving, and the soft down for lining pillows
or making candle-wicks.

Sunset was not for hours, but the mountain cast a veil over the last of the day's light. A lamp had been lit on the watermill, casting a glaring light down into a fenced yard. Orla found a gate and rattled it cautiously. It was locked, and strands of dead bramble had been twisted round the metal at the top. A sign on the gate said INKENBROOK: TRESPASSERS WILL BE SHOT.

Orla remembered Atlas's words: *Inkenbrook*. And she knew that she had seen that word before, not only on Ma's map, but on the side of the Hauler boat: INKENBROOK TRADING CO.

Above the gate, Orla spied a gap, just small enough for a child.

'They didn't think of that,' whispered Orla.

She climbed the gate and dropped into the yard. Winding her way through a jumble of buildings, she kept out of sight, her oilskin drawn tight over her nose to keep out the sharp, metallic smell that filled the air and caught the back of her throat. She was close to the steep face of the mountain now, and the air was cool and damp. She crept past bunkhouses and canteens, storage sheds and workshops, and between it all the sounds of the mill echoed – strange, clunking, mechanical – with the groan and rush of the waterwheel. Orla scanned the yard for signs of Idris and Ariana, and saw nothing but shadows.

When she reached the mill building, Orla craned her neck to see through the glass windows. The glow of a roaring furnace lit the enormous hall inside. The space was filled by a huge machine. Like a giant insect feasting on its prey, it pulled a belt towards its chomping jaws, where pistons worked up and down, crushing and hammering and grinding. Orla gasped as she saw black powder rolling beneath them. It was the sandy black rock that she had found in the river, she was sure of it. Beside the machine, Orla saw row upon row of glass bottles lined up, and a dozen or so workers, their backs bowed, watching as the machine filled the bottles with a dark liquid, before sealing them with a cork and stamping them with a label. Orla recognized the bottles. She knew that up close, those labels would read: ATLAS INK LTD.

Orla remembered Atlas's study, in Hind House, lined with glass bottles in a hundred colours. She thought of the dozens of bottles he was sending to Westharbour. So, those were not enough for him. She scanned the enormous hall. Here there were hundreds and hundreds of bottles, glimmering in the orange glow of the furnace. Atlas wanted more. He always wanted more – and he'd come here, to the mountains, to manufacture it.

Why not at Fleetwater? she thought. *There had been plenty of glass there once. Why here?*

'Cos he's a crook,' she muttered to herself. 'And whatever he's doing here, he's trying to keep it hidden.'

Orla squinted through the glass, but there was no sign of Idris and Ariana among the lines of dusty workers – and no sign of Atlas himself. Creeping around the mill, Orla peered in through each and every window. She saw machines and storerooms and a small office with a desk, and wondered if that was where Atlas had taken the plants. Chewing her sleeve, she looked at the wooden buildings that surrounded the yard. But where were Idris and Ariana?

There was a clang beside her, and the mill door opened, bathing the yard in orange light. Orla shrank back into the shadows.

'A ton of pitchstone?' said a voice. Orla recognized Bouchard's rough tone. 'You're joking.'

Pitchstone. The Hauler spat the word as though it were something awful.

'This is no joke,' came Silas's whispery tone. 'The guv'nor wants it loaded by dawn.'

He calmly lit his pipe. Orla saw his yellowish eyes in the flame.

Bouchard ran his hands over his beard and shook his head in disbelief. 'It's too much,' he said. 'The workers are fed up. Saying they were s'posed to be paid two weeks ago . . .' He turned back to the mill, looking over Silas's shoulder. 'I'll tell him we can't do it.'

'You won't tell him anything of the sort,' said Silas, blocking Bouchard as he tried to step back inside. 'Just load the pitchstone.'

'And what about the children?' asked Bouchard.

'Down in the mine,' laughed Silas, nodding his head towards the rocky face of the mountain. 'Getting a taste of Hauler work. Keep 'em in line. I'll see to Atlas.'

Bouchard strode off across the yard. Silas tipped the contents of his pipe on the floor and stubbed out the glowing embers with his toe. With a sigh, he turned back to the mill. The door swung behind him, sending beams of golden light into the yard.

Orla could not move. She felt as though her whole

body had turned to rock. Silas had as good as said that Idris and Ariana were down in the mine – and that the entrance was somewhere close by. Orla cast her eyes about. She'd seen it as she'd crossed the river, hadn't she? A dark mouth in the side of the mountain. Somewhere beyond the sheds and the mill and the yard.

Orla hesitated, looking back at the mill. The door was unlocked. She could sneak in now and look for the plants that Atlas had taken from the glasshouse, couldn't she? It would be easier on her own.

High above the mill, a bell began to ring. Orla jumped as she felt the earth rumble beneath her. A hundred men and women emerged from the bunkhouses around the yard, carrying shovels and buckets and pickaxes – and they were heading towards the mountain. Towards Idris and Ariana.

Her heart galloped. This was her chance.

Hurrying across the yard, she joined the crowd of workers. They funnelled between the wooden buildings, forming a line as they approached the foot of the mountain. Orla found herself at the tail end of the line, beside an old woman pushing a wooden cart. Ahead, she saw the workers lighting their lanterns and disappearing through a metal gate, into a hole in the rock.

Orla paused. Bouchard was standing sullenly beside the entrance to the mine, holding open the gate. Instinctively, Orla grabbed on to the cart of the woman beside her, and pushed. The woman did not seem to mind. She simply groaned with the effort, her eyes fixed on Bouchard, who held a bullwhip in one hand and a set of keys in the other. Orla swallowed and kept her head low.

Just as they were about to step into the darkness, she hesitated for a moment.

Something silver, right at the mouth of the tunnel, fluttering in the breeze.

It was a single stem of honesty, growing out of the dark rock, as bright and clear as those that grew in Orla's garden, its silver seed pods dancing like moons in the lamplight.

'What are you doing here?' she muttered under her breath.

The plant waved faintly. It whispered to Orla, its voice thin and tired.

You can do it, wise girl.

'Get in,' called Bouchard, his voice as sharp as metal on rock. Orla ducked into the tunnel, avoiding his gaze. At her side, the old woman lit a small lamp and hooked it on to the cart. Behind them, the gate clanged shut. The sound echoed in the dark tunnel ahead.

Orla turned, momentarily, but the plant had fallen silent. Bouchard's shadow filled the doorway. She had made her choice. Now, the only way was onwards.

29

Pennyroyal *Mentha pulegium*
Tea: for whooping cough; wrap in a parcel to rid a bed of
fleas and bugs.

The air in the mine was stale and dank, as though something had died below ground. The path rolled down before them, like the throat of an enormous snake. The lamp on the cart looked as small as a match in the gloom, its light barely reaching the dark walls of the tunnel. Beside Orla, the old woman pushed the cart with her back bent, her brow as furrowed as oak bark.

'He'll get what's coming to him,' she muttered as they followed the line of workers deeper into the mountain.

'What?' said Orla.

But the woman did not reply. She pressed on in silence, the little orange lamp jangling against the cart, winding down and down, until the echoes of their footsteps bounced further into the darkness, and Orla realized they were no longer in a tunnel, but an enormous cave. The lamps danced off into its far corners like sparks from a fire.

'Carts down to the water!' cried Bouchard, pushing past them.

The old woman wheeled the cart forwards.

Orla was startled to see the lamplight reflecting on the surface of a small underground lake. Rows of people shuffled at the water's edge, sifting through the mud and the silt with big round sieves.

The old woman brought the cart to a standstill and fished around inside it for a sieve. She bent down to the water and swirled it around, until dark lumps appeared in the silt. She picked them out and tossed them into her bucket.

'That's pitchstone,' said Orla, seeing how the rock seemed to drink up the lamplight. 'Where's it come from?'

The woman peered at Orla in the orange light. Then she nodded in the direction of another line of workers at the edge of the cave. They hung their lamps against the wall, took up their pickaxes and swung them into the wall with a clang, chipping away at the rock and tossing it into the waiting buckets. Small pieces of rock flew through the air and rolled into the water. A piece landed near Orla's foot, and she saw a curl of black spreading into the water, just like ink. It was the same black rock that she'd seen at the ford. A feeling of dread seeped through her then. The inky swirl did not just float on the surface of the water. It was spreading – *flowing* away from the water's edge and . . .

'Out to the river,' whispered Orla.

Now she knew.

Atlas was mining the pitchstone to grind into ink, taking it right from the heart of the mountain. This was no underground pool. The water curled out through the cave towards the mill, down through the rocky foothills and out into the forest. This was the very source of the river Inkwater. And Atlas had poisoned it.

Orla felt suddenly cold.

This was what had made Ma sick. *This* was what was making the plants sick, all the way down the river.

Orla stared at the broken rock, her mind racing. The river flowed down from the mountain to Fleetwater – to Westharbour. Not to Thorn Creek. The creek, with its own source, should be safe from the poison, unless . . .

'Unless he brought it there,' whispered Orla, thinking of the ink that the Haulers had spilt as they loaded the boats by Hind House; thinking of the pine trees close to Hind House, their roots and bark blackened from drinking up the poisoned water – the water that washed down the creek to Orla's garden. To *her* plants.

'He knew what he was doing all along,' said Orla through gritted teeth. She kicked the rock and the old woman looked over at her sympathetically.

'Don't they all,' she said with a shrug, still sieving the silt. As she worked, she hummed a Hauler song, low and steady.

'*Chantez, chantez, till the winter comes.*'

'Why don't you do something about it?' said Orla. 'And why are you singing Hauler songs?'

'They were our songs before they were Hauler songs, dear,' said the woman. 'And what am I supposed to do about all this, eh? We have no choice. Half of us are from Fleetwater, and there's not a penny to be made there, now the glassmakers are gone. I need the gold to send to my daughter in Westharbour. Jackson over there – his cabin was just eight miles from here. Haulers told him he had to work. And Siset, the old fellow with the pickaxe – he owed money to the Haulers . . .'

'But this *pitchstone*,' said Orla, feeling her face hot and red now. 'Atlas has cut away half the mountain for this. It's poisoning the river and everything along it!'

'You think I don't know that?' said the woman, drawing back her sleeve to show Orla the faint purple marks of the sickness spreading up her skin.

Orla stared. Deep down, she'd known that she would see it here – but her stomach turned at the sight of the purple marks on the old woman's arms.

The woman pulled down her sleeve.

'It's the *mapafoglia*, girl. Why're you staring? You look like you never seen it before.'

She reached out and snatched Orla's wrists. Her eyes widened when she saw them.

'You ain't got it,' whispered the woman. 'Why ain't you—'

'No *talking*,' called the Hauler, standing on a cluster of rocks that jutted out into the water. The woman cursed and went back to her sieving. But Orla turned in horror to watch the workers in the cave. Now that her eyes had adjusted to the dim light, she saw the faces of the people more clearly. They were not just tired: they were sick. Everywhere she looked, she saw the purple marks of the sickness. She saw people sitting down to rest as they worked. The Hauler prowling along to flick the whip at their feet until they stood and strained under the weight of the pickaxes. Others stumbled as they carried buckets – leaning on carts for support – tripping and falling into the water – crying out in pain.

'This can't be happening,' she said. 'These people are sick . . .'

The man called Siset stumbled and Orla saw the Hauler hurry over. His voice echoed through the cave. But the old man could not stand. Still the Hauler screamed at him.

'Get up, old man! Get up and do your duty.'

Orla shivered. The cave felt enormous and echoing, moving with indiscernible shadows. As she wrapped her oilskin around her, a memory slid into her mind.

Atlas. Standing in the lane by the garden, four years ago. His words faint at first, then echoing through the mist-drenched garden.

'Meddling too close to the wild. She only has herself to blame!'

The plants screaming out to her, louder than they'd ever been: Help us, Orla, help us!

A blur of Hauler arms; the stench of their blue coats. Ma, pale as birch-bark, her skin no longer hot with fever, but cold as frost on the rosehips. The Haulers carrying her out like a paper doll.

'Bury her out in the woods,' came Atlas's voice. 'Out there, among the plants that did this to her.'

Orla tried to steady her breath. The memory left her feeling dazed.

She realized that the old woman was staring at her.

'What is it, girl?' she asked softly. But Orla couldn't answer. The feeling was too big for words. It was Atlas – Atlas had given the order to bury Ma out in the woods, with no marker or name to her grave. Whenever Orla had taken Captain out into the Borderwoods, she had looked for Ma. But she'd never found her – never said goodbye. All because of Atlas.

Orla shook her head at the old woman, who shrugged

and went back to her sieve.

Atlas. It all led back to Atlas. She felt like there was a crack inside her, and each memory of what Atlas had done pried it further open.

And even then, four years ago, he'd told the same lie. He'd wanted everyone to think it was the plants that were the problem – plants, and the people that lived near them. Not the poison from his ink. He'd made up a lie to protect his business.

Orla pictured Castor cutting into the rock with his chisel and mallet. She imagined him coming here with hopes of earning a little more gold. And she wondered when he had noticed that he was falling sick. That *everyone* here was falling sick. She thought of the Hauler floating down the river.

And she knew at once that if she and Idris and Ariana stayed too long, they would get the sickness too.

She had to find them and get them out of here.

Snatching up the lamp, Orla pushed her way between the workers at the water's edge. She felt sick. Atlas knew what he was doing. His mine was poisoning the river, and that's why he wanted the cure. To cover up his own deceit. He'd destroyed this whole place, carved into the mountain – and for what? To make more money?

A bright flash of silver caught her eye.

She thought of the honesty plant, its pale moon seeds at the entrance to the mine. How had it survived here, when no other plant had?

Hurrying closer, Orla held her lamp aloft.

It was not a plant. It was a lace dress.

Ariana.

30

Lavender *Lavandula angustifolia*
A sweet oil for balms and salves; place a sprig in the pillow to comfort an anxious mind.

Her pale curls were pulled back in a scarf, and she had Idris's blue coat wrapped around her. She was digging through the silt, her eyes stoically focused, picking out pieces of pitchstone. But her arms quivered, struggling to hold the weight of the mud-filled sieve.

Orla's heart galloped. Did Atlas know the Haulers had found Ariana and brought her here? Had he decided to keep her in the mine, to keep her quiet – instead of sending her to Westharbour?

Before, she'd made fun of Ariana for being spoilt. But watching her then, Orla felt something strange – was it pity?

She hesitated. The last time she'd seen Ariana was when she'd left her – *abandoned her* – by the rapids. Orla wanted to say that she was sorry – that she hadn't meant this to happen. But she didn't know how. She felt like she was caught in a tangle of bindweed that was growing tighter and tighter around her chest until her eyes stung with tears. Ariana would surely never want to see her again. She took a sharp breath.

'Ariana,' said Orla. 'I—'

Ariana turned, and her eyes widened with joy and then immediately fear.

'Not here,' she interrupted, her eyes darting around. She led Orla away from the lamps and the Haulers, back into the shadows of the cave, where the walls of pitch-stone were jagged with carved edges and hidden places. There she pulled something out of her pocket: a tiny lamp made from a walnut shell, with a wick made from bulrushes.

'Idris,' she said, by way of an explanation, lighting the tiny light, just bright enough for them to see by – but not bright enough to shine beyond their little rocky shelter. Orla saw that the wick was neatly twisted. It was hard to get bulrushes to behave, and she felt a moment of admiration – and then concern – for Idris.

'Where is he?' asked Orla. 'Idris.'

'He's all right,' said Ariana, sounding a little breath-less. Her gaze was fixed on Bouchard. He was prowling among the workers, winding his way closer. 'I'll explain – but we don't have much time. Look.' She pulled a second object from inside the blue Hauler coat.

It was Ma's book, with its soft leather cover and faded gold lettering, its carefully stitched spine still holding the pages tight, the pressed leaves and flowers still poking out from the tops of the pages as though the book itself were alive and growing. It was all still there.

A feeling rose up in Orla then, a feeling she had not felt in a long, long time. It was a wave of warmth and hope, the feeling of sitting on Ma's knee, wrapped in a blanket by the fire, as Ma turned the pages of the book and ran her finger over the letters, showing Orla how to read the words. And Orla felt the tears in her eyes prickle again.

Ariana was watching her, her big eyes soft with concern. Orla bit her lip. Why didn't Ariana hate her? Why wasn't she shouting at her for leaving?

'I took care of it,' said Ariana quietly, handing Orla the book. 'For you.'

Orla still couldn't speak. She touched the cover, and felt as though Ma's words were flowing back into her. But she couldn't bear to open the book and see the ink running with river water, never to be read again.

Ariana reached out and gently opened the front cover. The blue of the river had faded a little, and so had the pinks and the purples Ma had used to draw the flowers.

The black writing was as fresh as the day it was written. Orla stared at it in confusion.

'Orla – the whole book – it's written in waterproof ink,' Ariana said. 'It's quite amazing how it survived the fall into the river.'

Orla's heart swelled with pride for Ma. She traced her fingers over the map.

'Waterproof ink,' said Orla. 'Atlas's ink?'

Ariana nodded. 'It's made with pitchstone.'

'But pitchstone is *poisonous*,' said Orla. 'It's in the river – it's—'

She stopped as the true horror of it all hit her.

She remembered Ma licking the nib of her pen to get the ink flowing. Waterproof ink she had bought from Atlas.

'No!' she whispered, clutching Ma's book. 'No – he knew it was poisonous and *he sold it to her anyway*!'

Rage burnt through her then, as though every ounce of her blood was made from boiling pine tar. She let out a sharp breath, her nostrils flaring, looking across the crowd of workers to the tunnel. All she wanted was to run to the mill, to find Atlas and . . .

'I know, Orla. It's awful, isn't it?'

Ariana's cold hand was on hers. She leant closer and Orla felt the calm radiating from her.

'Listen,' Ariana whispered. 'There's something else I discovered – I've stayed up all night.'

'You read it,' said Orla, feeling her face flush red. No one else had ever read Ma's book.

'I'm sorry, Orla,' said Ariana softly. 'I know that it's your book, but I had to. Orla, your mother *knew* about pitchstone. She knew about Atlas's plans to use it to make waterproof ink.'

Ariana opened the book carefully, its pages still damp, and turned to the end – to the point where Ma's writing dissolved into scribbles and scratches. Orla felt a pang of sadness then – she had never wanted anyone to see Ma's writing when she was sick. Ma was clever, Ma was a scientist. It wasn't fair to show her feverish scribbles.

Ariana blinked, her large eyes catching the lamplight. It was as though she'd read Orla's thoughts.

'They aren't scribbles,' she whispered. 'It's code.'

'What?' said Orla.

Ariana peered out. The Hauler was closer now, shouting at a young woman who had fallen in the water.

'I knew that if your ma had found a cure for the sickness, then she *must* have known about pitchstone,' she explained. 'She would have worked out why the stone was causing damage and how to stop it. So I searched through until I found it. There.'

Among the scribbles was a small, spidery word: *pitchstone*. Goose pimples prickled on Orla's arms. She felt a swoop of pride for Ma, knowing about this place. Ariana traced her finger over the swirls of ink, half-finished pictures of leaves and drawings of jars and bottles. There were numbers and symbols, fighting for space on the paper. *Code.*

'I'll explain it to you later, but right now we don't have long,' said Ariana. 'He'll notice we're gone.'

The young woman was still lying in the water. She was not moving. An old man had marched over to the Hauler and was shouting at him, red-faced. The old woman whose cart Orla had pushed was waving her bucket at the Hauler; another girl was wielding a pickaxe. Their words echoed through the cave.

'This isn't right – we need more breaks, more food.'

'And what about *medicine*?'

'And what about the gold he says he'll pay us?'

Ariana pulled her back into the shadows. 'Orla, listen. I need to tell you this in case – in case something happens.'

'Like what?' asked Orla, realizing her knees were trembling uncontrollably. 'Ariana, *where's Idris*?'

'In a moment, I promise.' She turned the page in Ma's book and began to read aloud.

Orla felt her whole body shaking then, to hear Ma's words whispered back to her.

'*I write in code because I am afraid that if Atlas discovers what I am doing, he will not share this medicine with those who need it. He does not want to help the suffering. He says that I can work on a cure using his laboratory, using his equipment. But he is watching me like a hawk. I fear he wants the cure, not just for himself – to make him immune to the rock – but to sell it – sell it at a high price that few can afford.*

'*I've worked out the composition of the pitchstone: it has properties akin to radioactive elements. It works its way into the body, by touch – by ingestion – by proximity. And over time, it becomes worse and worse.*'

'Touching the rock,' whispered Orla. 'Drinking the water.'

'*I do not have long,*' Ariana continued, her voice faltering. '*But there is a plant – a plant that binds itself to pitchstone and draws out the toxin like poison from a wound. The plants want to help. They know the pitchstone must stay in the ground. I gathered the seeds and I took them to Atlas's mine – hoping they would grow – for it is the only plant that can survive pitchstone – and it is our only hope.*'

Ariana stopped. She'd reached the end of the page, and the following page was blank.

'There's no more?' said Orla.

'It ends there,' said Ariana.

She closed the book and passed it back to Orla.

'Thanks for looking after it,' Orla said.

Ariana nodded. But she was looking around the mine, worried. The workers had fallen silent.

'Don't look,' she said.

It was too late: Orla peered out to see the Hauler dragging the limp body of the woman towards a wooden cart. She felt a sudden rush of foreboding, like a rabbit trapped in its burrow with dogs at either end. Digging her fingernails into her palms, she forced away the memory of the Haulers carrying Ma out of the garden.

She turned to Ariana, her voice trembling with fear and cold.

'We gotta leave,' she said, tucking Ma's book into the back of her breeches, so that it was hidden beneath her oilskin coat. 'We gotta find Idris, and we gotta leave right now.'

Ariana swallowed and shook her head in despair. 'The Haulers took him this morning,' she said. 'He's in the mill. With Atlas.'

31

Eyebright *Euphrasia officinalis*
For maladies of the sight.

Grabbing one of the wall lamps, Orla took Ariana by the hand and marched towards Bouchard, dust and pitch-stone kicking up from her feet.

'Hey!' she yelled at him. '*Hey!* You can't just leave her there. What about her family? What about her home?'

'She ain't got no home,' snarled the Hauler, looking from her to Ariana.

The workers turned then, sieves in hand, gawping at the girl hissing at the Hauler like a wildcat.

'You know this isn't right,' said Orla. 'You can't treat people like this. They're dying – dropping like flies. And for what – for the sake of *ink*? They're not even getting paid.'

She spat on the floor.

'My ma made better ink from oak galls.'

Bouchard glared at her. Then his eyes widened in recognition.

'How'd you get here?' he growled.

But the workers were gathering now, trying to see what all the fuss was about. Orla found herself surrounded by a whispering crowd.

'Isn't that Orla Carson?'

'Her ma came to Fleetwater—'

'*Elizabeth* – I remember her—'

'Wasn't it all nonsense, her medicine?'

'No – cured our goat pox; fixed my broken arm . . .'

'Enough!' cried Bouchard, trying to push through the crowd. Dozens of eyes were fixed on Orla.

'Castor,' she said hastily. 'Castor – from Thorn Creek – he escaped and made it all the way home to Thorn Creek to tell us that something was happening here, something bad. He escaped this horrible place – knew he had to tell everyone where the sickness was coming from.'

'Castor?' said a man.

'Aye,' said another. 'I knew Castor!'

'He *got away*,' said a woman holding a bucket. 'Headed downriver.'

The crowd were murmuring now – with a sound like the rising wind. Castor's name had sparked something in their spirits, and it was catching light like a fire in the forest pines.

'He was a sharp lad, that Castor – he had his head screwed on proper.'

'Maybe what he was saying was right—'

CRACK.

Orla jumped as Bouchard cracked his whip in the air.

'I said ENOUGH!' he shouted.

The crowd fell back. But as Bouchard marched towards them, Orla kept talking – speaking so fast that she was running out of air. She had to tell them.

'Castor made it back to Thorn Creek – he came to warn us—'

Bouchard was storming towards her, his arms outstretched, grabbing her by the shoulders – his arm around her, dragging her away from the crowd.

'This is WRONG!' yelled Orla. 'Atlas is never gonna pay you – no matter what he said. He's got a huge debt with the Marshall of Westharbour – he—'

'Back to work!' shouted Bouchard. 'We've told you before – there's a cure on its way. There's nothing to worry about.'

'Bet you tell them that every day,' said Orla. 'How many people gotta die before—'

Bouchard's hand clamped over her mouth. Orla bit down hard on his fingers, then spat at the metallic taste of pitchstone.

'You come with me, girl.'

'No!' said Orla, struggling against his grip. Ariana – she couldn't go without Ariana.

As though she'd read Orla's thoughts, Ariana stepped in front of the crowd. She spoke in a soft voice and for a moment Orla stopped struggling. Ariana's words made Orla's skin glow warm with admiration.

'Castor was really brave,' she said. 'You can all be like him – you can all get out of here.'

'Why would we leave? The cure's here, after all.'

'Atlas is lying!' said Ariana. 'It's all false promises. Do you think if he finds a cure, he'll give it away for free? No – it'll be for Westharbour folk alone.'

She paused, breathless. She was shaking, soaking wet, her hands stained black with pitchstone.

'Atlas doesn't care about you now,' Ariana went on. 'He won't suddenly decide to care about you if he gets his hands on a medicine. But if we find a cure first—'

'Silence, girl!' Bouchard shouted. Orla saw him signal to another Hauler, who was guarding the way out of the mine. Whispers were running through the crowd now, crackling like a sparking fire. Two women stepped in front of Ariana as the Hauler approached . . .

'Don't you dare touch her!' one cried.

'She's just a child!' said the other.

But the Hauler simply pushed them aside.

'Stop, you're hurting her!' shouted Orla, as the Hauler

seized Ariana and pulled her roughly through the crowd, ignoring the shouts and cries of the workers – whose sieves and carts now lay forgotten along the water's edge.

Bouchard growled in Orla's ear.

'You're going to the mill, missy,' he said. 'You and your little friend.'

32

Henbane *Hyoscyamus nox*
Deadly poisonous.

The searchlight flashed through the darkness as Bouchard marched them across the yard. Orla felt Ariana trembling beside her, quivering like a poplar tree. Orla's heart thudded with every step, joining the *thud thud* of the machines and the whir of the waterwheel, which grew louder and louder as they approached. When they reached the mill, Bouchard kicked open the door and dragged Orla and Ariana inside.

In the orange glow of the furnaces, Orla was hit at once by the true scale of Atlas's mill. Cables stretched a hundred yards from one end of the building to the other, either side of a central aisle, endlessly driving hammers and pistons fixed in wooden frames, rising and falling like the jaws of a great beast, crashing and grinding and spitting out smoke and powder on to enormous, moving belts that lolled like great tongues.

As Bouchard led them down the central aisle, Orla saw that the machinery moved as one: driven by the rush of the water into the wheel outside, crushing and pounding the pitchstone that men shovelled on to the belts. The powder was then stirred into an enormous vat, to be turned into a liquid that dripped out of a tap into rows of glass bottles.

Hundreds of bottles – to be sold to people in Westharbour and Thorn Creek and beyond.

It may as well be bottles of poison, thought Orla.

'Get on!' said Bouchard, dragging them towards the far end of the mill, towards the roaring furnace. Ahead, Orla saw a line of people. At first she thought they were warming themselves beside the fire. And then she saw Atlas at the head of the line, Silas at his side. And behind them – Orla gasped – the plants from the glasshouse, hung on a string in front of the furnace, limp and dry. She saw Atlas take a plant down and pass it to Silas, who ground it in a mortar set upon a wooden table, before adding a thin stream of liquid from a silver flask. Atlas paced up and down impatiently, his jaw set, a vein bulging in his temple, until Silas finished stirring and upended the container, pouring a dark liquid into a waiting glass.

'Batch 57: *Sloe*,' said Atlas, scribbling on a roll of paper.

Silas took the glass. Then he grabbed the first worker in the line: a man with cracked glass spectacles and purple marks spreading up his arms.

'Do your duty and drink,' said Atlas. The man drank eagerly, his face grimacing at the sour taste of the liquid.

'What is he *doing*?' hissed Orla to Ariana. 'Does he think – does he think he's making *medicine*? He's lost it! Those plants won't cure the sickness!'

Bouchard pushed Ariana and Orla to the back of the line. Atlas, however, had not noticed them. He was watching Silas process the next plant. Orla saw how carelessly he threw the whole thing into the mortar.

A moment later, 'Batch 58: *Woad*' was given to the next worker.

Orla shivered, though the furnace was kicking out a fierce heat. Atlas was watching the woman intently as she swallowed the concoction. A moment later, Silas lifted her arm to show the purple lines.

'No change,' he said.

Atlas sighed. 'It should happen *instantly*,' he said.

Orla watched, astonished. Few medicines worked *instantly*. Why did he think this one would?

Silas took down another plant – and Orla caught a brief shimmer of silver – but Atlas shook his head. 'Not that one – it's a weed.'

He tossed it on to the wooden table and picked up a

woody stem with purplish flowers.

'Batch 59: *Wisteria*.'

'He shouldn't drink that,' said Orla. 'It's nasty stuff –
scours your insides.'

But the next man in line was given the liquid. He
coughed in disgust, the concoction dribbling in faint blue
lines down his chin.

Blue. Atlas was working through all the plants that
looked even slightly blue.

But how did he know the colour of the cure?

Ariana grabbed her arm suddenly.

'Idris,' she said, pulling the Hauler coat he had lent
her tighter around her.

Idris huddled, shivering. His white shirt was stained
with pitchstone and he shuffled slowly forward.

'Why's he here?' said Orla.

Her blood ran cold when Atlas took down the next
plant – its petals were streaked with purple lines.

'Look,' he said. 'It looks just like the *mapafoglia*! That
cannot be a coincidence.'

Orla knew the plant. She remembered the label in the
glasshouse.

Hyoscyamus nox. Deadly poisonous.

'Batch 60: *Henbane*,' announced Atlas.

Orla watched as Atlas ground it up in the pestle and
decanted it into a glass beaker. Silas dragged Idris
forward.

He looked small there, among the others. Orla remembered him appearing in the garden at night, worried for Castor. All he wanted to do was help his brother.

Atlas held up the beaker.

'Surely this will be the one!'

'Wait,' said Idris. 'Wait, I'm *not sick*.'

'Of course you are, boy,' said Atlas. '*Everyone* here is.'

Silas yanked Idris towards the table. Atlas passed Silas the beaker.

'No!' cried Orla. 'It's *poison*.'

Atlas's eyes found her then.

'So,' he said, holding the glass. 'The Carson girl thinks she knows best. Got a secret from your mother, have you?'

'If I did, I wouldn't tell you,' said Orla.

'Not even to save the lives of all these people?' said Atlas.

'You're not saving their lives,' said Orla. 'You're poisoning them! First the pitchstone – then this – what do you think you're doing? You don't know how to make medicine. You just ripped those plants from the ground like you ripped open the mountain – like you destroyed the places where these people lived. My ma knew how to make medicines – but where do you think she learnt it from? She didn't make it up. People here have been making their own medicines for years and years – and they would still be able to, if you hadn't destroyed their land. And that's not enough – you're destroying them – in the name of selling better *ink* and making more money?'

But Silas tightened his grip on Idris.

'Let him go!' Orla said.

'This boy owes me,' Atlas replied coldly. 'His brother agreed to work to repay their father's debt and then he disappeared. If you want to save him – you trade him for that book. Search her.'

Orla ducked before Bouchard could reach her, and ran straight at Atlas, whose eyes glistened in the fire-light, the streaks of grey in his hair glowing like he himself had caught alight. Like a hawk Orla flew at him, sending the glass beaker smashing on to the ground.

Idris struggled free from Silas and stumbled into the machinery alongside them – narrowly missing a moving piston.

But Atlas struck back, grasping for the book.

'Give it to me!' he demanded, his eyes fierce, black dots in a sea of white. Instinctively, Orla shrank back towards the furnace, clutching the book.

'You want it?' said Orla. 'You want to steal one more thing? Well, you can't. I'll burn it!' she said. 'I'll burn it rather than give it to you! Ma would have done the same.'

Her voice echoed up into the rafters of the great mill.

The machines crashed around her, over and over. *Think*, she told herself, looking from the chimney to the pistons driven by the waterwheel. *There has to be a way out of here.* Panic rose in her chest.

'Stay back!' Atlas called to the Haulers. He prowled towards Orla, who held the book towards the flames with one shaking hand. 'You'll never destroy the book,' he said. 'Because, like everyone else, you are sentimental, you are weak. You are holding on to a memory – a memory of your pathetic mother. She wasn't clever, she wasn't a scientist – she was a fool! A fool to think she could help people and take nothing in return.'

Atlas's eyes flickered from Orla to Idris, Ariana and the fire. 'You do not know what is right and wrong in the world of adults. Sometimes people have to suffer for the world to work as it should.'

'But those people are never *you*,' said Ariana from the shadows. 'They're only ever those who are poor or struggling. It's not right. No one's life should depend on how much gold they have in their pocket.'

Orla took a deep breath. She couldn't let anyone else suffer the same fate as Ma, as Castor. She was starting to understand that now. If they found the cure, it wasn't just for Captain and the garden. It was for people like Castor, like Matteas and Magda. For the hundreds of people whose lives Atlas would ruin. Ma had known it. That's why she'd written her book. It wasn't just for Orla; it was for everyone who might need it. She looked at Idris, who was leaning against the machine. He looked exhausted – like he had lost all hope of saving his brother – of defeating Atlas. And the sight made the anger inside her flame even fiercer.

'You're the fool,' said Orla, stepping closer to the fire. 'The pitchstone was meant to stay in the ground, but you couldn't leave it there, could you? You wanted more. You as good as killed my ma, mining this horrible stuff, and now you're doing the same to everyone else. I can't let you do that.' She held the book close to the flames, watching the pages begin to curl at the edges, feeling the heat licking her skin. 'You blamed the plants,' she said, 'when they couldn't stand up for themselves – just like the people you've forced to work in your mine.'

'Orla, no!' cried Ariana. 'We need the book!'

'No, we don't,' said Orla, staring at the plant that Atlas had tossed aside. There was a flash of silver, like the glitter of falling coins.

Orla recognized the heart-shaped leaves, the seed pods like moons. And she realized the truth then. She had seen this plant the whole way up the river. It had been following her. *Ma had left a trail.*

She turned back to Atlas. 'Ma knew you were dishonest, she knew you were a greedy liar, so she left a trail of plants to expose you. It's all so clear now! You can't hide this any more – we'll tell the Marshall of Westharbour what you've done. He'll put a stop to all of it.'

Atlas laughed. 'The Marshall of Westharbour doesn't

give a damn what I do here, so long as I bring him a cure. And he certainly doesn't care what a *child* has to say about the matter. This is *business* – my business. And the Marshall of Westharbour needs ink just as much as the rest of the city. Now, give me the book and I'll make sure that everyone here has a dose of the cure.'

Idris spat on the floor and called the Marshall something incredibly rude.

'What do you know of it, boy?' sneered Atlas. 'Your brother was a weakling; he barely lasted a month at this mine before fleeing like a coward.'

Orla felt a burst of anger then, like a flood of water swelling and roaring, strong enough to break down the watermill itself. Atlas – the Haulers – and even the Marshall. None of them cared about the land, or the people that lived in it.

She lunged at Atlas, but Silas seized the back of her oilskin and she found herself scrabbling in mid-air.

'He's not worth it, Orla!' yelled Idris, his voice hoarse.

Silas flung her towards the table, but Orla did not let go of the book. Dazed, she pulled her hair out of her eyes to find herself right in front of the plant that Silas had tossed aside – the plant Atlas had called a weed. Its silver seed pods were stained purple from where it had drunk up the poison, like Ma had said.

Orla tried to shake the ringing sound from her ears. The furnace roared, the machines pounded, and, beyond it all, she realized she could hear the ringing of a bell – high and bright – and with it, the sound of a hundred footsteps, the sound of people shouting . . .

Atlas turned to the Haulers, as though to shout an instruction. But Silas and Bouchard were not looking at Atlas. They had heard the commotion outside the building and were watching the door, confused.

Bouchard moved to the side of the mill – and pulled a lever. The machinery clunked and stuttered and thudded to a halt. When the great room fell into silence, they could all hear it. The sound of a crowd thundering closer.

'Where's our gold?' came a shout from the yard.

'He's taken us for fools!' called another. 'He lied about the cure!'

'He's poisoning our homes!'

'Tear down the mill!'

'If I'm not mistaken,' said Ariana weakly, 'that's the sound of a hundred people who've realized you lied to them . . .'

With an enormous crash, the door came away from its hinges.

The colour drained from Atlas's face. He froze, his hands clenched so hard that his knuckles turned white. He stared at the workers with revulsion, as though a puddle of mud had decided to rise up against him.

'Get the children, you incompetent beast!' he shouted to Silas.

But the people surged forward as one, flooding into the building with a roar. They swept like a tide between the machines, battering the wood and metal with pick-axes and hammers, sending splinters into the air; tearing at the belts until they were shredded like ribbons.

Atlas looked on in horror.

'You must *obey*!' he shouted. But his voice was lost among the cries of rebellion and anguish. Six women seized a cart of crushed pitchstone and tipped it on to its side, scattering the black powder at Atlas's feet. The old woman Orla had helped in the mine hurried past her, reaching into the furnace to light a blazing torch.

'I've dreamt of this for a long time,' she said. 'Never thought it'd happen.'

She lifted the torch and set it down on a wooden machine. It burst into flame. 'Now get out of here!' she cried.

Orla did not hesitate. She knew what she had to do. Pulling Ariana with her, she raced down the central aisle, Idris at their heels.

She heard Atlas call out to Silas behind her. 'Saddle my horse!' he ordered. 'And follow those children!'

Black smoke was billowing into the rafters of the mill. Silas lunged at them, but the rioting workers, seeing that the building was now aflame, were fleeing towards the exit like a wave retreating into the ocean.

'This way!' Orla coughed as the smoke whirled around

them. There was a small window a little way from the door. She pushed it open and helped Ariana and Idris to climb out ahead of her. As they dropped down into the yard, Orla took one last look at the chaos behind her. Atlas was trying desperately to push through the seething mass of people, while Silas and Bouchard searched for the children.

'C'mon,' she said, landing in the yard. 'Get to the river. This isn't over yet.'

Struggling through a storm of ash and smoke, they made for the water. They raced across the yard and between the wooden buildings. It was as they passed the entrance to the mine that Orla skidded suddenly to a halt.

There it was: the plant that Atlas thought was no more than a weed. The plant whose seeds Ma had sown all the way up the river, from Thorn Creek to Fleetwater to the Inkenbrook mine. The only plant that could grow in pitchstone, and the only plant that could cure the sickness.

Honesty.

'Come on, Orla!' called Idris. 'To the river!'

The honesty waved its silver-coin seed pods, stained purple like the *mapafoglia*. Before her very eyes, Orla thought she could see the veins growing darker as they absorbed the pitchstone poison. Just as Ma had said.

'Orla, *quick!* Before they see!' called Ariana, ahead

now, and struggling to catch her breath.

Orla's eyes fixed on the plant. This was it. The plant they needed.

But it was all alone in the mountain. And it had a job to do.

'You stay here,' she told it. 'Keep on growing. Sow your seeds. Cover this blasted mountain with plants. We'll show Atlas.'

Idris looked at her, puzzled. Orla blushed.

'We don't need this one,' she explained. 'No – we gotta get back to Thorn Creek. Back home.'

'Back home?' said Ariana, pausing a little way ahead. 'What's there?'

'Honesty,' said Orla. 'My garden's covered in it. And it's more than enough for the cure.'

33

Honesty *Lunaria annua*
(Notes lost.)

At the water's edge they found the row of Hauler boats tossing and turning in the current. The river was a raging torrent now, and as Idris untied the first boat in the line, he had to strain against the rope to pull it close to the bank. With Orla and Ariana safely aboard, Idris jumped into his seat at the helm. No sooner had his feet left the jetty than the boat spun out into the middle of the channel. At once they were flying downstream, the grey smog of Inkenbrook disappearing behind them.

'We did it!' Orla said, scrabbling to light the Hauler lamp.

'You were right,' she said, turning to Ariana. 'Ma sowed the seeds deliberately – to show where Atlas had poisoned the world with pitchstone – and to try and stop it poisoning the river. It's honesty we need. Not from here – from Thorn Creek. We'll make the cure there, and get it straight to Castor.'

She opened Ma's book and turned to the page where Ma had drawn the honesty with its big green leaves and pinkish petals. Alongside it, she had drawn the seed pods too. She had labelled every part of the plant and she had even pressed several flowers between the pages. But there was no secret message written there – no hidden code to tell Orla how to use the honesty to make the cure.

'I don't understand,' she whispered. 'Didn't she write it down?'

Idris bent to look.

'The stitches are different on that page,' he said simply.

'That's just where it's come loose, when it fell in the river – oh, wait!'

Orla ran her finger down the centrefold of the book. Idris was right: the stitches seemed to be missing. Ma had shown her how to do this once, long ago. She'd made a hidden pocket in the book. Orla slid her finger inside and pulled out a slip of paper, three pressed honesty flowers, and three dried seed pods.

On the small piece of paper Ma had written just one line of code.

Ariana pulled out her pencil.

'Look,' she said, pointing at Ma's writing. 'Most of each letter is missing. She's only left the tiniest part of each, like the top curve of this *o*. If you weren't looking for a code, you certainly wouldn't recognize it as one.'

Orla flushed, ashamed that she'd never noticed this before.

'And she's not put the gaps between words, which is clever,' said Ariana, drawing a series of vertical lines among the sea of letters. 'See?'

'You're the clever one, Ariana!' whispered Orla, amazed.

'Here,' she said, filling in the rest of the letters.

'What does it say?' asked Idris, paddling steadily.

Ariana read aloud. '*For Orla*,' she began. 'Then – oh! – it's not words, it's a formula. Which means . . .'

She scribbled furiously in the space beneath Ma's writing.

'I don't understand,' said Orla quietly.

'Instructions. It looks like the honesty needs mixing with a number of chemicals to extract the medicinal properties – we have everything in the lab at Hind House. It's what your ma used – what Atlas uses for ink. Before all this.'

Idris looked over his shoulder at the mine in the distance.

'Orla, help me paddle,' he said, looking worried. 'It won't be long before—'

His face fell.

'Oh no.'

Orla followed his gaze. The moon broke out from between the clouds then, revealing the ghostly outline of the mine and the mountains behind them, along with a Hauler boat travelling fast towards them.

'Have they seen us?' gasped Orla, not daring to look back again.

'If they haven't yet, they will soon,' said Idris. Ahead of them the curve of the river straightened out, and they were faced with a long, open stretch of water. They were suddenly exposed, like ducklings leaving the nest for the first time.

The boat loomed towards them, closer by the minute.

'Silas,' said Ariana, looking fearfully back at the Haulers. 'Bouchard, too.'

'Don't worry,' said Idris. 'We're faster. I chose the lightest boat back there.'

'I hope you're right,' said Orla, as the trees flickered past, whipping and slicing at their faces. Idris paddled hard, though his eyes were bleary and tired. The hope of getting a cure for Castor had filled him with strength.

'Hold on tight,' he said. 'I'll get us to Thorn Creek. But it means going down through the rapids.'

34

<u>Scurvy-Grass</u> *Cochlearia officinalis*
Leaves: an ancient cure for scurvy, particularly useful for
voyages at sea.

They raced down the river a hundred times faster than they'd come up it. Behind them, Orla heard the shouts of the men that hunted them, and she gripped the side of the boat as they flew across the water like a skimming stone.

As they reached the maze of rapids, Orla held her breath. These were the jagged rocks that had snatched their paddles and torn their first boat in two. She remembered the heavy feeling of being dragged into the water and felt a wave of fear rise over her.

Idris guided the boat expertly through the current, as though it had been made for him. It swung easily between the rocks, lifting into the air like a leaping salmon as they travelled down and down through the white water. Rocks appeared at every turn, biting and snarling, threatening to pull them down into the deep. The water growled relentlessly. The trees of the Untold Forest had vanished now, swallowed by the familiar Fleetwater mist. Breathless, Idris steered them from the wild rapids on to the flat open river, but the current did not slow. It pushed them hungrily on, towards Fleetwater, and the gaping weir.

As the mist closed in on them, Orla clung to her pack, keeping Ma's book close. She could not lose it to the river a second time.

From somewhere in the gloom came a shout. 'Ahead!' cried a Hauler.

Out on the open water, the heavier boat was gaining on them.

'Pull in to the shore, Idris,' said Orla urgently. 'Anywhere, don't wait for the jetty. We have to hide!'

The mist was now so thick that they could barely see the riverbank. Idris steered the nose of the boat towards the shore, but Orla could hear the slap and swish of the Haulers' paddles. They were close.

Ariana huddled in the middle of the boat. She did not look well after the ride through the rapids.

Another shout came from the mist. 'Off the starboard bow!' boomed Silas. 'Full ahead!'

All of a sudden, a shadow loomed alongside them. Orla saw the sharp prow of a boat, like an arrow in the water, and Silas's bullish face peering at them, his enormous hands slicing the paddle through the water.

Idris swung his paddle to the right, trying to cut ahead of the Haulers and reach the bank. But the current was drawing them downstream.

Ariana screamed. Silas was alongside them now, leaning into the boat.

'All right, poppet,' he said to Orla. 'Give it here.'

'Get off!' yelped Orla as Silas reached for her pack. Orla lunged at Silas, hitting and slapping his hands. The two boats rolled and clunked together and Orla suddenly felt the pull of the current drawing them closer to the weir. She could hear its thundering roar.

'Idris!' she called. 'Get us away from the weir!'

'That way!' said Ariana, peering out into the gloom. 'The light – towards the light!'

'What?'

'Over there!'

Orla swung round – Ariana was right. Behind Silas, she saw a bright-green light – a glass lamp, glowing in the mist. Orla saw it flash once, then twice.

'Idris, *quick!*'

But Silas had taken hold of their boat now, and no matter how hard Idris paddled, they could not break free. A look of panic dawned on Idris's face as the two boats drifted closer to the weir.

'I can't!' he cried in horror. 'Help!'

Orla snatched one of the paddles from the Hauler boat, swung it behind her and brought it down on Silas's skull.

He slumped on to the deck, clutching his head.

Beside him, Bouchard, surprised, twisted to look at him, and Idris snatched the other paddle out of his hands. Then with one big boot, he kicked the boat, pushing themselves clear.

At once, Idris and Orla steered towards the green light.

But for Silas's boat it was too late. Already the current was pulling them towards the weir. Panicking, Silas reached overboard and tried to paddle with his hands – but the water was too fast – the boat was spinning out of control, pulled by the current like a leaf on the water. Orla saw a look of horror dawn on the Haulers' faces as they approached the dark line of the weir. Bouchard yelled in fright – Silas roared – and the boat disappeared over the weir, into the churning water below.

Orla gasped, but Idris did not stop to look. He was paddling fiercely now – parallel to the weir – towards the green light.

'The *lock*,' said Orla.

Through the mist, Orla saw the outline of a tall figure

holding the green lamp. Magda. She beckoned them nearer.

'That was close,' she said. 'Next time I'd recommend sticking closer to the bank, unless you want to end up dinner for the fishes.'

'We lost them, though, didn't we?' said Orla.

Magda bit her lip, narrowing her eyes at the weir. 'Maybe. They swim like otters, those Haulers. Can never be sure. Did you get it – the cure?'

'Almost,' said Orla. 'We just gotta get back to Thorn Creek.'

'All set!' called another voice. Another green lamp flashed into life and Orla saw Matteas by the entrance to the lock, using his back to push open the gates.

With a glance over his shoulder to make sure that the Haulers were truly gone, Idris steered them in.

As they pulled into the lock, Orla caught sight of the wide-mouthed weir, and the debris of the Hauler boat broken and scattered beyond. Dark shapes floated in the water.

Matteas and Magda each wound a lock handle and Orla felt the water falling beneath them. Beside her, Ariana was trembling. The Haulers had given them all a fright, Orla thought, but Ariana looked terrified. As the lock emptied, Orla dug the blanket from the bottom of her pack, which Ariana took gratefully. But she shook her head when Orla offered her the last two hazelnuts from her pack.

'You need proper supplies,' called Matteas. 'Hold on.'

He disappeared into a nearby house. A moment later, he threw a package down to Idris.

As the lock emptied, Idris unwrapped the package to reveal a stack of biscuits, each with a coloured sugar centre that looked just like glass. Orla crunched one hungrily, but still, Ariana would not eat. She closed her eyes and leant against the side of the boat sleepily.

'You bring that cure back, you hear me?' called Magda, when the boat reached the bottom of the lock.

Orla nodded, watching the gates open to reveal the river ahead. She could not shake the feeling that the Haulers were not quite gone.

Gathering her torn pack carefully in her lap, Orla took hold of her paddle once more. She barely noticed as Magda and Matteas waved them farewell, and Ariana curled herself up, exhausted, to sleep in the hollow of the boat. All Orla could think of now was getting the boat down the river: past the pine beach where they'd left the sick Hauler; past the cracking willows of Dead Elm Strand, and up the winding creek, back to Thorn Creek and the garden.

Three miles behind them, Atlas galloped along the river-bank, slicing through the trees. The old stallion was struggling now, his bay coat glistening with sweat and river mist, but Atlas urged him onwards. His mind was fixed on the Carson girl. She certainly knew how to slip away, he couldn't deny that. But despite her sly nature, the girl knew very little. Yes, she had somehow swept the boy into her games; and his own foolish niece too. But that did not worry Atlas. This was just like Elizabeth all over again. Everything would work out in his favour.

Racing past the roaring weir, Atlas looked up at the crumbling houses of Fleetwater and smiled to see the old glassmaking town empty. Yes, everything always worked out in his favour.

35

White Willow *Salix alba*
For pain.

Home again, wise girl.
   Long time lost.
   Back where the roots are deep, where the marshes grow wet.
   Rushes woven with spiders.
   And berries ripe for autumn.
It was like coming in from a storm to sit by the fire. As they pulled into the little wooden jetty below Hind House, Orla heard the plants shiver and waken into song, welcoming her home. She felt her whole body soften with relief, and as she stepped out of the boat on to land, she turned towards the garden.
   Wise-girl, wise-girl! they called.

You're safe for now, they sang. *Safe home.*

Orla's heart fluttered. There was still a chance that everything could go back to how it was.

'Come on, then,' she said, wondering why Idris and Ariana were still in the boat.

'Wait – Orla – no!' said Idris, his voice sounding much higher than usual. 'Orla, there's something wrong with Ariana!'

Orla felt suddenly cold. The world around her moved in slow motion as she turned to see Ariana slumped against the side of the boat. All the colour had gone from her face; she looked like a figure made from wax, her hair plastered to her face like waterweed. And from beneath the lacy cuff of her once-white dress, Orla saw on her wrist the blooming purple marks of the sickness.

'No!' she said in horror.

'Orla, help her up!' said Idris, kneeling on the jetty.

'I – can't . . .' said Orla, finding that her legs and her arms would not move. It took days for those marks to appear. How had she not noticed that Ariana was sick?

Ink in the water, murmured the plants. *Knives in the dark!*

Suddenly Orla couldn't breathe. It was as though an enormous hand had grasped her ribcage, squeezing it tight until all the air seeped out of her lungs. She remembered how Ariana had kept pulling down her sleeves; she had been hiding it – hiding the marks of the sickness on her wrists.

Orla forced a long, shaky breath. Idris was saying something – reaching down into the boat towards Ariana, but Orla could not hear him. The world was going dark at the edges. The sight of Ariana lying there, not moving . . . She should never have let her come with them. She should never have let her make tea, or help her with Ma's book. Because, just like Ma, she could be gone in an instant.

She flung herself away from the boat. Idris shouted her name, but she was already running. She saw Idris lift Ariana from the boat like a wilted plant, but still she did not stop as she raced along the hidden path. The plants around her cried out: *Help your friend, help your friend!* But Orla could not stop. She could only run, away from the horror, away from the world in ruin – back through the marsh grass, back through the myrtle.

What's wrong, wise girl? called the broom and the dock.

Where are you running?

Reaching the blackthorn hedge, Orla pushed frantically at the brambles, searching for the secret path. Ignoring their cries of alarm, she scrabbled through like a badger. Her arms were prickled and scratched, but Orla did not care. She ran into her garden, stopping beneath the apple trees, trying to catch her breath in long, shuddering gasps. Her heart hammered on and on. Visions of the purple marks on Ariana's arms flashed in her mind. Tears ran down her face.

'I should never have let her come,' she sobbed. 'I shoulda known she was sick.'

She pulled at the nettles, feeling their stings bite into her palms. It wasn't *fair*, Orla thought, putting her head in her hands. She'd been trying to do the right thing – trying to find the cure – and all she'd achieved was putting her friend in danger. She'd tried so hard to do what Ma couldn't, and it still hadn't gone right. She should never have tried. She should just have stayed in the garden. Perhaps, then, Ariana would not have fallen sick.

Orla gave a great, hiccuping sob and wiped her face with her sleeve.

It's not over, said the plants.

'It *is*,' said Orla, pulling at her oilskin.

The apple trees shivered in the breeze.

'Leave me alone,' she said grumpily.

Friends, they said.

Help.

Orla wiped her eyes.

'I know,' she said. 'You're trying to help, but I don't know what to do.'

A little distance from the apple trees she saw the stems of honesty dancing with their seed pods, rattling in the breeze.

Work to do, they said. *Keep on going!*

'It's too late,' she said, slumping back against one of the trees. 'I can't do it on my own.'

No, said the dock. *You can't.*

At last! said the bitter wormwood.

Friends, echoed the apple tree.

Orla found herself crying again, and felt annoyed at herself for caring so much.

She pulled up a dock leaf and wiped her face with it. Then she squashed it between her hands and rubbed the nettle stings. She blew her nose on another dock leaf and threw it into the long grass.

There was a rustle behind her, and a stocky figure appeared. It was Idris.

Orla quickly dried her face again.

'I told you once before, stop breaking into my garden.'

'Ariana's very sick,' he said.

'I can't help her,' said Orla. Her teeth were chattering. She gripped her knees to stop her hands shaking. 'I can't do it.'

'You got to,' he said simply.

'I couldn't help Castor,' said Orla, sniffing. 'I couldn't help Ma.'

'Are you ever gonna stop saying that?' said Idris. His eyes were red. Orla wondered if he'd been crying on the way to find her.

Afraid, said the nettles.

'I'm not afraid!' cried Orla.

'Yes, you are!' said Idris. 'You're afraid it won't work, so you won't try. You're afraid to trust me and Ariana, in case we let you down or run away to become Haulers. You're afraid to care too much in case we get sick and die like your ma. Well, guess what? *We're afraid of that too.*'

Orla's throat closed up, tight and painful.

'And you know what? It might go wrong. People might die – Castor might already be dead for all I know. But we can't let that make us afraid to try. We can't let it make us afraid to have friends or help other people. We shouldn't pretend we're not scared. Cos if we do, we're no better than Atlas. He thinks we shouldn't have feelings – that we should become hard as rock, because then we don't care when we hurt people. We don't care if we're killing other people in exchange for a scrap of gold. I don't want to grow up to be like that, Orla.'

'I know you don't,' said Orla, wiping her nose on her sleeve. 'You're not a Hauler like them.'

'Atlas was wrong,' said Idris. 'Those people at the mine cared enough to burn down the mill. Ariana cared enough to run away from everything she knew just to see if she could help people. You cared about your ma, but you mustn't feel guilty you couldn't save her. You were so small then. It's taken three of us to work out what she knew. So don't think about what you couldn't do before. Think about what you can do *now.*'

Idris looked away. He twisted a bit of grass between his fingers.

'The Haulers buried Ma in the woods, Idris,' Orla said quietly, looking out at the green spikes of the pine woods. 'I never knew where. They wouldn't tell me. I'm sorry I thought you were one of them. You'd never do anything like that.'

She wiped her eyes. Idris smiled gently.

'Castor's my only brother,' he said simply. 'I can't be on my own without him. And Ariana – she's our friend. So I'm asking you again, will you please help?'

Orla hesitated.

Idris and Ariana – they'd both looked at her with so much hope. What if she let them down? But there in her garden, she remembered making comfrey balm with Ma, to hand out to villagers with bruises and sprains. She remembered making ointment from the chamomile to soothe the bites of the creek mosquitoes. And she remembered fixing the wing of the little brown sparrow. They'd always tried to help, hadn't they?

She took a deep breath and looked Idris in the eye.

'I will try,' she said.

Idris smiled and pulled something out of his pocket. He threw it at Orla.

Watch out! called the plants.

Orla whipped her hand into the air and caught it – it was a dried plum. She broke it in half and tossed the stone into the bushes, then ate it in one. The sharpness made her feel a little more alive.

'Let's get Ariana to Hind House,' she said to Idris, feeling a little fire returning to her veins. 'Then you should go find Castor. To tell him it's going to be OK.'

Medicine, said the cow parsley.

Herbs, said the nettles.

Help your friend, said the hogweed.

Work to do, said the honesty.

36

<u>Feverfew</u> _Chrysanthemum parthenium_
Flowers: infuse in boiling water and allow to cool; for fever, headache, earache.

Ariana stirred as Idris lifted her from the boat.

'Do you have the plant?' she murmured, trying to stand up, but stumbling and falling on to the grass.

'I've got it, Ariana,' said Orla gently, kneeling down and scooping Ariana's arm over her shoulder. 'I've got it – don't worry.'

She tried not to look at the purple lines streaking up to Ariana's elbows. She and Idris walked Ariana up the slope towards Hind House, Orla carrying the bundle of honesty between the straps of her pack.

Keep hidden, said the river reeds.

Silent steps, said the ragwort.

Hind House rose out of the gloom. There were no candles lit in the windows, and the garden was untouched.

The roses snickered against the wall.

Back again, are you? they whispered.

'There's no one here,' said Idris quietly, trying the front door. It did not open.

'*No*,' croaked Ariana. 'That can't be right. Mother's here – the servants are here. Where would they go to?' She looked feverishly up at the glassy windows. Orla saw the whites of her eyes were lined with red.

The ivy on the walls rustled.

Stable gate, it said.

'Round the back,' said Orla. 'We'll find a way in.'

Ariana was holding tight to Idris's shoulder now, suddenly looking a lot weaker at the thought that her mother was not at home. They followed the stone garden wall, before squeezing in through the metal gate. Orla saw the neat herb beds, the roses trimmed and pruned, the soil so bare in places that it was hard and cracked. She glanced at the stables, but they were empty. Where was Captain?

'There's a cellar door,' said Ariana. 'Leads under the kitchen.'

They hurried across the stable yard. Close to the house, Orla spied yet more silver honesty seed heads and wondered briefly if Ma had sown the seeds when she came to Hind House. But then they were at the cellar door, beneath the kitchen window – and Orla was pulling open the wooden door, and helping Ariana down into the gloomy passage. There was not a sound from the rooms above – not a footstep, not a mouse.

Ariana looked worried, but she did not stop to wonder. 'His study's this way,' she said, leading the way in the dark without even a candle for light, Idris holding her steady. They climbed a creaking stairway and passed through door after door until they came to one that was locked.

Ariana's hands were shaking, but she pulled down a hairpin hidden above the door frame, and wriggled it around until the lock clicked.

The door swung open to reveal an unlit room. But in the dim light that came through the net curtains, Orla saw glass shimmering like frost on a cold morning. The walls were lined with a thousand ink bottles, in blues and greens and blacks. She ran her finger carefully along a shelf. There was ink the colour of nightshade berries, ink as dark as a moonless sky. Ink so pale and grey that it looked like water swirling beneath ice. All of it was beautiful. She bit her lip. Atlas could have made a fine living selling this ink. But he had wanted more. He wanted to be richer than all the men in Westharbour. No matter what it cost people like Ma and Castor. No matter what it cost his own niece.

Orla sighed. 'He'd better have what we need,' she said.

Ariana sank into the chair beside the bench and took a moment to gather her breath, before reaching for a pen and ink and a roll of paper. Orla laid Ma's book in front of her, and Ariana took out the slip of paper with Ma's formula written on it. She counted in a quiet whisper, making notes on the paper. Her hand kept slipping as she held the pen, and Orla could see beads of sweat on her forehead.

'Just in case I don't make it,' she said.

'You will make it!' said Orla, putting the honesty on the bench beside the book. 'Just tell me what to do.'

They wasted no time. Idris cleared Atlas's ink samples from the bench while Orla stood on a step stool and, with Ariana's instruction, pulled down the equipment they needed. One large glass beaker, perfectly cylindrical and impossibly thin. A metal tripod, and what looked like part of an oil lamp. Ariana arranged the tripod over the lamp, and placed the glass beaker above it. Then, she lit a match and held it to the lamp. A flame puffed into life, sending a bluish light into every glass.

'Pass me those goggles, please,' said Ariana, pointing to one of the shelves. Orla helped her to pull them over her eyes, so that only thin slits of glass shone through, glimmering blue in the light.

'Right,' she said, struggling into a pair of oversized gloves on the bench beside her. 'Pass me that container –

no, the one to the left – and that one – yes. Careful – the liquid is flammable.'

She stopped to catch her breath. Orla watched Ariana, impressed by how well she knew everything in Atlas's laboratory – but worried, more than anything, that she might collapse in a faint at any moment, despite her determination.

Idris helped Ariana to measure out the liquids, and tipped them into the glass beaker above the lamp. Ariana checked and double-checked Ma's notes, and then pointed to the honesty.

'We need to grind up the seeds,' she said.

Orla nodded, showing Idris how to peel open the paper-thin seed pods and lift out the round, flat seeds. They dropped them into a mortar and ground them to a floury paste.

'OK, stand back – and *don't* breathe this in.'

Ariana wrapped her scarf around her face and extinguished the blue flame, so that they were left with the light from the misted window. Then she tipped the honesty into the glass beaker above the burner and stirred everything together with a metal stick.

Orla held her breath, half expecting the mixture to explode like gunpowder.

'It's *quite* safe,' said Ariana, seeing Orla's concerned expression. 'We just have to wait for it to react.'

'What?' she said, alarmed. 'How long will that take?'

Orla slumped on her stool, chin in her hands, watching the liquid bubble. They were relying on Ariana's understanding of Ma's book, and, now that they were here, Orla was struggling to believe that it was going to work.

After what felt like hours, the liquid still hadn't changed colour.

'Why isn't it blue?' said Idris.

'Hold on,' said Ariana. She stirred the mixture again, her hand trembling so that the metal stick clattered against the glass. She checked Ma's notes again, but Orla saw that her eyes were struggling to focus.

'Ariana, are you all right?' said Orla nervously. Idris had turned pale, too. He kept looking towards the door and Orla could tell that he was worried about Castor.

'I'll just have to test it,' said Ariana quietly.

'I'm not letting you test it if it's not safe!' said Orla.

She picked up the metal stick from Ariana and stirred the mixture again. But it still did not change colour.

Orla's heart sank. The whole of their journey passed before her eyes: from Dead Elm Strand to Fleetwater, from the glasshouse to the mine. It was all wasted.

Ariana bowed her head. Orla clasped her hands together, her eyes stinging as she tried very hard to stop the tears of disappointment from spilling over.

'It's supposed to turn blue,' repeated Ariana, disappointed.

Idris kicked a cabinet, setting the whole glass shelf wobbling.

'Wait,' said Ariana. 'What if . . .'

She scanned the shelves and then sighed.

'Hmm.'

'What?'

'That one, there. It's a dye, really – it's found in purplish plants. Like blackberries and cabbage and . . . It's not an ingredient, it's a test. Your ma knew that if the solution turned blue, it was safe!'

'Cabbage,' said Orla, remembering Ma cutting up pounds and pounds of red cabbage. They used it for dye, for painting – and Ma had even taken it with her to Hind House.

'You're joking,' said Idris.

Orla shook her head.

'*Brassica oleracea*,' she said, scanning the shelves. 'There!'

A purplish ink in a large glass bottle with *Brassica oleracea* written on it in spiky handwriting. Orla climbed up and passed it down to Idris.

'There's only a drop,' he said, holding the bottle up to the light. 'Is it enough?'

'I hope so,' said Ariana.

Orla chewed her thumbnail. This was their last chance – their last opportunity to make the cure work. After that, she had no other ideas. She crossed her fingers and hoped that Ma and Ariana knew what they were doing.

Ariana dripped the purple liquid into the concoction. Orla held her breath.

And at once the liquid turned deep blue. It looked exactly as she remembered it: a swirling, inky colour, blue as a Hauler's coat.

Orla could hardly breathe. 'It's safe,' she whispered. 'Try it.'

'Bottle first,' said Ariana, reaching out her hand. 'We need to get it to Castor.'

Idris passed her a glass bottle, and Orla helped Ariana to pour the liquid in.

'And another one,' said Ariana faintly, filling a second bottle to the brim.

Holding the stopper in one hand, Ariana hesitated. Orla knew what she was thinking. *What if they were wrong? What if the mixture was poisonous?*

'You know what you're doing,' said Idris. 'I trust you.'

'Then go,' said Ariana. 'Quick – out the way we came.'

Idris nodded, took the little bottle and ran. Orla heard his footsteps echo down the hall.

Ariana turned off the burner, so they were left in golden lamplight. She sighed and rested her head in her hands.

'Come on, Ariana,' said Orla encouragingly. 'It's OK, you're going to be OK. Just drink the medicine.'

But Ariana was so weak that her hands fumbled, almost spilling the liquid. Her purple-stained arms flopped uselessly on to the bench.

'I . . .'

There was a thud somewhere in the distance.

Ariana looked suddenly worried.

'The front door – that wasn't Idris.'

'Drink, Ariana!'

Orla lifted the bottle to Ariana's lips. But before she could drink, a click came from the open door.

Orla jumped and swung round.

There, in the doorway, was Atlas, pointing a pistol directly at them. He had lost his hat somewhere on the journey, and his hair was wild and windswept. His gaze darted to the bottle in Ariana's hand like a falcon marking its prey.

'Very good, children,' he said with a smile. 'Now, hand it over. And the book, too.'

Ariana shrank back against the counter, but Atlas strode forward and snatched the bottle from her hands. She whimpered. Orla seized the burner and was about to fling it at Atlas, but he simply pointed the pistol towards her, lifting Ma's book from the bench with his other hand.

'You too, girl,' he said, twitching the gun towards Ariana. 'Come with me. Let's show the Marshall of Westharbour your marvellous medicine, shall we?'

Ariana looked at Orla then, her eyes pleading.

'She won't make it to Westharbour, you fool!' said Orla.

But Atlas swung the pistol back to Orla.

'I *will* shoot,' he said, wrenching Ariana towards him. She drooped like a flower in the frost, barely able to stand. Orla saw her knees buckle as Atlas backed out of the room, pistol raised. Orla froze. How could this be happening?

Atlas took one short step backwards, lowered the gun, and slammed the door behind him. Then he turned the key in the lock.

Orla flung herself at the door, screaming. 'You coward!' she shouted. 'You murderer! That's not yours to take! Come back, you monster!'

But it was no good. Atlas had vanished, leaving nothing but a draught against the door. He had left Hind House and fled. And now she was locked inside.

37

Ivy *Hedera helix*
Though it has no medicinal use, it will keep a garden alive,
for it feeds a hundred insects, and keeps bats safe in winter.

'It's over,' muttered Orla, sliding down on to the floor. She had lost everything.

She stared at the empty glass on the bench. Without Ariana, she could not make more of the cure. She did not know how the chemicals worked – not like Ariana did. Or Ma.

She looked hopelessly from the door to the window.

There was a curl of ivy pressed against the glass.

Don't give up! it called.

Wrenching herself to her feet, Orla yanked at the window. It was so overgrown with ivy that it did not shift.

'Let me out,' she whispered to the plants. '*Please!*'

She pushed the window with all her strength. With a *pop* the ivy gave way. She clambered out of the window into a damp flowerbed, just in time to see Atlas at the gate, mounted on a horse, Ariana draped like a rag doll in front of him.

A horse with bony ribs, a wonky mane and a patchwork coat.

Atlas was riding Captain.

Anger flooded Orla. He was riding *her horse*.

He kicked Captain and the horse stumbled into a canter. They disappeared out of the gate, out into the streets of Thorn Creek.

'Let me through!' cried Orla, scrambling out of the tangled flowerbed and flying across the garden.

Quick! cried the plants.

Fast, wise girl!

Run!

She raced through the undergrowth, scratching and tearing, until she reached the gate. She could just see Captain and Atlas in the distance, outside the grounds now – out on the cobbled streets of the village.

'Come back, Captain!' she shouted, breathless. 'It's me! Don't you *dare* go with him!'

At the sound of her voice, Captain tried to turn – straining and pulling against the reins. But Atlas whipped him on and forced him through the narrow streets.

Orla's lungs screamed. Her legs burnt. But she did not stop running.

'Stop!' she shouted. But there was no one to hear. Ahead, Captain was struggling between the crooked houses with their low-hanging eaves, his hooves slipping on the cobbles. They rounded a corner, but Orla darted through a gap between two houses, too narrow for a horse and rider, and appeared right on Captain's tail – shouting and swearing and panting. But Atlas held tight to Ariana and kicked the horse on, and Captain cantered out on to the main street, into the market square.

Go on! said the ivy, hidden between the houses in the gardens.

Not over yet! cheered the sorrel in the ditches.

Panting, Orla stumbled into the square, past the chapel and the tavern, past Dawson & Reed. Atlas was at the far side of the square now, approaching the gap between two leaning houses that marked the start of the Westharbour road. Atlas was making right for it, his gaze set on the great stone bridge at the edge of the village. He was trying to leave Thorn Creek with Ariana.

Atlas whipped Captain again, but this time the horse tossed his head in defiance. There was something in Captain's way – *something* was blocking the exit to the market square.

Orla ran, her pulse roaring in her ears as she drew

closer. Two horses stood in the road, their riders each bearing a stern expression.

It was Elias Dawson and Callahan Reed, Elias in his old work jacket on his grey mare, and Callahan Reed on his broad draught horse. They stood their ground as Atlas tried to push Captain onwards.

'Move aside!' Atlas shouted.

Orla sprinted closer.

Villagers were starting to emerge from the chapel and the tavern, drawn by the noise. Orla skidded to a halt behind Marianne Reed, whose arms were filled with sticks of wax.

'You look in a mighty hurry, Governor,' said Elias steadily. He did not move his horse.

'I must make for Westharbour,' he said. 'My niece is sick.'

'It's four days' ride to Westharbour,' said Callahan Reed, his voice deep and slow. 'Why not go by boat?'

Orla tried to scramble through the gathering crowd.

'My goodness, the poor girl!' cried a voice. Orla saw Agnes Dawson pointing at Ariana slumped in front of Atlas.

'Look at her arms!'

'His own *niece*!'

Atlas looked flustered. He raised his whip to Captain once more. Ariana stirred, groaned.

'Stop!' cried Orla, panting. 'Stop, she needs help!'

'Let me through, you fools!' said Atlas.

'No!' shouted Orla, struggling forward until she was in front of Elias's horse. 'She needs medicine – she needs it *now*!'

The villagers stared at Orla. Suddenly she realized how she must look to them all. She hadn't changed her clothes since they'd been to the mine. She was filthy. She must have looked like a street urchin: Orla Carson, the girl who lived down the swampy end of the village in that old woodshed, with her horse and her mother, who was never anything more than a fraud . . .

Elias eyed her carefully. 'Hello, Orla,' he said mildly, before turning to Atlas. 'I suggest you step down from that horse, Warden.'

Atlas did not step down from the horse. Instead, he kicked Captain. Finding himself still blocked by the other horses, Captain shied. Indignant, Atlas kicked him again and again, flapping his legs wildly, before raising his whip once more—

'Stop – stop hurting him!' cried Orla, trying to grab Captain's reins.

'Warden, be reasonable!' shouted Elias. 'You will step down from the horse, *now*.'

Atlas's face reddened. His jaw clenched.

'And why should I take orders from a *candlemaker*,' he said, once again raising his whip. The horse reared and tried to spin around – but the crowd had closed in;

there was no room. Captain tripped, and the crowd gasped as Ariana slipped sideways.

'Because we got worried about them children,' said Elias calmly, nodding towards Orla. 'Her and the young Hauler boy, missing for days. A Hauler boat gone too – and your fine stallion away from the stables? And that's not to mention the poor lad lying sick down by the river with no help at all – no medicine in this town, no boats to take him to the city for help.'

Orla watched Elias, astonished to realize that he'd noticed her gone. But then, she thought, he passed by her garden almost every day. Of course he'd noticed.

Atlas paused. Orla saw him grip Captain's reins tighter.

'Let us pass,' he said. 'I don't have time for this nonsense.'

'We're not the fools you think we are, Warden,' said Elias. 'You told us the grain was not safe to eat, but you sold it, didn't you? Hauled it to Westharbour for a pretty penny. You told us the sickness came from the wild. And yet this girl has fallen sick in your own home?'

'The grain *was* poisoned,' Atlas said without hesitation. 'It was *burnt*.'

A murmur ran through the crowd.

'Listen to me! He's lying!' shouted Orla, climbing on to the stump of the felled rowan tree. 'He blamed the plants for the sickness – but it was all lies! It's his *ink* that's made everyone sick – even his own niece. The waterproof ink. *Please* let me help her.'

Atlas swung round in the saddle. 'Foolish girl – she doesn't know what she's saying!'

'You know I'm no fool,' Orla growled. 'I know what I saw.'

The villagers fell silent, listening intently.

Orla took a deep breath. 'We discovered the truth,' she said. 'Atlas is mining a rock called pitchstone from the mountains north of Fleetwater – and he's using it to make this ink, which is poisonous. He's known about it for years, but that's not stopped him from selling it, or from spilling it in the creek by Hind House. Atlas's waterproof ink is what's making our plants sick!'

The crowd gasped. Orla felt her legs trembling – why should they believe her? She looked at Ariana, slumped lifeless on Captain's shoulders, Atlas gripping her dress with white knuckles.

'This is nonsense,' said Atlas. 'She's making up stories! Doubt the ignorant girl has ever been near a pot of ink in her life.'

'And it's not just our plants. Atlas's mine is poisoning the river upstream,' said Orla. 'Hundreds of people have died in Fleetwater. And in Westharbour, too. Cos the poison is in the *water* – not in the *plants*.'

'This is utter fiction!' exclaimed Atlas, holding tight as Captain stamped his feet impatiently. 'The girl doesn't know what she's talking about! Thorn Creek is safe, so long as we take the necessary precautions!'

Ariana's breath was shallow, Orla could see it.

'He is taking Ariana to Westharbour so he can prove the medicine works, so that the Marshall and all his friends know they're safe from the ink. He don't care about us – he won't bring it back, he won't sell it to people like us. He'll carry on mining the pitchstone and making his ink. And he'll make a pretty coin selling the cure to his Westharbour friends.'

Elias and Callahan moved their horses either side of Atlas.

'We've asked that you get down from the horse, Warden,' said Callahan. 'We will not ask again.'

'These are all *lies*!' said Atlas. Orla could see he was gripping the reins tightly. He knew he was trapped. But still he did not get down from the horse.

'For *shame*!' cried the innkeeper.

'Poisoned his own niece!' exclaimed Agnes.

'Poor girl,' gasped Marianne. 'Someone help her!'

At once five pairs of hands reached up and pulled Ariana gently from the horse. Orla saw Agnes lay her on the ground – she was not moving. Orla leapt down from the rowan stump, but she could not reach Ariana – Captain and Atlas were in her way now. And so were the villagers, swarming towards Atlas, a sea of hands pulling and scrambling to try and bring him down from the horse.

Atlas turned pale. In a panic, he swung Captain's head around, yanking at the bit, trying to force him through the crowd. Orla knew that was a mistake. Captain *hated* people pulling at the bit. He bucked, tossing his back legs into the air, and Atlas was jolted forward, clinging to Captain's mane. Then Captain dropped his head and Atlas slid to the ground in an undignified heap. Captain snorted, stepped over Atlas's crumpled figure, and nudged Orla's chest with his nose. He snuffled her carefully, smelling her coat and her jacket to see where she had been and whether she had any treats.

Elias and Callahan dismounted at once. Callahan lifted Atlas to his feet and pulled his arms behind his back, while Elias took hold of Captain's reins. Orla hurried to kneel beside Ariana.

'There's a bottle – in his pocket,' she told Elias. 'And a book – Ma's book. They're mine,' said Orla.

Atlas glared at Orla. 'The Marshall will hear about this,' he said. 'About what you and your *mother* have cost me.'

'Ignore him,' said Orla, holding out her hand to Elias. 'The bottle – it's the medicine she needs.'

Ariana was deathly pale now. She was fading . . .

Elias rummaged in Atlas's coat pockets and retrieved the little glass bottle.

He handed it over silently. Atlas growled.

Orla unstoppered the bottle and gently lifted Ariana's

278

head. Very carefully, she pressed it to Ariana's lips, so that a single drop of blue liquid spilt out.

'*Come on*,' whispered Orla, holding Ariana's hand.

Medicine, said the weeds beneath the drainpipe.

Hope, said the chickweed in the gutters.

Wise girl, said the moss among the cobbles.

The crowd huddled closer. Orla held her breath, cradling Ariana. What would she do if the cure did not work?

Ariana stirred slightly, but she did not waken. The pulse in her wrist was as faint as a bird's heartbeat.

Orla wiped her face, wet with tears. 'Please, Ariana,' she said. 'Please be all right.'

'Look!' cried Callahan, still holding on to Atlas. 'Look, the marks on her arms!'

Orla took her hand away from Ariana's wrist. There, right where her Orla had felt Ariana's pulse a moment before, the purple lines were beginning to fade, like a flood retreating.

'It's working,' she whispered.

38

Shepherd's Purse *Capsella bursa-pastoris*
Tincture: steep the fresh or dried herb in boiling water; soak cotton and use to stem a nosebleed. Also known as **Mother's Heart**.

A whisper ran through the crowd. 'The medicine works – the girl will survive! We will all survive!'

Orla saw Atlas then. He looked furious. How *dare* he look furious!

'You should be *pleased*!' she exclaimed. 'You should be pleased that she's alive!'

Someone was kneeling down beside Ariana, covering her with a shawl – but Orla could barely see through her rage. She pulled herself to her feet. It felt like a hurricane was rising inside her: she wanted to crush Atlas. She wanted to destroy him.

'You deserve to have the sickness. It should have been

you!' she cried, marching towards Atlas. 'You've spent all that time in the mine – and it was the innocent people who came to harm. You'd have thought—'

'You'd have thought I'd have caught the sickness by now?' suggested Atlas.

Orla stood face to face with Atlas. Her chest rose and fell in angry breaths, like a wildcat facing down a wolf.

Atlas blinked at her. 'It was a good thing your ma left me a little of the cure, then,' he said quite calmly.

A sudden pain seared Orla's chest, like thorns in her heart.

'Didn't you wonder how I could visit the mine unharmed?' he said. 'It's powerful stuff. One dose and you're set for life. Didn't you realize?'

No, thought Orla. *This cannot be possible.*

The crowd were whispering around them now, like a storm flickering into life. Orla remembered the dark shadow moving behind her as Ma gave her the cure to the sickness. A shadow with a broad-brimmed hat, just like Atlas's.

Atlas *had* had the sickness. He'd been there when Ma found the cure.

'It's a shame there wasn't enough left for her,' he said.

Orla felt as though the ground had fallen away. The corners of her vision were turning dark.

'You stole it,' she growled. 'You *stole* it!'

'Prove it,' spat Atlas, his hair flying into his face. Orla

saw Callahan's muscles straining with the effort of holding Atlas still.

'Because she would never have saved *you*!' cried Orla. 'She would never have saved you instead of herself. She would never have trusted you to make the cure!'

'Wouldn't she?' said Atlas. 'She knew that it was too late for her – she needed someone who had the money, the wits, the influence to make the cure and distribute it far and wide! She could see how useful I was. She wanted *me* to do what she could not.'

For a moment Orla believed him. Ma was kind. Ma *did* want to save as many people as possible.

'If you would just let me *go*,' he said, struggling against Callahan's grip, 'I can take you to Hind House, and I will show you that this girl is lying. I will show you how the cure is made. I know the details – I know everything.'

'You're lying!' said Orla. 'You lay in wait, just long enough to see that Ma's cure worked on me, and then you stole it. You could have waited – you could have let her save herself, and everyone else. She wanted to go back to Fleetwater – and you wouldn't let her. You wouldn't let her because she was trying to tell everyone what you'd done – just like you tried to send Ariana to Westharbour to keep her sickness a secret.'

Ariana stirred then, and Orla saw that it was Agnes who was cradling her in her shawl.

'But you were too late,' she continued. 'Ma had

282

already sowed the seeds all the way up the river. The seeds of the plant that would take the toxins out of the soil. And now that your mine is gone, that's what'll happen. You have my ma to thank for your life – yet you returned it by stealing her knowledge, using it to take a coin from dying men, and tossing her in the woods like she was nothing.'

'Lies!' hissed Atlas.

'I am telling the truth!' said Orla. 'And I can prove it. Give me the book.'

Callahan stuck his hand into the pocket of Atlas's greatcoat and pulled out Ma's book. Orla saw the flash of metal on the grip of Atlas's pistol, secured in a holster on his belt. Callahan handed the book to Orla, who opened it to the back pages, where Ariana had translated Ma's code, and showed it to the crowd.

'Ma wrote the cure in a code *so that he wouldn't see it,*' she said. 'Don't you think that if she'd trusted him enough to *save his life*, she would have freely shown him this book? Ariana's the one who decoded it . . .'

Elias pulled a pair of wire-framed glasses from his pocket, and placed them on his nose.

Orla's heart pulsed as she turned back to Atlas. 'It's all written here. Ma knew everything about your pitchstone operation. If it hadn't been for you, she would still be alive.'

The crowd held their breath. Elias looked over his

glasses at Orla, but she could not read his expression. What if all of this came to nothing?

'You know, your ma saved my life once,' Elias said, handing Orla the book. 'I got my foot caught in a trap – foolish, I know – and it started to rot. She visited every day. And Agnes—'

'She helped me through the most terrible fever.'

'She showed me how to grow sage and use it for tea!' said another woman.

'She fixed my horse's rotten hoof!'

'And she saved my life when Ariana was born,' said a quiet voice.

Orla turned – the voice sounded familiar, but fainter, weaker than she remembered from the days long ago in the little school house in the market square. It was Josephine Claw, her long white dress trailing through the dirt of the village. And standing at her side was Idris. His eyes were brimming with tears.

'Idris!' Orla said. 'Why aren't you with Castor, what's happened?'

Before Idris could answer, Josephine Claw fell to the ground beside her daughter, running her hands through Ariana's curls, holding the shawl tight around her and kissing her face. Orla felt her own tears welling up. She missed Ma – she missed her so much.

But then she felt a hand on her shoulder. It was Idris, bending down, his face streaked with tears – but his eyes were bright with joy and relief.

'He's all right, Orla,' he said. 'Castor's all right! Josephine was taking care of him. Our cure *worked*.'

There was a murmur among the villagers. Orla looked from person to person – from Agnes, shaking her head, forlorn, to the butcher, fixing Atlas with an icy stare. Perhaps, Orla thought, they'd not hated Ma as much as it had seemed.

Josephine spoke to the crowd then.

'We should never have listened to him!' she said, her voice quiet at first, but growing like a storm in the trees. She glared at Atlas, her face full of fury. 'It is because of him that we lost my husband, and because of him that we lost Elizabeth. And now, to risk the life of my dear Ariana, and Castor, too? He is a monster.'

She looked to Orla and Idris then. Orla saw the same ferocity she had seen in Ariana, back when she had addressed the workers in the mine. Josephine had been hurt, and so had Ariana. But there was a spark in them still, and Orla felt a rush of admiration for them both.

'These children have done what I could not. They've shown you the truth: Inishowen Atlas has destroyed this village. Elizabeth tried to warn us, and we did not take heed. We should have rooted him out, long ago. Isn't that right, Orla?'

A whisper of assent ran through the crowd. Orla took a deep breath. She could hear the forest pines shivering, the willows swaying in a rising breeze, the river gurgling as the rain drained down through the marsh grasses into the flooding creek.

Out, out, murmured the waterweeds.

Leave, hissed the nettles.

Orla nodded.

The plants wanted Atlas gone.

And so did the villagers.

'Take him to Westharbour,' they shouted. 'He must stand trial!'

'Let *me* deal with him!' cried another.

'He can't get away with this!'

Like a river in flood, the crowd pressed closer, their voices rising together in a thundering wave. Orla saw the sudden fear in Atlas's eyes. It was a look of pure panic, like a fox caught in a trap. Atlas knew that he'd lost, and he was afraid. With a sharp twist, he broke free from Callahan's grasp and scrabbled through the crowd, pushing past Captain, past Idris, tripping as he went.

'No!' cried Orla. 'Stop him!'

But he was off, racing towards the Westharbour road – and flying away from the village as though the very river was surging after him.

39

Nettles *Urtica dioica*
Leaves: for tea. The plant has strong fibres that can be wound into cord for string, ropes and fishing nets.

Orla dived into the crowd – struggling, scrapping as she chased after Atlas.

To the bridge! called the beech in the hedge.

Faster and faster, cried the thistles.

Heart pounding, Orla raced to the bridge. She was gaining on Atlas now – close behind him as he reached the high grey bridge that arched its back over the creek. Atlas skidded to a halt at the edge of the bridge, eying something below. But Orla was behind him – lunging at him as he tried to climb the stone parapet. She could not let him escape.

'Don't you dare!' Orla cried. Her first grasp missed –

he was climbing over, his eyes set on a row of Hauler boats moored below.

'I'm not letting you get away!' she gasped.

Atlas swung around then, grabbing Orla by the collar – and suddenly she was dangling in mid-air, with Atlas holding her out over the churning water.

Help her! cried the plants, as the water curled and writhed beneath her.

Help the girl!

Orla struggled, but Atlas held her firm, glaring down at her.

'What are you gonna do, throw me in?' she said. Her tinderbox tumbled from her pocket and plummeted down towards the water.

'You've cost me everything, girl,' said Atlas. 'Just like your mother wanted.'

Orla growled and twisted, trying to pull free. But Atlas only tightened his grip. Below the bridge, the Hauler boats clunked together in the floodwater. If she fell, she would hit them – or the water. She didn't know which was worse. No one would survive the creek in flood. Her mind went blank. The plants were roaring, the nettles crying out, the river weeds . . .

We need you, wise girl!

Set her free, set her free!

Orla gasped. She couldn't breathe . . .

'Perhaps you should end up in the wild like her,' Atlas

said, eying the water. 'This world has no place for women like—'

Orla kicked out – and Atlas gave a cry. In an instant, Orla's mind cleared. She reached for Atlas's belt and found what she was looking for – his pistol. She pulled it from the holster and tried to remember what Atlas had done back at Hind House. *There was a catch somewhere . . .*

But Atlas was no longer crying out in pain – he leant forward, his eyes on the river, his decision made.

'Goodbye, Orla Carson,' he said.

The gun clicked and Atlas froze.

'Oh, I don't think so,' said Orla.

'You wouldn't dare,' said Atlas.

Orla's hand was trembling. Maybe he was right . . .

'She wouldn't,' said a gravelly voice. 'But I would.'

There was another click – louder this time.

With difficulty, Orla turned her head to see the enormous figure of Silas. His coat was soaking wet, his eyes yellower than ever. And he was standing in the middle of the bridge, pointing a hunting rifle at Atlas.

Atlas stepped backwards, away from the edge of the parapet. Catching hold of the stone wall, Orla pulled herself upright, but she did not lower the gun.

Atlas held his hands up in surrender, looking between Silas and Orla.

'Step back, poppet,' said Silas. 'He's ours.'

'Steady on, Silas,' said Atlas, trying to sound calm. 'I have the money, I have the cure! Let me take you to Westharbour – we'll meet with the Marshall – we'll sort something out.'

'I don't believe you,' said Silas. 'You took too long. We don't care about the Marshall. He's just another one of you lot. You don't understand our way of life, and neither does he. We've had enough of following orders. We'll take our business elsewhere. You'll be lucky to find a Hauler that'll set foot in Thorn Creek while you're around.'

There was a shout from below. Next to the boats Orla saw Bouchard bedraggled and river-soaked. He'd survived the weir, too, like Magda had warned. His eyes were set on Atlas, fierce as a wild dog. Beside him were half a dozen Haulers Orla vaguely recognized: men who had worked the boats in Thorn Creek and beyond.

'I can pay you,' muttered Atlas. 'I can pay you all.'

Silas paused for a moment, as though considering the offer. Then, he strode forward and stretched out a hand to Atlas.

Orla groaned.

'I knew you'd come around,' said Atlas, his eyes narrow.

'Did you?' said Silas. 'Then you don't know nothing 'bout Haulers at all.'

In one quick move, Silas yanked Atlas forward,

swinging him towards the stone parapet.

Atlas teetered, his eyes wide as he saw the creek flooding below. He waved his hands hopelessly, trying to steady himself. But Silas was right behind him.

'Let's see if you're waterproof,' he said. And with a shove, he pushed Atlas over the edge of the bridge and into the churning water.

Orla gasped and rushed to look over the parapet.

There was no sign of Atlas.

Silas grunted. Then he spat on the ground. He did not look at Orla. He simply nodded to the Haulers below, and the Haulers nodded in return.

Orla fell to her knees, exhausted. Her fingers found the soft moss that grew on the stones of the bridge, and she closed her eyes. Atlas was gone. Thorn Creek was safe.

Down by the waterside, she heard the Haulers singing. It started softly, joining the murmur of the moss and the beech trees, the river reeds and the swaying pines, and rose as they unmoored their boats and set off down the river.

Il est mort, le loup
Qu'on a chassé sans arrêt
En hiver, en hiver
Quand la pluie ne cesse pas.

40

Meadowsweet *Filipendula ulmaria*

For brightness and light, strew about the house. Aromatic
and pleasant to flavour beverages and soothe the stomach.
The roots will make a black dye. Also known as Queen
of the Meadow.

At dawn, when the birds started shuffling their feathers
in the blackthorn hedges, Orla woke and went out to
examine the garden. She walked around each and every
plant, checking who had been hurt by the Haulers and
who had not, who was growing well, who was gone, and
who would need extra care. Some plants had been cut
and trampled, but mostly they grew strong and determined, telling her not to worry, and pestering her to
check for aphids and keep Captain away from their
newest leaves, now that the black marks of the sickness

were starting to fade.

Once Orla had checked the garden, she tidied the woodshed, and soon it looked like Atlas had never been. Then she heated water for a tub and scrubbed herself by the fire until she was clean, as Ma would have wanted. Afterwards she pulled on her dirty breeches and oilskin, because she was still Orla, and never enjoyed washing clothes.

She was too tired to make breakfast, but the autumn plums were ripe and had not been stolen. Captain was snuffling around in the long grass, trying to find those that had already fallen. Orla pulled a handful of mint from the riverbank to distract him from the plums, and he snuffled it up gladly. While he dozed beneath the plum tree, Orla combed his mane and picked out his hooves; she was glad to see that the pine tar really had done its job, and there was no sign of rot in Captain's foot. When she was done, she climbed on to Captain's back, so that she could reach the clusters of purple plums hanging above them. Then she rested her head on Captain's shoulders and hugged his warm, dusty body as she ate. Captain sighed and chewed the grass, moving carefully so as not to disturb his passenger. Orla let her arms and legs dangle down. The garden was already regrowing, she thought. There wasn't much that could stop that.

*

A little while later, Orla climbed one of the apple trees in her garden and surveyed the village. Down by the river, she could see Idris casting his net into the water.

'Perfect,' she whispered to the apple tree. Shimmying down, she went to collect the little parcel that she'd made up the night before, and hurried along the lane to Idris's home by the river.

'Is he still fishing?' she asked the bulrushes.

Down by the water, they said.

Net made of nettle stems, spun into thread.

'Good,' said Orla, approaching the little house. She hadn't noticed before, but the thatched roof was so overgrown with plants that it looked as if it were part of the riverbank itself, growing happily up into the sunlight.

She gave a gentle knock on the door, before creeping inside. Idris had said to visit any time – he *hadn't* said that he needed to be home.

'Hello?' she whispered. 'Castor?'

Castor had been sleeping peacefully in a bed by the stove, but he opened his eyes when Orla arrived. With care, she placed the parcel beside him on the bed, noticing that the purple lines had faded from his arms. His face still looked gaunt and thin, but the medicine had worked.

'Here,' she said. 'Honey balm – from Elias's bees. Vervain tea. And a bit of pumpernickel bread – you could have that with smoked fish. And there's some comfrey, for the bruises. There.' She looked over her shoulder, nervous that Idris would come back. She wasn't used to people seeing that she cared.

Castor smiled faintly.

'Thanks,' he said croakily. 'For helping Idris.'

The reeds in the roof sang.

Friends, they said. *Family*.

Orla patted the parcel.

'He helped *me*,' she said.

Castor shrugged. 'In Thorn Creek, we gotta help each other,' he said, as though it was the most obvious thing in the world.

When she returned to the garden, Orla gathered up Ma's book and went to sit on her favourite patch of grass down by the water. There was a dampness in the air, as there always was in Thorn Creek, but that afternoon the sun was unusually bright. The last of the flowers in the garden – the last that would bloom before autumn really took hold – were turning their heads up to the sun. Opening the book, Orla was amazed to think that, even now, she had not read all of the pages. There were so many medicines here, so many secrets about how the world worked. As she translated the scribbled code using the key that Ariana had made, it was as though Ma was whispering in her ear.

When she thought about the darkness of the mine and

the deserted streets of Fleetwater, there was one place that Orla could not shake from her memory: the glasshouse. She wondered how her ma had got those delicate panes of glass up the river and through the forest – or had someone from Fleetwater built it long ago? She wished she'd been able to ask Ma where all the plants had come from. And she felt sad that Atlas had destroyed it before she could visit it again.

Leafing through the pages, she found an ink drawing that Ma had made of the glasshouse. Somehow, she'd made it look like the glass was shining on the page, catching the sunlight as Orla moved the book. And inside, she'd drawn some of the plants that Orla had found there: the wolfsbane, the angel's trumpets, the nightshade . . .

Turning the page over, Orla noticed a scribbled paragraph that she had not read before – for she hadn't known that Ma was writing in code. Using Ariana's method to decipher the words, she read aloud to the plants.

'*People have lived among the plants for as long as there have been people. They have harboured us in storms, made our clothes and our nets to fish, our medicine and our shelter. They have kept a watchful eye on us for thousands of years. But how do we shelter them, when the world is so enormous and so full of danger? How can we truly keep them safe? Perhaps a glasshouse is the start. It may not hide the biggest redwoods, or the greatest forests; but it may just hold the seeds to spark all kinds of new life.'*

Orla closed the book, watching the dragonflies dancing over the water in flashes of blue and green. Ma had never stopped imagining new possibilities. She'd gone on dreaming about the glasshouse – dreaming of a way to help the people around her, even when the villagers scorned her medicine, and Atlas dismissed her cause. She'd believed that science and plants and medicine could help everyone to live better lives.

Orla felt a stirring, a feeling that she imagined the plants felt when they grew towards the sun. She had felt a lot of sadness for Ma, and a lot of anger. And she knew that it would never fully disappear. But it felt like something was growing out of the sadness, like a seed that was starting to shoot. It was a feeling a little like hope, and pride, and it felt like the spark of an idea.

She spent the afternoon tending the garden: harvesting the plums before they fell, sweeping the porch and tying the ivy back to its proper perch. Now and again she could not help glancing expectantly at the gate, hoping that it would not be long before someone came to visit.

In the late afternoon light Orla watched a charm of goldfinches feeding on the teasels at the end of the garden. She grinned as they flew off in a cloud of gold and yellow, shouting in alarm. There was someone in the lane.

As Orla was washing a handful of plums, there was a call from the gate. It was Idris and Ariana. Idris had not washed, or changed, but Ariana was sparkly clean in a cotton dress and bonnet. Orla opened the gate, making sure there were no brambles to tangle into Ariana's skirts, and Idris helped her into the garden.

They sat in the long grass in the sunshine, and ate their way through the honey-sweet plums. Soon Idris and Orla were dripping with plum juice. Ariana's dress was miraculously unspoilt.

'You know, there's a caterpillar in every plum,' said Orla.

'That's rather fascinating,' said Ariana. 'Is it a moth?'

Orla nodded, licking the juice from her fingers.

Idris frowned at them, and started eating the plums a bit more carefully.

'As soon as Castor's better,' he said, 'we'll go up to Fleetwater. He wants to meet Magda and Matteas. Thought we'd help them to start rebuilding things up there. You could come . . .'

'I've had enough journeys for a while,' said Orla. 'But tell Castor I said thanks. And tell Magda and Matteas that they can come here too – if they want.'

'Castor's proper grateful, Orla,' said Idris. 'Elias came to visit. He said that Castor can come and apprentice in the chandlery. But only if he likes. Castor's great at building boats, so maybe he'll go that way . . . when

Pa comes back . . .'

Idris drifted off, chewing his plum contentedly.

'Sounds good to me,' said Orla, putting a piece of plum aside for the wasps.

There was a rustle from the hedge, and Orla heard the blackthorn whispering about intruders.

Standing on tiptoe, she could see the top of Elias's head. She recognized his flat cap and Agnes's bonnet alongside it. They came to the gate and stood looking awkwardly into the garden. Elias coughed apologetically.

Orla wiped the plum juice on her breeches. 'What're you doing?' she said, frowning.

Ariana flicked her leg. 'Be nice!' she hissed.

'If it's medicine you're after – we're doing the rounds this afternoon,' said Orla. 'If anyone's been *anywhere* near Atlas's ink, they get priority.'

'We saw what you did for Castor and for wee Ariana here,' said Elias. 'But no, it's just a little sage we're wanting. We've come to see if you're willing to trade for some eggs.'

Orla knew very well that they had plenty of sage growing by their back step, but she didn't mention it. She managed to say a curt thank you to Agnes for the half dozen eggs, and in exchange gave them a large bunch of sage leaves.

'Dry 'em,' she said. 'They taste nice fried, too,' she added with a half-smile.

'Thank you, love,' said Agnes. She shoved a small parcel into Orla's hands, and scurried off towards the village. Orla unwrapped the parcel. It was a batch of honey biscuits, the kind she had made with Agnes up at Dawson & Reed just after Ma had died. Before Orla had run away in a tantrum, swearing at Agnes for not having a proper garden. She felt a strange burst of fondness for Agnes then, and vowed to take her some flower seeds for her bees.

Orla didn't have a chance to start the biscuits, because before long a steady stream of villagers appeared at the gate, hoping to trade their produce for plants from the garden. Orla ended up with sacks of carrots, a skein of red-dyed yarn, a full round of goat's cheese, and even a fat hen in a basket. After a while, she had to set a limit.

'I'll show you how to grow 'em!' she said to the disgruntled crowd. 'But right now you're stripping my garden bare. Like locusts!'

Ariana put a sign up on the gate, saying that anyone wishing to trade could come again tomorrow at eleven, and then she helped Orla to carry the honey biscuits and the cheese to the willows by the riverbank. The hen followed them, pecking at crumbs and scurrying beneath Captain's feet. The horse looked very bemused.

'I've got an idea,' said Orla, sharing out the biscuits.

'Atlas destroyed the glasshouse. The plants in Fleetwater were barely surviving. Those places could have held the secret to curing a hundred illnesses – but they're fading away. We gotta find a way to protect the plants.'

Ariana dusted the crumbs from her fingers and the hen chased after them. 'A place to keep things safe,' she said.

'I think we could build a glasshouse in Thorn Creek,' said Orla. 'We could grow a hundred different plants – more than I can fit in my garden!'

'Well, we should use Hind House,' said Ariana decisively. 'The garden needs work. And there's certainly some glass Atlas won't be using any more. We could turn his study into a laboratory! Then we'll really know what we're doing. Mother will be glad to help – really, she will,' she added, seeing Orla's expression. 'She has some seeds – seeds from your ma, she said. But she never dared plant them while Atlas was around.'

Orla blushed, thinking of how she'd judged Josephine and Ariana for hiding away at Hind House, too good for the rest of the village – too good for her and Ma, when really it was Atlas who had forced them apart.

'We can even write a book about it!' said Ariana. Suddenly her eyes widened and she rummaged frantically in her skirts. From a pocket she pulled out a wrapped paper parcel and handed it to Orla. 'For you!' she said. 'If you're going to write out the cure properly, you'll need a pen.'

'And the ink *is* safe,' Idris added with a smile.

Cautiously Orla unwrapped the parcel. Inside was a wooden pen with a silver nib, and a glass bottle of ink. She held tight to the gift, wishing she could tell Ma what they were planning.

'Come to tea tomorrow,' said Ariana. 'We'll find the best place to build the glasshouse. It could be enormous,' she said dreamily. 'And I can introduce you to all the plants in the garden.'

Orla didn't tell Ariana that the plants spoke back – but then, she thought, the whole world spoke back if you listened. Ariana understood numbers and calculations just as if they were speaking to her. Idris knew how to spin thread from the plants, and how to stitch things tighter than anything. Elias knew how to spin wax into candles; and Agnes sang to her bees. Perhaps everyone had a language that they knew.

They fell quiet, munching the honey biscuits and cheese. Orla listened to the waterweeds in the river, quieter now that Idris and Ariana were around. But they were still there, keeping her company, muttering and swirling in the current, telling her that the pike were swimming down this way to hunt the minnows. Telling her the sun was shining and the world was bright, and that the river was growing wild as ever. Their voices would never fade completely, even if she did have other friends to talk to now.

That evening, Orla took a lamp into the garden and sat with Ma's book on her lap. In the twilight, the new hen pecked excitedly around Captain's hooves, and the plants whispered, calling the moths and night insects to their flowers. Orla turned to the empty pages at the back of the book, and pulled out the pen and ink that Ariana had given her. Then she began to carefully write out the cure for the pitchstone sickness.

She copied Ariana's notes on Ma's cure word for word, adding what she knew about where the plants grew and how they should be used. She drew the honesty in fine detail, just like Ma would have done – every tiny hair, every fine stem. She labelled each part of the plant and what it should be used for. And when she wrote, she did not write in code. She wanted to share what she had found, so that anyone who needed it might know how to use the plants. She drew until the stars came out, and the plants hummed and shuffled in the breeze of the night. Then, satisfied, Orla closed the book. The cover was a little worn and river-stained, blotted with ink and smudges of green where she had left it among the grass in the garden. While the plants whispered their evening song, Orla took her pen and retraced the faded title on the front cover so that it stood out, blue as the night:

Plants and their Medicinal Uses
by
Elizabeth Carson
&
Orla Carson
With help from her friends,
Ariana Claw and Idris Romero

Epilogue

The Forest in Spring

One morning, the following spring, Orla rode Captain into the woods in search of mallow flowers, to mix with honey for Ariana's birthday. They crossed Pike Ford, where minnows nibbled Orla's bare feet, and wandered through the trees, snacking on bright-green beech leaves as they went. They followed the winding paths between the grasses and tall pines, and listened to the sound of new things growing.

Sun and springlight! called the dog roses, reaching up into the sunlight.

Wake up, winter flowers – wake, sleeping roots! sang the cowslips.

In the middle of a cluster of hawthorn trees, Captain stopped suddenly.

'There's no mallows here,' said Orla, urging him onwards. 'Keep going.'

But Captain stamped his foot. Orla looked down. In the middle of the glade there was a grassy mound, dotted with pink honesty flowers.

Orla felt a sudden goose-prickling on her skin as the plants whispered gently to her.

Healing hands, healing plants, healing seeds, they said.

Safe seeds, they said. *Medicine seeds*.

Orla slid down from Captain's back, holding tight to his mane, and felt her heart fluttering like a thousand petals in the wind.

'Ma?' she said quietly.

She stumbled through the long grass and knelt beside the plants. She knew at once where Captain had brought her. This was Ma's grave, and the plants had grown from the seeds in her pockets.

Gentle, wise girl, said the plants.

'We made a cure, Ma,' she said, tears brimming in her eyes. 'We made it from your book – me and Ariana and Idris. We did it. And we're gonna make a glasshouse too, Ma. To keep the plants safe – so there's medicine enough for the whole village.'

Orla wiped her face with her sleeve, but she did not stop herself from crying. She stroked the long grass and thought of Ma, buried here beneath the roots, her life ended but never quite gone.

'We'd never have done it without you, or your book. You kept us safe, all along.'

Wise girl, said the plants, in a voice that reminded her of Ma. *Wise friends.*

Orla hiccuped and wiped her nose. Captain snuffled in the grass beside her.

'I got so much to tell you,' she said, lying down among the dancing flowers.

Hours passed. She told Ma about Ariana and Idris, and how they'd ordered the glass from Fleetwater and the iron from the blacksmith in Westharbour. She told her about Magda and Matteas, who had looked after the woods around Fleetwater, and who had started to rebuild the village there, little by little. She watched the hoverflies and the day moths skipping around the flowers on the grave. And she stretched her arms up to the warm dappled sun, like a flower drinking up the light. By and by the sunlight turned deep gold. Evening had come, and Captain trod gently through the glade to rub his nose on her face. It was time to go home.

'I'll come back,' said Orla. 'When the plants are in seed. I'll keep them safe. And I'll tell you everything that's happening, I promise.'

Wise girl, said the plants in chorus. *Safe home.*

Orla touched the petals of the honesty, bright and

alive, and she felt something settle deep inside her. It felt like liquid gold, like rosehip tea, like Captain's reassuring snuffles in the darkness. It felt like comfort and kindness. It felt like home. Climbing on to Captain's back, Orla nodded goodbye to the plants and to Ma, and let Captain carry her back down the sunset path.

It was a path that would be trodden many times over a lifetime, Orla thought. Year on year, the flowers would come, as would the seeds. And all the while, the plants would whisper, for the people who listened.

Acknowledgements

For as long as we have existed, human beings have used plants as medicine. Many of our modern treatments originated from plants: painkillers from willow, heart medicine from foxgloves and cancer treatment from yew trees. Even animals have been known to use plants medicinally: from the starlings that put yarrow in their nests to keep parasites away, to the brown bears that rub their fur with wild parsnip as an insect repellent. This book is, first of all, for them: plants that provide our food, our medicine and our shelter.

While Orla's story is set in a world a little like modern Europe, where few people use plant medicine, this book owes an enormous debt to the people around the world who have kept traditional medicine alive into the modern day – in particular, the indigenous communities that safeguard around eighty per cent of our planet's biodiversity. We have so much to relearn and to protect.

I started writing *The Map of Leaves* long before the pandemic, but most of the editing and rewriting happened during the ups and downs of lockdowns, temporary housing and narrowboat life. This book could not have been written without the kind-hearted canal community (Tara and Miranda especially) or the support of my friends and family in Southampton. I owe special thanks to Carol and Verity (along with Jake and Ben the rescue cobs, who both lent their personalities to Captain) for teaching me the herbs that keep horses well, and to work with persistence and grit, even in deep mud. Thank you also to Nazneen, for tea and story wisdom; to Jake, for socially-distanced football; to Sally B, for advice and encouragement; to Jon G, for always helping; to Clare at October Books, Lynne C and Louiza, who it was always a pleasure to see dropping by the HB House-boat in the early stages of writing this book; to Steve, for housing me last minute during lockdown and letting me tackle the apple trees; to Frances and Jon, for their constant support and kindness – and to Deb, for being the heart of the community and teaching me what it means to bring people together.

An author starts with the seed of a story. Without my team of kind and experienced story-gardeners, *The Map of Leaves* would be nothing but a struggling shoot. It has been such a privilege to work with two wise women: firstly, my wonderful agent, Jenny Savill, who took this tangly story and guided it into a thriving adventure, and secondly, my editor Rachel Leyshon, who is extraordinarily talented at seeing what I'm trying to do and helping me to do it better. Thank you to everyone at Chicken House, in particular, Laura, Jazz and Olivia – and Barry, for seeing the magic in talking plants. Thank you to my copy-editor, Daphne, for being so clever about boats, and to Andy Winfield at the University of Bristol Botanic Garden for keeping a close eye on the plants – in particular the irises! And thank you to Marie-Alice Harel and Helen Crawford-White for the incredible illustration and design work. Thank you also to my writer pal, Anya Glazer, for her constant enthusiasm for cake and discussing the tricky bits.

Finally, this story would never have come to life without my MA tutors, Elen Caldecott, C. J. Skuse, Joanna Nadin and Steve Voake, whose wisdom and teaching took my understanding of storytelling to a whole new level. I will forever be learning, because of them.

A special thank you goes to the plant lovers in my life: Hazel, for her love of climbing tall trees and growing things; Susannah, for running in gorse bush tunnels with me; and Tiff, for her love of long grass and wild gardens. Even more gratitude goes to my mum, for her collection of remedy books and herbal teas; and to my Dad, for carrying seeds in his pockets and curiosity in his brain. And finally to Dom, for his endless patience and love, and not minding too much when I come home covered in mud and brambles.

There are so many more people I have to thank for my stories, so I suppose I must write a hundred more books to thank you all.